BUY ME LOVE

BUY ME LOVE

♥

Martha Cooley

🐔 Red Hen Press | *Pasadena, CA*

Book design by Mark E. Cull

Library of Congress Cataloging-in-Publication Data

Names: Cooley, Martha, author.
Title: Buy me love / Martha Cooley.
Description: First Edition. | Pasadena, CA : Red Hen Press, [2021]
Identifiers: LCCN 2020056795 (print) | LCCN 2020056796 (ebook) | ISBN
  9781597091206 (trade paperback) | ISBN 9781597098748 (epub)
Classification: LCC PS3553.O5646 B89 2021 (print) | LCC PS3553.O5646
  (ebook) | DDC 813/.54—dc23
LC record available at https://lccn.loc.gov/2020056795
LC ebook record available at https://lccn.loc.gov/2020056796

The National Endowment for the Arts, the Los Angeles County Arts Commission, the
Ahmanson Foundation, the Dwight Stuart Youth Fund, the Max Factor Family Foun-
dation, the Pasadena Tournament of Roses Foundation, the Pasadena Arts & Culture
Commission and the City of Pasadena Cultural Affairs Division, the City of Los Angeles
Department of Cultural Affairs, the Audrey & Sydney Irmas Charitable Foundation, the
Meta & George Rosenberg Foundation, the Albert and Elaine Borchard Foundation, the
Adams Family Foundation, Amazon Literary Partnership, the Sam Francis Foundation,
and the Mara W. Breech Foundation partially support Red Hen Press.

First Edition
Published by Red Hen Press
www.redhen.org
Printed in Canada

Acknowledgments

To my family and friends, at home and abroad, thanks for sustenance of all stripes. I have been buoyed by you in countless precious ways.

This book's been awfully long in the making. Along the way, its maker received practical help. I am grateful to Adelphi University for sabbaticals in 2012–13 and 2019–20, and to the Siena School for Liberal Arts in Siena, Italy, for respites in the summers of 2006 and 2007. My gratitude goes as well to the Corporation of Yaddo for my stay there in 2008.

The Red Hen team has been superlative from start to finish. To all, my deepest appreciation.

To Deborah Schneider, my agent, heartfelt thanks for believing in this book, and in me.

To the Bennington Writing Seminars: thanks for past and ongoing gifts of collegiality and fellowship.

To Daniel and Oana Muntean and Raffaella Paoletti for warm company in Castiglione del Terziere.

To Mark Matousek for wise listening.

To Askold Melnyczuk for spurring me at a tricky juncture.

To Fiona Maazel for clear-eyed encouragement.

To Anne Germanacos for urging adventure.

To Sheridan Hay for generosities of spirit.

To Susie and Jim Merrell for friendship and aid in Sag Harbor.

To Lynn Whittemore for always helping me straighten up and fly right.

And to Antonio Romani, my beloved, *sempre*.

For Antonio

BUY ME LOVE

... it's the surprise of change that makes good fortune and bad luck feel the same.

—Anne Pierson Wiese, "Discovery"

ONE

Trio, Quartet

1

Not a scrap but a square, the size of a woman's handkerchief. A square of paper, small and white, pinned against the underside of an iron grate beneath Ellen Portinari's feet—detained there by an updraft of cool air, its scent moldy, metallic: Eau de Subway.

All but blank, that square. Its sole markings a few numbers printed by hand. Ellen would've missed that little flag of white, failed altogether to notice it, were it not for a fear that halted her midstride.

Was her wallet where it ought to be, in the scuffed satchel now slung over her shoulder? Maybe not . . . still loitering, perhaps, in the green suede clutch she'd sported the evening before? (A going-out purse: elegant, impractical.) And why'd she bothered switching, anyway? As if a different bag could've altered the evening's chemistry, fizzed it . . . dumb, dumb.

Standing atop the grate, she patted the side pocket of her satchel.

No familiar bulge there. Yet the wallet couldn't still be in the green clutch—she'd emptied that bag of its contents. Unzipping her satchel's center opening, she reached in and felt around. The evening's chemistry? Hardly explosive. Two long-married couples (not close friends of hers, merely acquaintances), a newly divorced middle-aged male, and a fifty-two-year-old single woman—herself—had made for a practiced restraint. Potentially intriguing domestic concerns (fidelity and infidelity, erotic malaise) were not likely to arise in conversation. Her dining companions had stuck to benign topics, though when the subject of real estate cropped up, she'd had to suppress an urge to bolt. ("Do you own or rent?" was a question she dreaded like no other; even "Seeing anyone?" felt less toxic.)

Still, the whole thing could've been much worse. They'd eaten at a Smith

Street bistro serving its own take on pot-au-feu, overly salted but good, especially when paired with a Côte du Rhône that the newly divorced man had termed "velvet-y"—prompting her own descriptor, "sateen-y," which had led to his counter-offer ("moleskin-y") and a flurry of what he'd termed fabricated adjectives ("damask-y," "grosgrain-y") from their fellow diners. Everyone at the table had been witty. There'd been sufficient laughter. And another social encounter with the newly divorced man, whose hands had been long-fingered and expressive, might prove mildly entertaining. Yet by its close the evening had felt like nothing so much as a game of musical chairs, with none of the players fully confident they'd wind up in the seat of happiness.

2

Pawing now through her bag (balanced on one uplifted knee), Ellen felt the initial stirrings of panic. Where the hell *was* the damn wallet?

Unpleasant to contemplate its loss. Not just because of the cash (precious little), but the hassle: credit card companies to call, a new driver's license to procure, the organ donation ID to renew. And the irreplaceables—a dried four-leaf clover, a dog-eared photo of the nearest-and-dearest at Dale's for his fiftieth . . . Plus that line from *Merry Wives*—*Money is a good soldier, sir, and will on*—scribbled by Anne on a matchbook cover when they were roommates at NYU. *If money go before, all ways do lie open!* They'd given up cigarettes and chocolate to save funds; to keep their spirits up, Anne had spouted Shakespeare quotes. As for the wallet itself, hadn't it been a gift from one of the nearest-and-dearest? Yes—Sophie and Hank. Buttery yellow it was, and just the right size. O fuck if it were lost!

Or stolen?

She took a deep breath. Of course the wallet hadn't been filched, not during these few minutes as she walked from home to this spot. Impossible. She'd passed only a handful of people and hadn't bumped against a single one, had she? No, no. And even if the wallet *had* been lifted somehow (by an extremely skilled pickpocket), that'd hardly be a tragedy. *Who steals my purse steals trash*: another of Anne's offerings. '*Tis something, nothing; 'twas mine, 'tis his . . .*

Underfoot, a stream of dank air began venting through the grate.

It riffled the hem of her skirt, sending spurts of itself up to her knees. On her bare calves the air was a caress, swift and clear. Not warm yet welcome; like happiness, perhaps, arriving as it ought to—cool fingertips probing, laying claim?

That stray thought arose in the air-fondled instant before her hand, still groping in her satchel, met up at last with the missing wallet.

Belowground, an F train rumbled rhythmically toward the Seventh Avenue station. It whined as it slowed, its noise fading to a hum.

Ellen glanced down. Although the draft of air pushed upward by the incoming train had ceased toying with her skirt, the white square of paper pressed against the grate held steady: the air was sustaining its loft.

She stooped, peering. The piece of paper lay flat, seemingly glued into place. It wasn't wholly white, though. Strings of numerals were hand-printed across its middle.

She crouched closer. Most of the numerals were too messy and tightly spaced to distinguish, but one neatly rendered cluster stood out. The first five numbers—a six, a three, an eight, another six, a zero—weren't hard to discern; the last two were smudged.

Seven numbers: 6-3-8-6-0-something-something.

She straightened, frowning. Familiar, that sequence, but from where?

As she bent over the iron cross-hatching once more, the piece of paper shimmied a little, then rocked gently downward on its cradle of air. In a few seconds it was gone.

3

Reshouldering her bag, Ellen continued uphill. She crossed Fifth Avenue, her legs and lungs registering the incline as Ninth Street steepened. Trudging—Prospect Park her goal—she waited for memory's tumblers to click into place.

That seven-numeral sequence: her childhood phone number. How weird was *that*?

She'd memorized that number with Walter's help, when she was in, what, first grade? Tapping two pencils together, he'd sung in his lustrous baritone: *Six, three, eight . . . there's your trio.* And then, after a pause: *Six, oh, three, three . . . there's your quartet. Trio, quartet. Easy.* A seven-note song, each note a numeral.

Now you sing it, he'd ordered. *The whole thing, so you won't forget.* His hand on her neck, cool fingers and thumb at either side of her throat. Lightly assessing her phrasing. *One more time.* He'd accompanied her then, an octave below: their first and only father-daughter duet. His voice magnificent, hers a wisp of aural smoke. Nola had been there too, yes?—leaning against the doorsill, sipping her drink: *la mamma* half in the bag already, though it was only mid-afternoon.

And Win must've been around as well. Probably upstairs in his room, teaching himself how to notate—having by then squirreled away a stack of Walter's staff-paper, plus a metronome from the music department at school, pencils from art class, plastic binders from the homeroom closet . . . Bit of a klepto, the brother used to be. Not that anyone noticed, what with Walter making as if his son didn't exist, and Nola too sauced to care, and Win's teachers barely aware of that boy who seldom spoke but was always drumming his fingers on his desk.

He wasn't a petty thief, though. Win would nick only what was necessary: supplies for his secret life. *Composition*, he'd murmur as they walked to the school bus stop. Varying the word's rhythms, pitches, stresses—*com-po-si-tion* . . . Not a social animal; always his own best company. Off by himself, staring into space, humming.

Why d'you hum to yourself, Win?

I'm practicing.

For what.

For being a composer. That's what I am. Walter sings, I compose.

Oh, Edwin . . . what to *do* with the bro, what to say to him, how to get him back on track?

Such a good composer. Such a waste of talent.

Leave him be, he's gotta figure this out for himself: Sophie and Hank's advice. Hang in there, he'll come round: Anne's counsel. And her partner Giselle's: grief holds you hostage til it's ready to release you.

Yeah, but it'd been over two years since Madrid. And Win more isolated now than ever, his drinking even worse.

Dale took the realistic view, as always: Win's gonna do what he's doing til he doesn't need to do it any longer. Just keep letting him know you won't walk away. Put the oxygen mask on your own face first, though! Don't get consumed by his mess.

Win was a classic loner. Never easy to be around; not as a kid, not as a grownup. That gaze of his, so impassive. Like the gaze of a cat who knows there's no such thing as a second life, let alone a ninth, so you better do it now—whatever matters to you—since if you delay, you might get blown up. As in, by a bomb. As in, Madrid.

All right, Win. But did *whatever matters to you* have to include buckets of booze?

4

The time? Seven forty-five. She wasn't running late, for once. Hence there was no need to pick up the pace, not in this heat.

Everything made music, according to Win. Your body walking, of course. Plus ordinary objects, plants and animals, thoughts and feelings, ideas, dreams. The world was an orchestra playing nonstop; its instruments didn't rehearse, had no conductor or score. They simply improvised. *Just listen*, Win used to say. *That truck's a bass. When the kettle boils, it's a piccolo. Roses are oboes.*

And composers, what did they do?

They listened. Then wrote down whatever they heard during a given stretch of time. *Notation*, such writing was called. At first you made a mess, but then came the fun part: trimming and shaping, playing with time.

How?

By speeding or slowing it. Bending it, stretching it.

How d'you know you're doing it right?

The music says. You just have to listen.

Like following orders?

More like remembering a dream.

5

Side-swiped by a long-haired dog, Ellen halted. The creature sailed past, owner huffing in tow.

Good lord. Who had whom by the leash there?

If music be the food of love, play on! Walter'd sung that, when? *'Tis not so sweet now as it was before . . .* at a wedding. Some Belgian patron of the arts had set some bits of Shakespeare to music, then hired a couple of big-name singers to perform the bits at his nuptials. Walter had been flown to Bruges on a private jet. There'd been a dog aboard, a dachshund with a red velvet collar. See what crap I have to put up with, he'd fumed when he returned. You kids don't have a clue, and neither does your mother. While I'm off singing for some fool with a lapdog, you're freeloading.

Off singing. Then he vamoosed for good, a few months after the incident with the lost score. At 5:00 a.m. a cabbie had beeped out front, and *poof*—Signor Portinari and his two leather suitcases were gone. To Cremona, Italy, of all places, where a lover, a man named Bruno, awaited him. Somewhere near Milan, Cremona was. A gorgeous medieval town, according to the guidebooks. Stradivari and Guarneri used to make violins there, and Bruno happened to be one of Cremona's best instrument-makers, and Walter one of the great baritones of his day. And a guy named Bruno Walter used to be one of the best conductors of the mid-twentieth century. Now wasn't life just a happy heap of coincidences?

Oh, and Bruno Walter's daughter was murdered by her husband in a fit of jealousy because she'd fallen for an Italian singer. Ah well.

Poof. The sound of Walter disappearing.

Had Walter recognized Win's talent?

Of course. How could he *not* have noticed that his firstborn had perfect pitch? Or that by the time the kid was five, Win could hum a bit of Bach he'd heard months earlier, without missing a note? Or compose a piece of music on the spot, prompted only by the sloshing of gin in his mother's glass?

Walter knew. But after the disaster with the lost score, none of it mattered to him. And once he'd turned against Win—cutting him short whenever the kid addressed him, acting like Win occupied a negative space that could simply be stared through—nobody could get him to ease up. *Walter*, Nola used to mutter now and then, *knock it off.* As if Walter would ever cease believing Win had actually planned the whole absurd business. As if Nola had ever had the slightest sway over her husband. As if that ten-year-old boy could ever have found words to defend himself— Win, who spoke mainly in monosyllables and preferred to hum.

As-if as-if as-if as-if as-if: iambic pentameter.

Family, fiasco: in the dictionary, why weren't they listed as synonyms?

6

Green at last!

Not that it made any difference. The traffic light at the corner of Ninth Street and Seventh Avenue was merely a suggestion, especially at rush hour.

Looking both ways, Ellen skittered across the avenue. A car-service sedan squealed round the corner, nearly clipping her. Safe on the far curb, she took a deep breath, then glanced downward. A big fake dollar bill . . . no, a *hundred*-dollar bill, stenciled in red on the sidewalk. It looked like a real C-note, too, except for its missing portrait, the one that was supposed to sit in the central oval. (Of some president, or was it Ben Franklin on each bill?) In place of the portrait was a three-word phrase: *You are here.* Below, the usual "In God We Trust" was replaced by *in confusion.*

You are here / in confusion. How bizarre.

She scraped her heel along the edge of the image. Not a mark, not even a smudge.

A few yards away, a group of riders emerged from the entrance to the F train. Dozens of feet trod over the C-note.

A lanky man was the last to ascend. In one hand he held an open can of soda.

Look, Ellen said, pointing.

The man glanced downward, frowned, then tipped his soda over the C-note and rotated his heel across the image, grinding hard. The liquid had absorbed; nothing happened to the C-note.

He shrugged. It's all yours, he said. Better spend it soon, though. Use it or lose it!

His accent was British but not posh, laced with . . . was it mischief, derision? He saluted her, then loped away.

7

Her cellphone, belching. A text from Dale.

Can't do tomorrow, it's date night—this one's a grad student in medical anthropology, WTF is that? Wish me luck! How about Tues after 7?

One good thing: Dale never proselytized about dating. Was fine with the fact that although his old pal Ellen might possibly be going out for the eve with some acquaintance, or maybe might've arranged to spend a few hours with one of the guys she occasionally slept with, or could perhaps be doing her shift at the food co-op—while some such thing *might* be happening, it was much more probable she'd be at home, playing paper-ball soccer with her two cats.

Tuesday's fine, you choose film, I'll order takeout. Have fun w/date!

Coffee, coffee? Damn. She'd walked right by the place, two blocks earlier.

Was there enough time to go back? She glanced at her watch: eight o'clock sharp. Nola in the living room, singing softly to herself first thing in the morning, cradling a coffee mug . . . that image still so vivid. Her voice, too. Something odd: though never recorded, Nola's voice was easier to recall than Walter's. There were plenty of recordings of *il baritono*, of course. And occasional pictures of him, too, in the *Times*'s Arts section, grainy black-and-white photos from music festivals in Salzburg, Vienna, London . . . After he retired, the visual evidence ended, yet the man himself was still over there in Italia. And right now it must be lunchtime in Cremona. Hence two elegant octogenarians would be having prosciutto and melon, with a glass of *prosecco* to wash it down. Espresso afterward. Then a brief stroll and a nap.

Nola meanwhile consumed by worms.

And speaking of things long gone: why'd they arisen now, those seven numerals—6 3 8 6 0 3 3? Like birds from nowhere, startled into flight?

Nethermead

1

The artist responsible for the C-note: Blair Talpa.

Born and raised in Brooklyn Heights. Twenty-four years old, short and lithe, with cropped wavy hair, strong hands, broad feet. A recent graduate of a visual arts program in San Francisco, to which she'd sent herself after accumulating the necessary funds.

During her twelve-month tenure there, the big western sky had been troubling. It gave off a false sense of freedom, as though the people living beneath it felt authorized to do whatever they wanted, without having to pay for it. Back east, the sky-roof was less expansive but offered more reliable cover. Under it, she'd prepare to commit artistic acts. Sort of like committing crimes—same level of risk, different scales of judgment and punishment.

Albert Camus: the only good reading she'd done in San Francisco.

The Stranger was a book worth the trouble. And the essays. Most of the other reading assignments for school had been dull things written by a bunch of windy art critics. Camus, though—he got it. Especially about respect: if it's based on fear, it becomes despicable. Action was the only basis for respect. And action always implied reaction, hence rebellion. Camus was right about rebellion, too. It wasn't noble by itself, he said; only its demands were noble.

Art's sole purpose was to increase the sum of freedom. Making art meant deranging orbits, forcing minds into new directions and patterns. Of course people would resist. Human beings, Camus said, are the only creatures that refuse to be what they are. They betray themselves, refusing the new, caving in to the familiar. But an artist still had to try.

School in San Francisco had been unexceptional. Not a surprise; she'd expected as much. After all, who could teach derangement?

Yet she'd learned what she needed—techniques and craft, ways and means. Her main accomplishment was an invisible performance piece called "Tabula Rasa." Twenty-four weeks of secret, deliberate self-annulment. Like gestation, but not of a child; rather, of a nonself, a nullity. She'd pulled it off, lent absolutely no impression. Paid the tuition bill, attended the classes, did the assignments as ordered, and almost never spoke. To teachers and students alike, she'd been essentially nonexistent.

Annul: reduce to zero. Zero being the most powerful number.

2

The C-notes, her first attempt at street art, were a step in the right direction. There'd be more such experiments; mistakes, too. Part of the process, a warning to herself.

Like the thing with the kid. An error she'd make only once.

Camus said freedom was a chance to be better. There'd be no one to stop her; nobody would care. "Tabula Rasa" had proved it was possible to be invisible—like a current of air that moved freely yet unseen, pushing people slightly off-kilter, then more, more, til they couldn't maintain their usual mental orbits any longer.

At which point they'd think differently; they'd *have* to. And act and react differently as well.

3

Returning from San Francisco to Brooklyn, she found an apartment, a small studio. It was near the Gowanus Canal, on the top floor of an old brownstone. The canal's rank odors wafted through the windows on warm days, but the space was quiet. There was no one bothersome in the building, no one curious to know who or what she was.

Soon enough, she landed a job in an arts supply store in lower Manhattan.

The work was menial—stocking shelves, mopping floors—but required little interaction with customers. Though the pay was crap, the hours were flexible. And lifting the small stuff she needed (brushes and paper, paints, charcoal) wasn't hard; nobody noticed.

Having few acquaintances and no close friends made everything easier. There was nobody to report to. Nobody to whom something was owed.

The parents were both remarried now. It was no longer necessary to hear their rants and sob-stories. Both of them earned good salaries; they spent the money on their ugly homes in New Jersey, their Club Med vacations, meals in tacky restaurants, lousy Broadway shows. They couldn't care less about what was happening outside their self-congratulatory little worlds.

Now and then, one or the other would ask her to coffee in the city. It wasn't hard to field their questions and lob a few bland answers: yeah, the job's okay, Brooklyn's fine, they're cleaning up the Gowanus Canal. No, I don't need money, thanks. Take care, see you.

The parents didn't recall how she'd spent her adolescence in Brooklyn Heights. In her bedroom, mostly—reading art books while they yelled at each other and at Keith. She'd read, slept, and checked the news: the first Gulf War, Bush's stolen election. And done some drugs, too; mostly pot, occasionally hash. No coke or crack or meth or smack, though. And not much booze. No getting into real trouble, like Keith.

4

Stay off everyone's radar: rule number one.

The parents made that easy. Before their divorce they'd been on each other's backs so often, they'd barely noticed her. And they'd been caught up in blaming her brother for everything they weren't heaping on each other. Now they were absorbed in their new lives. And Keith was gone.

He'd be thirty soon. Hard to recall the details of his body. Long hands and feet; thin hair; a scar on his right elbow from when he'd been shoved off his bike by a fourth-grade bully. As a kid he'd almost never laughed or smiled. Behind his blank expression, though—inside his head—there'd been so much going on . . . School meant nothing to him. Right from the start, the parents had shrieked at him about his grades, insisting he was lazy, uncooperative. Why couldn't he make friends, why such a loner? It was wrong, they said. Whatever he was doing was wrong.

The truth was Keith only liked animals: dogs, cats, birds. Once, he set a bird's broken wing. He was patient even with nasty animals, like the stray dog who'd snapped at kids in the neighborhood. He fed it, got it to lick his hand. Said the dog was just scared.

He'd had trouble reading, a learning disability of some kind. No one could figure out how to help him deal with it. When he hit seventh grade, the parents got him a tutor, a preppy college kid who treated Keith like an idiot. The tutor kept hissing *you stupid shit* when the parents were out of earshot. In high school, kids called Keith other names—dogfucker, pussy-cat. His answer was to steal things. Nothing valuable at first, mostly crap from kids' lockers and neighbors' houses, or stuff he'd find in cars when someone forgot to lock the doors. Once he took a sapphire ring from a neighbor's kitchen counter and chucked it in the trash. The woman who'd left it on the counter was so stupid, he said, that she didn't even know her own son was nicking bills from her wallet.

That had to be true; Keith didn't lie about stuff like that. He noticed things other people didn't.

Then there was the neighbor with the BMW. She'd gone inside with groceries, and her phone rang and she forgot about the keys tossed on the passenger seat. Keith hopped in, drove the car to Floyd Bennett Park, piled trash from garbage cans into the back seat, and set the whole thing on fire. Fucked it up, and himself, too: burns on his arms, a jail sentence. He'd just turned nineteen.

Once he was taken away, the parents wouldn't even mention his name. They just kept fighting, mainly over money. As for their second kid—herself—they'd figured she would go to college and get some sort of job. Not as an artist, they'd never imagine that. And then some guy would come along and lift the remaining sack off the parental shoulders.

5

Talking was mostly a waste of time.

In high school, people turned away when they didn't understand stuff, such as being a boy in a girl's body. Keith always knew. When she was six, he said look, this is how boys do it, you need to know. He'd shown her a few times; slowly, not too hard. This is how we do it, he said, but don't tell anyone I'm showing you. When you want to do it to someone, you can use a finger instead, in either place. Boys mostly do it here with girls. And here with other boys. But you can do it however you want.

From watching animals, he said. That's how he knew, how he'd learned.

When he got out of jail, he disappeared. He must've figured out how to get past it—the shit that was stopping him from being who he was. No one had heard from him since.

Become so free, said Camus, that existence itself is an act of rebellion. That was the goal; hers, anyway.

As for other artists, the ones in the street-art world talked a good game, but all they really wanted was money and fame. Like that guy Neck Face, the one who did those black-and-white stickers on billboards and lamp-posts. He'd begun as a nameless slacker, then became famous for a little while, then a boring sellout. And what about those graffiti artists from a while ago, the ones who'd used subway cars for canvases—Keith Haring's entourage—where'd they all gone? At least they'd managed to fend off the SoHo and Chelsea pimps for a while, til Basquiat came along and people started paying millions for his canvases.

Pitfalls like that could be avoided, though. It just took discipline. Eat well: no meat, plenty of fruit. Go easy on booze, and no hard drugs. And deal with sex, not let it get in the way. On that score, Camus wasn't great; he had a bunch of lovers and a messy marriage. But what mattered was his writing. That way he had of getting straight to the point: you're alone.

Things were starting to fall into place.

People were basically distracted. If you stayed quiet, or made dumb remarks about the weather, you'd be left alone.

Art's lonely, her fifth-grade art teacher said once. He'd come up to her while she'd been finger-painting, off by herself in a corner of the art room. Out of nowhere he'd leaned over and whispered: *Art's lonely. Get used to it.* He'd spoken to her as though she'd been a grownup, not some girl dragging a thumb sideways through blue paint.

He'd patted her on the shoulder, then turned away. Message delivered.

Her first C-note, the one on the sidewalk in front of her middle school— she'd made it in his honor. Gradually it would fade. But it'd still be there, doing its work of derangement.

6

Memory could be a problem. Yet with practice anything, even forgetting, got easier.

On awakening, for instance, it was often hard to recall the thoughts she'd had before falling asleep. Or the face of whoever she'd had sex with, a few hours earlier. Or even where the sex had taken place. Of the act itself, a few meaningless details stayed in memory for a few hours, then vanished.

One thing was certain, though: whatever had happened, she'd been on top. No sex with anyone, male or female, unless they accepted that rule. And no negotiating. The rule came from experience.

When someone's on top of you, it's hard to get out from under that person unless he or she cooperates.

And when someone's on top of you and suddenly stops sucking your chest and mumbles something like *I don't feel well* and stops moving—so at first you think she's kidding, then realize she's not—when that happens, it's even more difficult to get out from under. Because that person now weighs a ton. She's five-foot-ten, at least a hundred and fifty pounds. All her weight seems to be right on your solar plexus. You're suffocating, but you can't say *get off me, I can't breathe*, because she won't—can't hear you. Her head's turned to the side, by your shoulder; you can't see her face. All you can do is squirm til you finally get free and take a deep breath and realize this person isn't breathing. It's not a joke, she's not playing with you.

Not an experience to be repeated. And not easy to delete certain details from memory—like the questions asked by the EMT guys, along with the answers you had to give: *I don't know who her husband is* (true), *I'm a new acquaintance of hers* (also true). *I stopped by to pick up a book and she told me to wait, she was about to take a shower, then she dropped onto the bed* (sort of true; they were in bed before she stopped breathing).

The EMT guys said she'd died of heart failure. Just like that, no warning. Only one thing to do afterward: answer the questions and get out. Leave that stranger lying there on the bed, some woman you'd encountered by chance a week earlier. Just get out.

They'd been in Prospect Park, walking in opposite directions along a path deep in the woods, nobody else around—that's how they'd met. Mid-week, on an empty trail.

The woman had given her a look, paused, and murmured *wait*. They'd stared at each other. Then the woman had scribbled an address on a scrap of paper and handed it over. *I'm home during the day. No one's around.* That was it.

A week later, the woman had answered her knock at the door. Smiled a little. Then led her directly to a bedroom at the back of the apartment. All fine, the way things ought to go, no small-talk beforehand. There'd been decent art in the bedroom. A couple of copper-wire sculptures, simple and clean. And a small painting of a ten-dollar bill with a bird at the center, instead of a human portrait. The bird's wings glinted. It was a strange painting—strange in a good way. There'd been a few other canvases, but the one with the bird was the best.

The woman had stripped her, then taken off her own clothes. The woman came first, then got on top, lay there for a moment, mumbled *I don't feel well*. Then stopped moving.

No one on top during sex, ever again.

The police had called a few days later: the husband wanted to talk with her. She'd told them no; they said okay, it was her choice. So it ended.

7

Three in the morning, and perfectly silent in the station.

Her next project would be an unsolicited contribution to Arts for Transit, the city's public-art program. The makeover of the Eastern Parkway station didn't amount to high art, but it did mix old and new in a smart way. Along the corridor that linked the station's two entrances were ornamental fragments, sections of old lintels and cornices and some gargoyles, which had been set into a bright-blue mosaic. With their thin gold borders, they looked almost giddy against the wall's white tile.

Actually, just a few of the Arts for Transit installations were memorable. The wall of opaque glass designed by Robert Wilson for the Coney Island terminus—*that* was pretty great. Photos and sketches had been embedded in the glass, as if in jello. The prehistoric creatures set into the walls and floors at the Museum of Natural History's station were good. So were the theatrical figures at Lincoln Center, and the terracotta beavers at Astor Place. Also the border motifs in Canal Street's N/R station, inspired by ancient Chinese designs. And those little brass humans and animals at Fourteenth Street on the A line—they were strong comic sendups of money-grubbers.

But that mock-geologic stuff in the connecting passage between Fifth and Sixth Avenues at Forty-Second Street didn't work. Nor did the mural of flowers at Lex and Fifty-Ninth Street: too eye-catchy. The hats at Twenty-Third Street's BMT station were a dumb attempt at coyness. As for those tiled eyes on the walls of the Eighth Ave. platform on the downtown side (at Canal, was it, or the old World Trade Center stop?)—their gaze was just silly, especially after 9/11. Somebody ought to vandalize that station.

Best installation? A mosaic mural on both sides of the passageway leading from the A/C platforms at Thirty-Fourth Street to Penn Station.

The mural told a story. A father wearing a suit and tie, returning from work, enters a kind of magic circus. He tosses away his briefcase and becomes a performer on stage. Yet he's still a man greeting his wife and baby, an ordinary father transformed into a juggler of roses—a companion of trapeze artists. He's living a secret life that his family will never know about.

At least the artist had managed some actual strangeness. Art should shake people up, rattle them like ragdolls. Else why bother? She'd done that once: rattled someone. While living with the parents, commuting by bike to Brooklyn College before dropping out in the second term . . . That was back when the parents were fighting all the time. And drinking more than their usual too-much. Ramping up for the divorce. The babysitting job she'd landed had been a way of staying out of the house. A whole summer with just one kid, five days a week, six hours a day, seven bucks an hour. An easy gig, for the most part.

That one day, though, the kid had behaved like a tyrant. Kept trying to tackle her, push her onto her back. Wouldn't stop laughing when she told him to knock it off. Poked at her with fingers, his eyes bright like some ugly animal's. Kept calling her a fake. You think you're a boy, don't you, he kept saying. But you're not, you're just a girl.

During the shaking, he'd passed out for a moment. Dizzy when he came around. Complained of a headache for the rest of the evening. But he'd understood: his only option was silence. For a six-year-old, he was smart. A few days later he'd been taken to the hospital, stayed there for several days—some sort of difficulty with balance . . . his parents weren't sure what caused his symptoms, maybe a fall from the jungle gym at school? They'd never questioned her about it, though.

The kid was basically okay, it seemed.

A close call.

8

Exiting the station, Blair walked to Grand Army Plaza, turning into the park. A few hundred feet in, she stood and listened.

Middle of the night, and not even a bird's rustle.

Continuing along the park's ring-road, she turned right at Center Drive. Soon she stood on the Nethermead Arches: a stone bridge spanning a low, rocky stream that descended from the Ravine. Chain-link fencing ran the length of the bridge. Squared off at both ends, the fence created a narrow, rectangular work-area whose fourth side was the bridge's parapet. Caged inside were sections of stone under reconstruction.

No clip of horse's hooves, no whir of bike-wheels. Good: no park police.

She walked beneath the bridge, where the darkness magnified the water's burbling. Emerging on the other side, she clambered up a steep incline, then slipped through a small gap between the fencing and the parapet.

The stonemasons had been at work. The parapet's arabesque was badly chipped, and the masons' plan (posted at one end of the fence) was to maintain and repair the original structure. The apertures were evenly spaced, shaped like three-leaf clovers. A good design, elegant and spare. Not trying too hard.

From her backpack she pulled out what she needed: a retractable tape-measure, a roll of butcher paper, several pieces of charcoal. A bottle of water.

The park was much cooler than the streets. A relief to be away from the Gowanus's fetid air, from her apartment, the streets, the workplace. Other people.

The indifference of the world, Camus called it. Everyone babbled about connectivity, but that was a mirage. Indifference was real.

Massaging her hands to warm them up, she set to work.

Birdsong

1

Ellen shifted her bag from one shoulder to the other. Which one bore the weight better, the right or the left? Hard to say: both ached.

At Eighth Avenue the light turned red. She shifted the bag again, then let its strap slide off her shoulder and into her hand. Time for a knapsack? Like Lena Horne said—it's not the load that wears you down, baby, it's how you carry it.

Stand up straight! Pretend there's a string attached to your breastbone, tugging lightly upward.

To think it was only June, and well over ninety degrees already. Could the soles of sandals melt?

Imagine how much worse it'd be, commuting daily by subway instead of on foot. At least there was Prospect Park to walk through each day. It was always cooler under the trees' canopy. Deep in the park every sound traveled differently; you could go there, close your eyes, and things would sound softer—not muffled but gentler. Even with planes overhead, what you'd mainly hear would be wind and water. A woodpecker tapping, now and then. Squirrels, their manic chatter. Doves in the morning. Somebody's dog carousing.

Best sound ever in the park? That light thwap-thwap of snowflakes falling slant-wise through the trees.

Ah well—six more months or so til snow-time. And maybe by then Win would be better. If not, how to get him into some sort of counseling? Christ, was he even paying his bills? And did he think *she* could, if he wasn't? That wouldn't be like him. He'd get himself into trouble, but never put her at risk. And he wouldn't take any money from her, even if she had it. Which of course only increased the pressure to help, though he'd keep resisting her. Total cross-purposes.

A heavy truck rattled by.

She shut her eyes for a beat or two, then opened them. Blinked a few more times. Dark, light, dark, light: the mind's theater, with eyelashes for curtains.

Another truck. Dear potholed Park Slope, dear Brooklyn, dear NYC. This intense affection for the city, when'd it begun? Must've been the late seventies, while sharing that tiny two-bedroom in the West Village with Dale. That was right after NYU, when she'd worked as a copy editor for Macmillan. Anne had already moved to France to be with Giselle, yes? And Sophie and Hank were on the Upper East Side. Earning good money, too, right from the start.

Housing chronology was the only way New Yorkers knew how to narrate their lives. So: first, that little place with Dale; then a bigger apartment on Thompson, also with Dale, along with his serial girlfriends—Kim, Ruth, Jean, Sue, those one-syllable women. Then that dump of a studio on the Upper West Side. Then Arnie'd become the boyfriend in 1979, and wow, what a nice place he'd had. On Hicks Street, with a view of the Twin Towers. Brooklyn Heights had been heaven, til it could no longer be denied that life with Arnie was tedious.

Then solo to Park Slope after that breakup. Her first apartment on Carroll Street, back in the mid-eighties—lovely view, leaky windows, the pleasures of solitude. And then the move to Sixth Avenue, with Paul.

Paul-and-El . . . like a pair of old shoes, loose and comfy, yet each day losing more traction.

It'd been easy to live together, yet as a couple they'd been doomed. The problem wasn't dullness. It was quietness tipping into silence tipping into a stalemate over mutually canceling desires: Paul's for a family, hers for a marriage sans kids. No wonder Paul'd recoupled within a few months of the divorce. Such a sense of failure she'd had, after that split—waking up each morning thinking, what the hell'd you *do* with those years, girl?

Not a fair question, Dale said. You're discounting the value of the experience.

True, sure, but so what? The marriage had bombed.

Though not like in Madrid. So: don't look back.

2

A train rumbled belowground; the sidewalk vibrated in response.

Her forehead felt slick. Another hot flash, the humidity, both?

Several yards down, a heavyset man waited as his gray-whiskered dog urinated on a lamppost. The man checked his cell phone, squinting at its tiny screen. Only connect, eh? Or disconnect, in Win's case. Sometimes he'd take himself to a hole-in-the-wall bar in Sunset Park, a dive where no one would look for him. Otherwise he'd sit at home with headphones and a bottle of Stoli. The only person he was regularly in touch with was the delivery guy from the local liquor store. Now and then he'd have a drink with some musician in town for a gig. But he'd dropped whatever friends he'd had, pre-Madrid, or they'd fallen away. What were they supposed to do— wait for years til he'd passed through all five stages of grief? Til he stopped dicking around and resumed his career as a composer?

He'd call soon, though; it'd been two weeks. Not to seek aid or comfort, merely to tug on the string. Useless to ask how he was; he'd just say something barbed to throw her off. *Don't worry, El, I'm dumping all my toxic waste into my music.*

The heavyset man lumbered down the street, dog in tow.

Who knew, maybe the dog suffered from depression and the man was grouchy. Perhaps they were able to put up with each other only while walking outdoors. Still, neither canine nor human spent his days digging out from under heaps of rubble . . .

For God's sake. Flags would surely fly at half-mast every March 11, in Madrid if not in New York. What had happened there wouldn't be forgotten, so why did Win keep obsessing over it?

Because of the nails stuck into the dynamite, to inflict greater damage when the bombs went off.

Because *not* obsessing over it would be tantamount to denying Mel's existence.

As if that were possible.

As-if-as-if-as-if-as-if. Say it fast and it's almost like crazy.

3

Cellphone burping again . . . Dale was probably thumbing a message while sprinting to work. One of these days, the guy would fall down an open manhole.

Daley, the dearest of the nearest-and-dearest. Without a partner or kids, but awfully good at concealing his sorrow. Never letting himself grow bitter or discouraged. A stellar guy. He was acting a bit nutty these days, though. First-time buyers of real estate tended to go bonkers for a while. Well, a mortgage must be terrifying. Renting was easy, and having no money was easy, too. Only one thing to worry about: getting some more—not what to do with it, since that was obvious: pay the bills, buy food, and fantasize about putting something aside for retirement.

Another text from Dale. *How about we watch something cozy & domestic? Like maybe* Fatal Attraction? At least he hadn't lost his sense of humor. *Or how about* Pacific Heights, *that one w/Michael Keaton where the couple buys a house and their tenant destroys their lives?*

Too bad Dale's romantic life was a series of tragicomic train wrecks. If ever a guy deserved a break! Ah, Daley-Dale . . . Why did *fat chance* and *slim chance* mean the same thing?

Oh wait, El, I just realized I can't do Tuesday, I've got another date . . . Sorry. Wednesday, maybe?

Nope, that's my Co-op shift. Lemme know when the dating dust settles.

OK. Til soon.

4

Ascending Ninth Street, coffee nearing. Just another block . . .

Her current abode was pretty much perfect. Close to the F *and* the R; small but not cramped, and serene, with good light. Top floor, hence quiet. And (value added!) the other tenants were willing to take care of Girl-Cat and Boy-Cat for a few days.

The apartment had been her home for almost twenty years now. Far longer than anywhere else—including the childhood manse, that clapboard house on King Street in Morristown with its morose gray shutters, those opaque panes of etched glass in the front door . . . Walter's parents' place, once upon a time. Rather Addams Family–ish, except for those massive rhododendrons out front. Each May they'd sprouted enormous purple flowers that the first strong rain turned to vivid mush.

Those bushes made music, Win used to say. Like a cornet pitched at B-flat. And what exactly did a cornet sound like, Win? Like a trumpet, but mellower. Did anyone actually play the thing? Yep, Bix Biederbecke used to play it. He made music like those bushes, only better. And was his first name really *Bix*? Nope, it was Leon.

How many other sixth-graders had even heard of Bix Biederbecke, let alone known his real name?

Underfoot now, a slight trembling. A very mild earthquake, or someone with a jackhammer? Neither. Merely the F train hauling up Ninth Street.

5

Ellen paused for breath. Someone was warbling from a second-story window, off-key but loud. Whoever whistled Bach these days?

Walter used to sing Mozart arias while cooking. Then he'd whistle Bach after dinner as he walked from the dining room to his study, leaving the cleanup to the kids—Edwin the dishes, Ellen the trash. *Can one of you remember to feed Clef, since your mother will surely forget? And change his litter, too, or am I the only one offended by the stench?*

Beautiful baritone birdsong.

Occasionally on the radio he'd be singing Schubert lieder, some Deutsche Gramophone recording from the early seventies. Most likely "Die Forelle," that chilling little caprice: *So lang dem Wasser Helle, nicht gebricht . . .* or a few minutes of Wagner, perhaps Tristan's duet with Isolde in Act Two: *wie sie Fassen, wie sie Lassen,* how to grasp it, how to leave it, this bliss?

Walter, Walter—like the call of a vireo: *listen now listen, listen now listen . . .* in the house on King Street he'd flit from room to room, singing. Had the man ever done anything *but* sing while living there? Ever treated the house as anything other than his own private birdcage? Indeed he had. Each night in the kitchen, he'd donned an apron and executed his cooking rites as though they were holy acts. Not that he'd ever ventured to church. Really, he asked once, you want to go someplace to listen to *God*? You can hear God in the living room—just turn on the stereo. One night he'd hummed some Bach while Win tapped his fingers on the table in soft accompaniment. Then he'd issued one of his pronouncements: God is Bach, the guy who wrote that music. Don't let anyone tell you otherwise.

Walter cooking, Nola drinking. Domestic sounds, scrape-scrape, clink-clink: *eine kleine Nachtmusik.*

At the table, Walter would hold court. *What have you been up to? Ah, I see. And this will be confirmed by your report cards?* Supervisory daddy, laying down the law. *Last month's bill from Epstein's was ridiculous, Nola. Did you simply stand aside while these two heaped clothing into shopping carts?* Scornful daddy, rebuking the spouse. *You don't run a tab at a department store, my dear. That's for bars.*

Win's fingers drumming the table.

And yet: on the wall by the kitchen door hung an old-fashioned telephone. So weren't the four of them part of the outside world, too? Yes, of course. Across that phone's rotary dial were seven digits, the household phone number, which did get called regularly—by conductors, accompanists, musicians and musical directors; by the occasional journalist or music critic; by one of the taxi services that ferried Walter to and from

JFK or Newark; by the dry cleaners, reminding Nola to pick up one of Walter's tuxes; by the liquor store, asking when to deliver.

And by Nola's parents, once in a blue moon. The sole grandparents—Walter's progenitors having been long gone by that time. What a pair, Nola's! Living like moles in the shabby apartment in Cleveland where they'd raised their only child. Poppa Herb was a mechanic, Momma Tillie a Higbee's saleswoman; neither of them could tell Bach from Bacharach. Yet they'd always called on Christmas and July Fourth, inquiring when Nola was coming to visit so they could meet the grandchildren.

They're demented, Nola would announce after each call. For they *had* met their grandchildren—just once, at Easter-time, when Edwin was nine and his sister five. Win had vomited across Pennsylvania. Nola's parents had forgotten to reserve rooms for them in some cheap motel in their neighborhood, so upon their arrival in Cleveland, they'd had to decamp to the only hotel available on a holiday weekend, the ultra-pricey Renaissance. Walter knew it well; he always stayed there when performing at Severance Hall. The hotel's massive lobby had enchanted Win, at least til he managed to get both hands stuck in the grand staircase's fretwork. The concierge had to grease Win's wrists in order to yank them free.

Walter hadn't been around to witness that. He'd gone to the room of some good-looking male musician he'd encountered in the lobby. *To talk shop*, he'd said. *Be back in a bit*, he'd added as he sauntered off. *Right*, Win had muttered. *Back soon, sure thing.*

Things one recalled of childhood, shards of a mosaic: Win's reddened wrists, Nola's silences . . .

So. If all you know of your father, whom you haven't seen since you were eight, is his disembodied voice on the radio or CD player; if you've forsworn all videos or YouTube clips of his performances; if you've elected not to show up on his Italian doorstep because you know you'd be rebuffed (else wouldn't *he* have shown up on your Brooklyn doorstep by now?); if you lack concrete proof of his ongoing existence, not having validated it in a whole bunch of years; and if, in any case, you long ago took your few tactile memories of him (his hand around yours while crossing King Street, his palm on your forehead that time your fever spiked) and squeezed the juice out of them—if all this is as it is, then whenever you hear a recording of Walter Portinari singing, is it really your father you're hearing, or just some guy who happens to bear his name?

6

Glistening on the ground: an old subway token. Worth nothing, of course. Although perhaps a token found on the street was a good luck charm?

Pick it up, then, and rub it between thumb and forefinger. For what, precisely, was luck needed? Well, getting Win into either therapy or AA would require a great deal of luck. So would snagging a decent freelance gig for September. Summer was taken care of, but autumn and winter were looking pretty barren. Two of her regular clients had just hired in-house editors; another, a nonprofit arts school, had recently lost its main donor. New trees would have to be shaken.

Dale might have some contacts. He knew the think tank world really well; maybe he could set her up with something temporary. But that'd probably mean having to commute weekly to DC for project meetings, and Washington was loathsome—crawling with Bush sycophants and war supporters. And who'd feed Girl-Cat and Boy-Cat for a whole week? That'd be asking way too much of a neighbor.

The best luck of all would be getting tapped on the head by a poetry-wand.

A pathetic wish, that.

Real poets wrote poetry, period. They didn't need tapping or prodding, didn't let the failure of a first book knock them sideways, didn't fall into endless funks. Real poets went back in the ring and threw some more word-punches til something happened—the bell rang, a new poem was won, that bout was over, another could start.

Consider the bro. He was always composing; nothing stopped him— not booze, not even Mel's death. He did it differently now, but he was still at it. In that sense, he was just like Walter. The two of them never left the ring.

As for herself? Like Nola, only without the drinking. Sitting on her hands.

Nola was the one who'd turned Win on to booze.

Each late afternoon, the waning daylight used to lure Clef the cat to the living room. He'd stretch out beneath the Steinway and knead the rug with his claws, and as evening advanced, Nola would join him. They'd sit there—Clef with his paws tucked neatly under him, Nola with her bottle of gin at her side—and as dusk fell, *la mamma* would start singing to herself. *Just in time . . .*

She'd known the lyrics of an awful lot of songs. Her voice was like Judy Garland's, with less kitsch in the vibrato. Now and then she'd snap out of it, notice her son and daughter, attempt a bit of encouragement. *Go ahead and write a sonnet, Ellen, why don't you? Edwin, go compose a sonata. When you're done, put them in the kitchen drawer. I'll look at them when I have time.*

Right. As though she went to work each day.

Actually, from mid-morning on, Nola did have a destination to reach. *All roads lead to Bombay, don't they, dear,* Walter used to taunt her. *May I top off your drink? More tonic or more gin?—let me guess.* And when Walter wasn't there, Win did the topping off. And took nips for himself.

7

A soft click overhead: the walk sign downshifting.

Ellen moved quickly across the intersection.

No dillydallying! Nola used to say that, propelling herself and her kids across the Green in Morristown. Amazing how she managed never to bob and weave. And rarely yelled. She was almost never nasty. A bit of a nag now and then, with Walter. Fifteen years in the closet with one's not-yet-out husband would make anyone snappish, though, wouldn't it? She'd lacked Walter's rapier wit, couldn't slice quick-quick then walk away.

Easy to say she should've been the one to leave. But how—an unskilled housewife with no scratch of her own? Walter would never have agreed to joint custody; she'd have been stuck with the kids in any case. At least he left her the house, plus enough money to live on. And funds for the offspring's educations.

Urgent drum-roll: incoming train.

The sidewalk hissed softly in response, like a cymbal being brushed.

Somewhere there's music, how near, how far . . .

It was crazy that Nola and Walter had ever met, let alone married. The meeting had happened in Cleveland, when Nola was twenty-two and jobless. One of those classic newspaper tales: her old music teacher had given her a ticket to one of Walter's performances, and when it ended, Nola passed by the side entrance of Severance Hall just as *il baritono* was emerging from his dressing-room. A journalist snapped a photo of Walter Portinari and a young female fan, smiling at each other in surprise.

Walter'd been smitten, but by what? Probably by Nola's body, so like a teenaged boy's: lanky, lean-hipped. Not to mention her willingness to submit to his take-it-or-leave-it proposal. He'd needed a wife. He told her he'd move her to the house in Morristown, where she'd set up base-camp and create a stage-set for his life. It'd all work out fine as long as she didn't ask questions about where he was going, what he was doing, or who he was seeing.

Had she given a thought to motherhood prior to meeting him? Apparently not. Yet the prospect hadn't unnerved her. For herself as well as for Walter, the kids would be props for the stage-set. But then the gin took over, and Walter's sexual proclivities were no longer overlookable. So when Nola started acting snippy on a regular basis, Walter leveled his verbal guns at her. *You've got no money of your own. You're a stay-at-home drunk. Make the kids do what they're supposed to; I'll handle everything else. And stay out of my study.*

Cause of *la mamma*'s death? There was an official story—an unfortunate accident—and the untold one. Plus a question:

If, one day in your late fifties, after your husband's dumped you to live with a man in Italy, and your kids have left home, and you're living alone in a studio apartment, drinking your way through your days; if, one afternoon as you're thinking *my God, I'll be sixty soon*, you consume so much gin that you trip and hit your head on the edge of a chair and lose consciousness and lie on your back on the floor and don't wake up again and are discovered almost a week later by the super of your building because your mail's piled up and you're not answering the doorbell—if you die after all this happens, then haven't you truly drowned in Bombay, even if the stated cause of death is accidental blunt head trauma in New Jersey?

Tumbling Woman

1

A life-sized bronze statue went on display in the lower concourse of Rocke-feller Center in Manhattan during the fall of 2002. Called "Tumbling Woman," it depicted a naked woman "plunging from a Trade Center tow-er," according to the newspaper.

Actually, the sculpture didn't include a tower, or anything else but the woman's body. But in an interview, the sculptor spoke of the fate of those who'd fallen or jumped from the Twin Towers a year earlier. Viewers could thus draw their own conclusions.

"Tumbling Woman" wasn't on display for long; numerous protests result-ed in its removal midway through its two-week run. Before taking it away, Rockefeller Center officials covered it with a cloth and hid it behind a screen.

The sculptor spoke about his creation shortly after he'd reluctantly permitted its eviction. "The thing is," he said, "if you look at the piece it-self, it feels like a dream in which somebody is floating. There's no weight there . . . sending the crushing, rippling current back through the body as it hits a solid mass. It feels more like tumbleweed, even though it's a mas-sive sculpture. So somebody else looking at it might say, 'God, it reminds me of falling in a dream right before I wake up.'"

2

To fall like that . . .

Blair blew on her hands to warm them.

Weightless as tumbleweed. To fall through life that way, bobbing care-lessly through the air, would be ideal. People spoke about moving through life—moving steadily, evenly, as though life were a conveyor belt. But what really happened was falling. You were born and you started falling, and you fell and fell til you hit bottom, which was death. You could fall in all kinds of ways—slowly or quickly, smoothly or roughly; it was partly up to you, partly up to your luck. In any case you had to try to make yourself light. To strip away things other people thought of as necessities. To be loved and admired, to be paid attention, those weren't necessities. Seeking what is true, Camus said, is not seeking what is desirable. Choice was the only real necessity: the ability to choose how to fall through your life. Like a tumbleweed.

People referred to her as if she were a girl. But that didn't matter. Her choice had always been to ignore labels. To be invisible, as a boy, as herself. Keith knew. That was enough.

She swept her hands lightly over the parapet.

It was surfaced in concrete, neither too fine nor too rough. Rubbing it wasn't like rubbing slate or granite. Every material required its own special type of *frottage*. It took time to learn the right way to press and rub. Too hard and the paper would rip; too lightly and no clear details could be captured.

She lay a piece of butcher paper on the top of the parapet and worked the charcoal evenly across it, keeping the pressure uniform. Soon its surface looked like roughly napped suede. She measured one of the parapet's regularly spaced apertures: eighteen inches wide, fourteen high. Using a thin sheet of cardboard, she made a tracing of its clover-shaped perimeter, cut it out, and lay it between two sturdier sheets. At home she'd make a stencil by stretching lightweight mesh across a square plywood frame and fixing the cutout to the center of the mesh. A long wooden handle would complete it. The frame would look like a square tennis racket with a paper clover in its middle.

The mesh would have to be built up. She'd sprinkle dirt and gravel across it, apply a fixative, let it dry, and test it. If all went well, the paint sprayed through the mesh would deliver a texture visually similar to that of the parapet's surface.

Getting the texture right would be the tricky part. After all that she'd be ready, armed with a template and a tray of magnetized block letters. And the same red paint she'd used for the C-notes—her trademark color.

3

Had there ever been a time when the parents had accepted Keith as he was? If there had been, she couldn't recall it. They'd always objected to him. He violated some rule simply by being himself.

It was a good thing they didn't know he'd shown her how to be a boy. They probably would've kicked Keith out of the house—and considered her a bad seed, too. As it was, she was overlookable. They'd prattled on about getting good grades, getting ahead, as if it were indisputable that she'd want a life just like theirs. And what was theirs but a prison? And now each of them was married again, to money-grubbers like themselves.

They weren't worth thinking about.

There is no such thing as great suffering, great regret, great memory, said Camus. *There is only a way of looking at things, a way that comes to you every once in a while.* Keith had his own way. You and I are animals too, he said that first time they did it. But don't talk about it. No one will get it. You're my pup, he said—not my bitch but my pup. I'm showing you how pups do it.

She rolled up the butcher paper and put it in her knapsack.

Pick Seven

1

Didn't you say you're working in a print shop, El? So why do I hear
honking?

She sidestepped a trash can. Nearby, a garbage truck stood double-parked;
traffic was backing up as horns blared.

I'm on the street, Win, I'm heading to work. It's the garbage truck
you're hearing.

So *that's* the growling sound. You're late, right?

Yup.

Remind me again where this print shop is?

It's a printing *department*. In the Brooklyn Museum.

Ah, yes. Are the offices swanky?

They're in the basement, actually. Tell me what's up. Are you composing anything new?

Are *you*?

Don't bait me.

Just wondering when you'll go back to doing your thing. Poems, I mean.

2

They wouldn't get into it now; not over the phone, anyway.

Over drinks, eventually. Easy to visualize the scene: they'd meet at
a bar, and Win would down several vodkas in a row while she nursed
a beer. If she inquired nonchalantly enough, he might hum something
for her. Perhaps a few measures of a counterpoint for one of the preludes
he'd composed, shortly before Melody left for Spain. Beautiful, those preludes—prickly yet tender. Several had been recorded a few years back. The

string quartet had wanted to record the counterparts as well, but there was a problem: the counterparts weren't actually *written*, because Win had stopped scoring. He no longer wanted people to read his scores. He wanted them to *see* the music instead, then *recompose* it, in their own heads. How were musicians gonna do that? By using the nonrepresentational sketches he was doing now. Each one was roughly the size of a normal score, but with nothing recognizable from any system of notation. Which wasn't a problem, Win claimed. If the players looked at his sketches closely enough, they'd be able to hear his counterpoints. They wouldn't need any notation.

So let's get this straight: seeing's a kind of hearing, and hearing's a way of seeing. Composition is recomposition, with the listener (the viewer, that is), not the composer, carrying the ball over the finish line. Welcome to Win's world.

Of course it'd all made little sense to the musicians and musical directors Win had worked with before Madrid. What could they do but turn away in frustration?

Hence no commissions since Mel's death.

For over two years he'd been digging himself into an ever deeper hole. He'd written almost no arrangements or advertising jingles like he used to do. And word had traveled: Win Portinari was doing wacky experiments in notation, so-called drawn music. Silly shenanigans, especially for a composer who'd already established a name for himself.

Good grief, Win. No, *bad* grief. A take-no-prisoners kind of grief.

El? You still there?

Yep.

So tell me, how *are* the work conditions at the museum?

Crappy wages. But I have free rein with my schedule, more or less.

He snorted softly.

And you're doing what, exactly?

What I always do—editing copy, proofing copy . . . right now I'm working on the text for some exhibition tiles, plus a few wall treatments. Illustrated didactics, they're called.

Who knew you could perform such tricks?

And you, what are you doing?

Right now? Listening to my tinnitus.

Your what?

Tinnitus. The sounds inside my head.

Like, when your ears ring? I didn't know you had that. How'd you get it?

Dunno. Nobody knows what causes it. It can come and go, or it can be there all the time. In my case it's constant.

But why? There must be some cause.

Silence for a moment, as if the call'd been dropped.

Win? Can you hear me?

Yep.

So is there really no cause for tinnitus?

Sometimes it's brought on by loud noises, or by stress. Sometimes it just happens. No one can say for sure.

Have you seen a doctor?

Nope. I've read up on it, there's nothing to be done. It's not a disease, it's a condition. You live with it. With me, it started after . . . anyway, I wear headphones to block out other sounds; that way, I can focus on the tinnitus. I've started sketching it.

Jesus . . . but isn't it just one sound, like a whistling?

Actually, no. It varies in pitch and volume, even in rhythm. I hear two layers of sound. There's a background *whoosh*, kind of like the sound of traffic. And then there are a couple of lines in the foreground, one sustained, the other choppy; their distance varies. The thing about tinnitus is, at first everything seems to be happening on just one plane, and then you realize it's totally three-dimensional.

He paused. Was winding down, would sign off in a moment. Had to be snared now, or he'd slip away.

Let's make a date, okay, Win? Hang out together for a few hours?

Ice cubes dropping into a glass. That tinkling noise—did he hear it as the bubbling of a creek? Or did it bang on the insides of his head, like sound waves of an explosion boomeranging between Madrid and New York?

I'm no different, El.

Different? In what sense?

From the way I've been. So there's not much point in our getting together.

Listen, you can't keep going like this, staying alone all the time, turning down work . . .

We'll talk in a bit, okay? Gotta go. You too, eh?—you've got your freelance gig. Take care.

3

What dumb game was Win playing? Drawn music, recomposition—escapist tricks.

The seat of happiness, would Win ever get to sit in it? Happiness's hassock. Not a footstool or ottoman, and not at all leathery . . . A swing-seat, suspended by a brace of unsnappable cords reaching up to the clouds—a swing-seat upholstered in blue-and-white ticking, with downy cushions and plush velvet armrests.

The sort of seat a canny dog would make his own.

What would it feel like, sitting there? You'd close your eyes and settle in, locomoted by a steady breeze, the ceaseless air of *here and now;* and as the seat swayed, you'd accept everything—uncertainty, terror, shame, loss, the whole existential kit—and your mind would expand languidly as the gas of *rien*, invisible and odorless, filled it; and best of all, you'd no longer be thinking! You'd have slipped the Cartesian noose and entered a state of . . . what, exactly?

Splendid guilt-free carelessness.

Once you were in that seat, there'd be no more warbling of songs about failure, no sleep-banishing mantras—*did I say something wrong, do something foolish, miss some boat?* No fear of irrelevance, life thinning out. Just easy swaying, all the day long.

But there was a hitch. You couldn't simply be hoisted into the seat; you'd have to clamber up there by yourself. En route, you'd take wrong turns and backslide down tricky slopes. That wasn't all. If you spoke openly about wanting to reach this perch, you'd seem on a fool's mission—since as everyone knew (though nobody liked to admit it), the seat of happiness had an eject button, which sooner or later its occupant was bound (accidentally-on-purpose?) to push. Thus *getting there* was only part of the challenge. The other, harder part: *staying put.*

So you just had to hope you'd arrive somehow, occupy the seat, and not blow it. Because this wasn't the kind of thing you could do over and over. You wouldn't have endless shots at it. You'd be lucky to get just one.

4

Coffee at long last, after sweaty backtracking . . . there it was, across the street—on the corner of Sixth Avenue.

Monday through Friday, the best brew in the Slope could be found in a dumpy bodega. *Slope Shop* was the name printed crookedly across the bodega's front window; inside, a ceiling fan whirred in all seasons. By the cash register lay a tiny ancient dog that slept all the time, grunting as it dreamt. And in the air was the scent of really, truly good joe. None of that overpriced yuppie shit.

Merchandise? Shelves of this and that, mainly useless junk. Dust bunnies in all the corners. Expiration dates long past. Throughout, a sense of pleasantest sloth.

What *was* it, the smell of the interior of the Slope Shop? Apart from coffee, of course. Some childhood scent, ineffable.

Yes: behind the Morristown house, in a far corner of the back yard, the scent of a circle of earth beneath a droopy pine tree. On summer evenings the two of them would slide under the pine's lowest branches, crawl inward, and sit cross-legged at the base of the trunk. If Walter wasn't around, they'd wait out the half-hour during which Nola would try summoning them to supper. Once she'd given up, they'd stay a bit longer so Win could use pinecones to scratch little designs in the soot. Signals to enemies, he called them. Little notes of warning.

He'd whistle as he scratched. Recomposing, maybe? Once he got bored, he'd hum an all's-clear and they'd crawl out, slip into the kitchen, and eat supper, now cold, by themselves. Then clear the table. Then wash the day's dishes. Then go to their bedrooms—Win to compose, herself to commune with Clef, whisper a poem to him.

5

Jaywalking across Sixth Avenue, Ellen opened the bodega's brass-handled door.

Ah, that scent . . . With an overlay of freshest coffee.

The proprietor, a short, oval-faced man, raised both hands in greeting. The dog by the register raised its head for a moment, then dropped back to sleep.

Morning, the proprietor said in a gruff cheerful voice.

Morning, Mr. Reyes.

He gestured in the direction of the avenue she had just crossed. A car sat in the middle of the intersection, waiting to turn. Immediately behind it, a beat-up black Lincoln honked aggressively.

Car services! Idiots, those drivers! Why can't Brooklyn have regular taxis, like in the city?

The Lincoln's driver leaned out of his window and began yelling at the driver ahead of him. Mr. Reyes clucked his tongue.

One of these days, he said, you're gonna walk against that light and get mowed down. Those guys can't drive to save their *own* lives!

Oh, I'll be fine. But thanks for worrying about me.

Your usual? He reached for the coffee pot.

Please. And one of those cookies your wife makes. They're *so* good.

I haven't put them out yet. First have some of this . . .

He handed her a paper cup filled to its brim; she sipped cautiously.

Hot, strong, reassuring.

She fished a ten-dollar bill from her pocket and handed it over.

Anything smaller? asked Mr. Reyes.

Oh, sorry—hang on a sec . . .

Reaching into her bag, she pulled out her wallet, attempting to open it with one hand while stabilizing her coffee with the other.

Put that cup down, said Mr. Reyes. You're gonna spill all over yourself!

Setting the cup on the counter, she spread open her billfold and walked the tip of her forefinger through its contents. No singles, just larger bills.

No dice. I just went to the bank last night, all I've got are twenties . . .

Rich lady, eh? Mr. Reyes chuckled.

I wish!

You could be.

What, rich?

Yeah! You should play this new lottery game. Win big-time. *Really* big!

Like what?

Like, a hundred million, he smiled. That's the jackpot.

She sipped more coffee. But I never play—I mean, I've never even bought a lottery ticket. Too complicated, all those rules.

Complicated? Nah, it's easy! You just pick seven numbers. See?

The printed form he handed her had seven empty squares in the middle. Tiny text swarmed across the white spaces above and below the squares.

Squinting, she reached into her bag in search of her reading glasses. Mr. Reyes pointed to something like a cash register sitting on the counter, near the dog. A modest white box with a small keyboard.

Don't bother reading anything on that form, he said. It's all automated! All you gotta do is pay your dollar and pick your numbers. They can be single or double digits—it doesn't matter. I'll punch them into that little machine, and you check your TV tomorrow to see if you're the winner.

I don't own a TV.

Really? His brows rose. You don't get bored?

I *do* get bored. That's why I don't own a TV.

He laughed. Ah well, I can't make it through a day without watching a little soccer. Plus the news. You know, if something should happen . . .

If something should happen, I've got a radio, so I'd know.

Yeah. Sometimes I wonder why we need to *see* everything. Who wants to watch buildings fall down over and over?

Exactly.

Or car-bombings, suicide attacks . . .

We've got ourselves into quite the mess over there, haven't we? Hard to believe we've been at war over two years already.

Ayudanos! Listen, you really should try the new lottery. It's called "Pick Seven." These crazy times we live in . . . I just have this feeling one of my customers is gonna win big. I'll even say a prayer for you!

She laughed. Who will you pray to, Mr. Reyes?

A divine figure, of course. Jesus, Mohammed, Buddha—I rotate them each week. Today's Monday . . . I have to check my calendar.

You rotate them? Really?

He nodded earnestly.

To increase the odds, he said. Look, buy a ticket! And bring in your numbers tomorrow—that's when the drawing is. I'll tell you if you're a winner. Even if you don't hit the jackpot, they're giving out lots of smaller prizes. Wouldn't you like a few extra grand in your bank account? Or a trip to Barbados with your boyfriend?

He smirked in a friendly, non-lascivious way.

Hah, she said. Right, my boyfriend, Casper the Friendly Ghost.

Ah . . . Well, escaping to Barbados by yourself wouldn't be so bad, would it?

The coffee had cooled to just the right temperature. A reprieve—a few instants in the seat of happiness.

The lottery form: seven empty boxes, waiting to be filled in.

You'll get a cut if I win, right?

You bet! Mr. Reyes's smile elongated, revealing a pair of gold-capped incisors.

All right, then. Here's a buck. Pray to whomever you like. I'll take whatever help I can get.

He grinned, gold teeth glinting.

You'll get it! Oh, your cookie—wait—I almost forgot . . .

I wouldn't let that happen.

Mr. Reyes disappeared into a small room at the back of the shop, returning with a plate of nut-studded cookies. Selecting the two largest, he wrapped them in a paper napkin.

Here you go: two for one, he said.

Thanks for the extra. And tell your wife she's a terrific baker. My mornings have become unthinkable without her cookies.

Don't I know it! Mr. Reyes grinned. She should go into the dessert business, I tell her. What do you do for work?

Me? I'm a writer and editor. Pausing, she added: a poet, actually.

A poet! You earn a living that way?

No. I earn a living editing stuff for other people.

You get any of your poems published? Like, in newspapers, or wherever they print poetry these days?

Not recently. You read poetry, Mr. Reyes?

Oh, I used to, in school . . . I still read some Neruda now and then, since I'm Chilean. It's tough being a poet, isn't it? Neruda did other things, too, didn't he? Wasn't he a mayor or something?

An ambassador. To France.

Then at least he had a salary! My niece says she wants to be a poet. Dreamy kid . . . I tell her go right ahead, but it's no way to buy a house!

You're a wise man.

He shrugged amiably. So, you own your apartment?

No, I rent.

He nodded. Yeah, who can afford anything around here? A doghouse is out of my range! That's why I live in Sunset Park. Still not cheap, but better than *this* neighborhood . . .

My brother lives in Sunset Park, too. His rent's lower than mine, and his bathroom's a lot bigger.

Hah. Well, what can you do. Okay—here's a pen, go ahead and fill in your numbers . . .

Staring at the lottery form, she pictured a large glass barrel on its side, rolling in some sort of metal cylinder. Hadn't such a contraption been on TV, years earlier?

Yes, and there'd been a blonde in a sequined gown who'd turned a crank that set the barrel spinning. And a dapper little man who'd opened the barrel's side-door and pulled out a single slip of paper from amongst the thousands stuffed in there. *And our winner is . . .*

She took the pen Mr. Reyes held out to her. Seven numbers. Why not *trio, quartet?*

She filled in the seven squares and handed back the form.

I wish you luck, Mr. Reyes replied, tipping forward in a bow.

He punched her numbers into his machine and gave her a small piece of paper.

Don't lose this ticket, it's your new life!

I won't . . . Thanks!

Folding the ticket in half, she shoved it into her bag, her fingers tunneling down til they touched leathery bottom. Then, coffee in hand, she continued her uphill hike.

6

What might be done with an unexpected influx of cash?

That Mr. Reyes, what a salesman . . . A cup of joe and a lottery ticket, for God's sake.

On the street, she sipped her coffee. An unexpected influx, okay—but what amount? Not just a couple of thousand, or even a couple of hundred thousand. Or a million, or several million. A *lot* more. A hundred million, say. A fairytale trove, pie in the sky, pot of gold. An honest-to-God windfall.

What to *do* with it? If one already had a bit of money, a windfall would surely mean something different than if one were broke to begin with. So what was *a bit* of money? In her own case: sixty thousand bucks. For oil sheiks and Bill Gates, that was chump change. For the very well-off but not truly rolling-in-it, that'd be merely a little something. For the comfy-but-not-wealthy, a decent but unexceptional amount. For a whole lot of working folks, a helluva lot. And for hundreds of millions of humans around the globe, sixty thousand dollars would be a truly vast sum. When it came to money, nobody was ever talking about the same thing. A person could have twenty bucks to her name and feel safe, or a million and feel vulnerable.

As for that sixty grand of hers, where might it be found?

Molting in an ordinary savings account.

And apart from those so-called life savings, what other assets were at hand?

Hah. No stocks, no bonds, no 401(k) (or whatever the right letter was), no Roth IRA (was that one named after Philip, Henry, or Joseph?), no wads of dough stuffed into a mattress. Her checking account balance? Rarely more than five hundred bucks. Hovering at three hundred just now, in fact. Additional valuables? No real estate. No car. No fine art. No fancy furnishings. No expensive jewelry. No coin or stamp collection. No first editions or rare books.

Rich relations? Nola'd left twenty grand when she died—a stack of bills in a safe-deposit box. Cash she'd literally forgotten about. The key to the box had been in an old, zipper-less purse in Nola's closet—found by accident. Hence ten grand for herself, ten for Win. Spent long ago, of course.

What about other relations—grandparents, aunts, uncles, some familial hero to the rescue? Uh-uh. Not a single relative would come crawling out of the woodwork or the grave. The buck had already stopped.

And the paterfamilias?

Impossible to say how much Walter might've socked away—euros in an Italian bank account, dollars in New York . . . A nice chunk of change. The man had been gainfully employed for decades, after all. But none of his money would land in his progeny's laps. He'd probably leave it all to La Scala, his favorite concert hall. Or to Bruno, who in turn would bequeath the money to some good-looking Italian boy he'd start up with after Walter's death, to assuage his grief. Then fall pathetically in love with. And get ripped off by.

Opera buffa. Singspiel.

7

Onward, freelancer!

She proceeded up Ninth Street.

Where'd her piddly income gone each year? Into poetry, mostly. Hardcovers, paperbacks, chapbooks, series and anthologies, translations, special editions. Loads of books and journals. Dale liked to say she spent more on poetry than a wino did on plonk.

Other expenses? Occasional music or theater performances. Drinks or meals with friends, though not often. Now-and-then shopping sprees. (Biggest splurge in months? A pair of second-hand Armani flats for a mere thirty bucks. Thank God for Upper East Side thrift shops.)

Freelancing was a choice, though. Nobody'd strong-armed her into it. And she'd gotten by. It wasn't really a matter of living modestly; it required magic tricks of the mind. Negative capability. And hope, the thing with feathers, Emily Dickinson's mute little bird . . .

How about that earlier question: what would an unexpected windfall actually *do* for the recipient?

It would make that person a believer. In what? In this: after all the practical impediments were dealt with, the sluicegates would open and happiness would flood in, filling all the cracks and crevices and creating a sunlit, pearl-bottomed, tranquil lake of blessedness to swim in, for ever and ever amen.

But the real impediments wouldn't be the practical ones, would they?

No, dear, they wouldn't.

Oh, come on. People in Uzbekistan weren't complaining about the non-practical impediments! In Haiti and Sudan, they weren't griping about obstacles in their *heads*. They were looking for the next meal and some drinkable water.

True. All the same, it's your own desert places that mess with you most.

At Eighth Avenue, she passed a heap of cardboard on the curb. Someone was moving in, or out.

Dale fretted about something his economist colleagues called the housing bubble. There was a big one now, they said, and it'd pop soon, and all hell would break loose. But wouldn't real estate in New York City be immune from bubble-popping? Dale said no, but in any case the issue was irrelevant for him. He'd turn blue at the gills if anyone took him out of his urban pond. And now, despite being partnerless and kidless, he was getting what he'd always longed for—a Lower East Side fixer-upper. A place of his own. Which was more than could be said for his buddy across the bridge in Brooklyn, with her rented apartment and a paltry sixty grand in her piggybank.

Dear girl, Dale would say, your real problem isn't money. After all, you'll collect Social Security when you stop working, and you can always sleep on my couch. Your real problem is you sit on your hands. Write some more poems!

Fecha Límite

1

She'd be going underground soon, into a subway station. Her next project would be called "Euphemisms."

In the art supply store, Blair stacked cans of turpentine. She'd need a roll of stencil paper; it'd be a little tricky to lift, but she could slip it into an empty carton of cans, take it to the storage area, and transfer it to her backpack when no one was around.

A guy came in wearing an American flag pin. She turned away. He could find someone else on the floor to help him. Americans were cowards, snug in their homes while people in Baghdad had nowhere to run or hide. Refusing to admit they'd been tricked by their own leaders. What did the ordinary Iraqi know or care about weapons of mass destruction? There weren't any; it was all a lie.

Keith always said animals didn't have wars. They fought, but it wasn't war. Dogs didn't send other dogs to fight on their behalf. No dog ever made a profit on a dogfight.

Right and wrong were beside the point, in any case. Art was beside the point, too; it meant nothing in and of itself, was merely a stone skipping across water. What mattered were the ripples: getting people to do something they wouldn't normally allow themselves to do. So they'd become strangers to themselves.

Keith was like the guy in *The Stranger* who said to be free, you had to make a wild run for it. That was the phrase Camus used—a wild run.

Why hadn't Keith let her know where he'd gone? Did he figure she'd tell someone, talk about how he'd shown her how to be a boy? No, that was between them. Talking was pointless.

He'd turn up. She'd have to wait, was all. You're a good pup, he'd say if he were here. Just keep quiet and wait.

2

Daylight broke as she was packing up.

On the path that led from the Nethermead to the Long Meadow, early-morning dampness muffled her footsteps. A few birds stirred; the stream made the only other sound, a low steady burbling. Next time she'd bring a sleeping bag and spend the night in the Ravine. The park police would never find her.

The time? She checked her watch: almost six. Too early to go to work; the store didn't open til nine. Go home, get a bit of sleep? Not worth it; by the time she reached home, she'd have to turn around and go out again. Might as well stick around the Slope, have some breakfast, get the newspaper. See how the fucked-up war was proceeding.

Exiting the park, she headed down Ninth Street.

There were several coffee-shops on Seventh Avenue, but the R train was on Fourth. There'd be a diner somewhere on Fifth.

At the corner of Sixth Avenue and Ninth Street, the proprietor of a small bodega was opening his shop's metal gates.

Morning, he said as she entered. You're my first customer. Coffee?

No thanks, she said. Just the *Times*.

Cookie?

No, thanks.

Taped to his cash register was a penciled notice: *The Slope Shop has a winner! Announce yourself!*

What's that about? she asked.

The Pick Seven jackpot, said the proprietor. They announced the win yesterday—a hundred million! And the ticket was purchased right here in this neighborhood. I got a notice from the Lottery Commission; that's all they'd tell me. But I'm sure it's one of my customers.

Anything's possible, she said.

The man shook his head soberly.

When I have hunches, he said, they're almost always right.

Almost isn't a hundred million bucks.

Again the man shook his head.

That's true, he replied. But it's also true you must trust what you know, here.

He tapped his diaphragm. Even, he added, if there doesn't seem to be a reason.

Yes, she said, that's true.

The proprietor regarded her in silence.

I believe in fate, he said finally. So if you learn who the winner is, tell that person there's a *fecha límite*—a deadline.

In his sternness, he reminded her of her old art teacher. The word "deadline" sounded better in Spanish than in English. More like a challenge, less like a threat.

I will, she said.

Man and Boy

1

Seven in the evening: prime time at the Ninth Street gym. Worst possible hour—every treadmill taken. No cross-trainers available, either.

Ellen proceeded to the Balcony. Mounted twenty feet up the walls of the basketball court, the Balcony was an overhanging track, a gray cast-iron oval ringed by sturdy railings whose banked surface was covered with ratty carpeting. Four warmup nooks were located in each of the Balcony's corners. The one major drawback was noise: basketball players' cries from the court below ricocheted off the high walls, and on some afternoons, nursery schoolers made an unholy racket during their play-hour. Still, the Balcony offered privacy. No serious exercisers went there.

She stretched out and began her jog, glancing downward. Half the court had been covered with tumbling-mats: an evening gymnastics class was about to start. Its participants were middle school girls, all storks' legs and long necks. They gabbled noisily, awaiting their teacher.

A man's voice summoned the class to order. A new hire, presumably. Ellen looked toward the doorway below. There he was, beckoning the girls.

All set? C'mon, let's go!

The girls lined up neatly at one end of a long padded runway.

Okay! Who wants to try a flip?

Ellen slowed down in order to watch the blonde-braided girl at the head of the line began to sprint. As the girl's hands went down and her feet flew upward, one of the man's hands reached for her stomach, the other for the small of her back. He moved with the girl as she inverted, releasing her after she'd flipped all the way over. In a few seconds she was upright again, balanced on the balls of her feet. She gave a formal curtsy.

Nice! said the man, giving one of her braids a friendly tug as she passed him. Next! he called to her successor, shorter but more muscular. Come on—you call that *running*?

The second girl picked up speed. Down-over-up, down-over-up: two flips in a row. Each time, the man's hands were where they needed to be, to protect her.

Excellent! he said after yet another girl had done a flip. See what happens when you pay attention?

The girls gathered at the center of the court as the man explained the best way to go from a handstand to a bridge. To demonstrate, he took a few quick steps and inverted himself, toes pointing pertly at the ceiling. Slowly his feet fell backward; his knees followed. Over he went, feet touching ground, torso forming a perfect upside-down U. Then, kicking off lightly with one foot, he reversed himself: torso skyward, feet touching down again. Now into a crouch. Finally rising, bowing, his students clapping.

Who did this guy resemble? Somebody in a novel . . . Yes—Emma Bovary's lover. Not the man from Rouen. The other one, the guy who took Emma horseback riding and got her to gallop.

Actually, this guy seemed more like a grown-up Peter Pan—to the girls, anyway. Now they'd formed two groups. Roy, called one girl, it's my turn, will you flip me?

Roy. Latino, was he? Mediterranean, possibly Arabic? His features and coloring were ambiguous. Not swarthy, but definitely not northern European, too olive-toned for that. Slightly wavy, dark-brown hair.

A good face.

2

Resuming her jog, Ellen paused every few minutes to look down at the court.

After forty minutes or so, the man made the girls perform a final set of stretches, then dismissed them. They filed off the court, voices rising as they entered the hallway. A door closed; the court fell silent. The man stood at its center, not moving. As though listening for something.

Roy, called a voice. A kid's, a boy's.

Ellen craned over the railing.

Roy! the voice repeated urgently.

Yeah, answered Roy. Speaking quietly into the air before him, he added: You okay, En?

En? Was that an actual name, or the first letter of one?

Ennio! Roy spoke again, sharply. *En-ni-o!* Come out now!

No, replied the voice, firmly.

Just come out, okay?

I told you, *no!*

The voice was coming from within some stuff in a corner—tumbling mats and rubber runways rolled like bales of hay.

Now a rustling sound.

You've got to come out, Ennio, said Roy. We can't stay here.

More rustling, then a small form shot out from behind one of the rubber bales: a child, not more than seven or eight years old, dressed in dark shorts, a yellow T-shirt, and sneakers. He flew across the court and through the open door at the far end. Running to catch him, Roy failed to stop the door before it clanked shut. He pulled it open and stepped out of sight.

Where were they headed? Toward the locker rooms, or the gym's front lobby? Or they could be in the stairwell connecting the basketball court and the Balcony.

Ellen jogged toward the Balcony's open door.

Footsteps: someone ascending the stairs.

She made it to the doorway just as the boy reached the top of the stairwell. Sprinting to her, he pressed against her, locking his arms around her waist. Then he moved behind her, clutching the waistband of her sweatpants.

Roy was approaching, his footsteps rapid, deliberate.

The boy's sharp jaw was now against the small of her back. His breath felt warm. Then Roy materialized in the doorway, showing no surprise at her presence. Or at the fact that a young boy was pasted against her back.

Whose kid is this, she asked.

Mine, he answered.

His eyes a deep hazel beneath straight dark brows. His gaze unwavering.

The small body behind hers stiffened slightly. As if the child were drawing himself up, trying to make himself leaner.

No, he's not yours.

Yes, he is.

His tone was calm and direct, with no hint of pleading or anger. Addressing the child hiding behind her, he dropped his gaze to her midsection.

Ennio, he said softly, listen to me. If you want to be safe, you've got to come with me.

What's going on here, said Ellen. What are you doing with this kid?

Roy dropped into a squat, his face on a par with her knees as he murmured to the boy.

En, you have to leave this lady alone, he said. Come on, gimme your hands . . .

The boy didn't respond. Roy sprang forward, planted a shoulder against one of her thighs, and wrapped one arm around her legs. With his free hand, he grabbed the child behind her. His head was nearly in her crotch. Softly and rhythmically, he began crooning the boy's name: *Ennio, Ennio.*

She raked her fingers through Roy's hair. It was thick enough to gain a purchase; one sharp tug drew his head back.

Let go of the kid!

His arms loosened. As the boy began to pull away, Roy slipped sideways and dropped onto the floor, his left shoulder bearing the impact of a body-roll. So fluid, he was—how'd he gone from stooping to sitting? Or from being in front of her to behind her?

En route, he seized one of the boy's ankles. The child landed softly in Roy's lap, legs splayed like a ragdoll's. As if the whole maneuver had been choreographed? But it hadn't been. Roy's face communicated relief, the boy's was unreadable. Hopeless, resigned, scared?

None of those. Lost, it seemed. As if stuck inside some happy-painful memory.

Now the boy wound both arms around Roy's neck, burying his face in his chest. Sobbing quietly, he chanted: *It's not safe!* Roy lowered his mouth to the boy's ear and murmured *yes, it is*. Putting his hands under the child's armpits, he urged him to his feet.

The boy began quieting, tears still glazing his cheeks. His hands fisted and unfisted at his sides.

Better? asked Roy, tousling Ennio's hair.

The boy inhaled deeply, then nodded. He was calmer now. He directed his gaze at her.

Are *you* okay? he asked solemnly.

Me? Yeah, I'm fine.

Don't ride any trains, all right? Only subways. Only the ones that stay underground. Those are safe.

What?

Thanks, Roy said to her, as though the child hadn't just uttered something nonsensical.

Look, she said, you need to explain what's going on here. Don't think I'm just gonna—

—I understand, Roy replied evenly. I'll explain, but not here.

Let's go downstairs. I want you to prove to me that you're this kid's parent.

I will. The director will vouch for me. He's in his office now.

3

The director confirmed Roy's words. And Roy was apologetic.

Sorry I scared you, he said.

The boy stood to the side, gazing out the front windows of the gym.

He seemed entirely tranquil, as though nothing out of the ordinary had happened.

Well, you have to admit it was a pretty weird scene up there with the two of you.

Yeah, for sure. Looked at from the outside, I mean. Are you a regular here? I don't think I've seen you before. I've been working here a few months.

Yeah, I am, though I don't come as often as I'd like. I guess I'm an irregular regular.

There are plenty of those. And we interrupted your jog, didn't we?

Don't worry, I was about to call it quits.

Hey, said Ennio, moving to Roy's side. Can we go outside? Let's go to the park.

He smiled, revealing a pair of dimples, the left more pronounced than the right. With the smile came a lifting of his eyebrows, dark and straight like Roy's.

The park? Ellen repeated.

Yeah, the boy said. Before it gets dark. Why don't you come too?

Saying no might risk more tears, but saying yes meant risking—what? Nothing, in all likelihood. Dusk wouldn't arrive for another hour. At the park's Ninth Street entrance there'd be plenty of people around, in case anything felt strange.

Okay, she answered. I'll meet you out front. Give me a minute to get my bag.

4

Like a pair of obedient dogs, boy and man awaited her on the sidewalk.

You need to tell me your names, said Ellen.

Roy Lince, said the man, placing a hand on his chest.

Ennio, said the boy, mimicking the gesture.

Ennio what? Roy nudged him.

Iandoli! he replied, grinning.

Ennio Iandoli. That's a mouthful. How old are you, Ennio Iandoli?

Eight and three-quarters, he answered.

Pushing nine, said Roy.

Yeah, pushing nine! And *your* name?

Don't point, said Roy, it's rude.

I'm Ellen Portinari.

You're Italian, too!

Sort of. Half Italian and half from other places—Ireland, England . . .

She's a mongrel, said Roy to Ennio. Like most everyone in this borough.

We're purebreds, said the boy. All Italian.

Is that so? Ellen said. I never met one of those.

Well, now you have!

They walked up Ninth Street. At the corner of Eighth Avenue, Ennio pointed at the sidewalk.

You are here, he read confidently. *In confusion.*

The three of them gazed at the red C-note stenciled on the sidewalk.

You read well, said Ellen.

I learned to read when I was three and a half, Ennio stated.

Really?

Yep. I can speak and read Italian, too. In Italian, this would be, um . . . *Sei qui, in confusione.*

His accent was beautiful. Not Bensonhurst but the real thing.

Good for you! Ellen said. What about Spanish, you speak Spanish, too?

The boy leaned into Roy. No, he said softly, no, not Spanish.

Ellen glanced at Roy, who shook his head. *Later*, he mouthed silently.

She shifted her bag from one shoulder to the other. Below, a train's arrival: light screechings, then silence.

There it is again, said Ennio, turning his face into Roy's side.

It's okay, buddy.

Listen, Ellen said. Instead of going to the park, why don't I buy each of you a glass of chocolate milk?

5

I love this drink, announced Ennio. Love, love, *love* it!

He punctuated his refrain by flapping his elbows. Above his upper lip was a milky light-brown mustache. They were sitting in a booth in a new café on the corner of Ninth Street and Eighth Avenue. Three glasses of chocolate milk had cost a ridiculous twelve dollars, but the place was quiet and clean.

Me too, seconded Roy. It's really good.

There was a small dip in the middle of his upper lip, a delicate indent. Picking up his glass, he drank in small sips, like a cat. Outside, the street-corner was busy with commuters returning from Manhattan.

You like the park, right? Ennio asked. 'Cause *we* think it's great.

Of course. I live in Park Slope, how can I not like the park?

He grinned.

Do you live in this neighborhood, too, Ennio?

Nope, we live in Bay Ridge. But we come here for the park. And the gym. *He* teaches there—Mr. Big-Shot!

He poked Roy in the shoulder; Roy poked back. A flurry of poking ensued.

So d'you take the subway here, or a bus?

The subway! Not the F, though . . .

Let's see, for Bay Ridge you'd take the R, right?

Yep. It stays underground.

We don't like above-ground subways, Roy said quietly.

Only subways that stay in tunnels, said Ennio. We never take any others.

Underground trains are best, Roy added. Not subways that run aboveground. Or regular trains. We don't like regular train stations, either. Subway stations are fine, as long as they're underground.

His gaze held hers without flickering.

Ah, she said. Okay . . .

Listen, Ennio—Roy tugged at the boy's sleeve—do me a favor and pop out to that blue box on the corner. See it? It's got newspapers inside. Get me a copy of a paper called the *Village Voice*, all right?

The boy peered out the window.

I see the box, he said. Won't I have to pay for the paper?

Nope, it's free. The *Village Voice*. Two *V*'s.

I know, and two *L*'s in village! You think I can't spell? I'm in third grade!

6

The boy scooted out the door and to the box. A woman and a small collie stopped to get a paper; the dog and Ennio introduced themselves, their shapes soft-edged in the dusk.

Ennio's father died, said Roy as he stared out the window at the boy. My sister's husband. Just before 9/11, that August—in a train accident.

Oh, Christ . . .

Outside, the boy was stroking the dog's thin muzzle.

I don't normally tell people about all this, right off the bat. But what you saw up on the Balcony—it's related to that accident.

Where'd it happen?

In England. Ennio's father was traveling by train from London to Manchester. He was going to a conference. The train derailed.

Was Ennio with him?

No, but he's got a vivid imagination. The other day, I was watching the news at my sister's, and I didn't realize Ennio was in the living room. There was a short segment about terrorism, bombs in public places, images of trains . . .

Trains?

Yeah. Two years ago this past March, some commuter trains were blown up in the center of—

—Madrid.

Roy paused. You know about it, he said.

Yes . . . the story was all over the news.

True, but people don't always remember. For some, it's as if 9/11 is the only terrorist event that ever happened. Anyway, those news clips really set Ennio back. He's kind of edgy these days. I take him out of the house a lot, to distract him. We go to the gym, the park . . . It helps.

He sipped his milk, gazing downward. Outside, the boy was shaking paws with the dog. Ellen pointed at him.

He's very sociable.

Sometimes. He does like to chat with dogs and their owners.

So, was Ennio's father a native Italian? Is that why Ennio speaks the language?

Yeah. Renzo came to the States when he was ten. Gina and I are Italian, too, but we were born here. We grew up in Bay Ridge and went to high school there. So did Renzo. That's where he and Gina met.

Lynch—that's your last name? I figured Irish.

Roy nodded.

Most people do, because we pronounce it that way. But it's L-i-n-c-e. That's Leen-chay in Italian.

Ah. What part of Italy is your family from?

Near Lake Como, in the north.

She nodded. My father's family was northern, too. From Turin.

You've still got people there?

No, but my father moved back to Italy many years ago. He lives in Cremona now. It's about an hour from Milan.

Must be nice to visit.

Never been there, actually.

Really?

I haven't seen my father in decades. He left when I was . . . right around Ennio's age.

And your mother?

She died when I was twenty-two.

That sounds . . . not easy.

Yeah, well. It's past.

Finishing off his chocolate milk, Roy blotted his mouth with his napkin before speaking again.

I've never visited Italy either. But my paternal grandparents spoke Italian at home, so I grew up with the sound of it.

You're lucky, I wish I'd had that advantage . . . So Ennio and his dad used to speak Italian together?

He nodded.

The kid misses that, he said. Along with everything else.

7

Outside, the boy was waving goodbye to the collie.

Thanks, Roy said quietly. For dealing with what happened at the gym.

What *did* happen? I mean, what exactly freaked Ennio out?

It was the noise of the subway—you know, under the sidewalk. Just before we got to the gym, we walked across one of those sidewalk grates, and the F train made a loud sound, like when the cars go around a corner. Ennio can handle the usual rumbling, but not those shrieks. As soon as we walked into the building, he went for one of his secret places. He's got several tucked-away spots where he feels safe. I decided to let him hide during class.

But then he didn't want to come out?

Yeah. He can be . . . strange.

The boy began moving toward the diner's door, one foot directly in front of the other, as if on a tight-rope. Tottering, then righting himself. A little game.

I imagine we must've looked like an odd pair, Roy added.

There are lots of weirdos at the gym. You're not the winners of *that* contest.

But you had every right to wonder. Hey! Roy called out to Ennio, now entering the diner. It's time to vanish, bud. We gotta let this lady go home to her supper—it's almost nine o'clock.

We ate already, Ennio said to Ellen. We always eat early before going to the gym. Not too much, though. Mr. Big-Shot doesn't like to work with a full stomach.

It's *on* a full stomach, not *with*.

No, *with*!

Another flurry of poking.

You be the tiebreaker, said Roy to Ellen.

Hate to tell you, Ennio, but Roy's right.

Ennio mock-pouted, then asked: What're *you* having for supper?

Depends what my cats want. I have two.

Due gatti! You eat what they eat?

No, she laughed, but I try to take their wishes into account. Um, I think we'll have . . . leftover salmon.

Ennio grinned. D'you ever try putting napkins around their necks?

Nah. My *gatti* are greedy, they gobble their food. It'd be a waste of napkins.

What if they choke on the bones?

Cats never choke on fish bones, said Roy.

You're right, said Ellen. But *I* did, once.

Ennio's eyes widened. Really? What happened?

Well, I got a small fish-bone stuck in my throat, and I couldn't cough it out, so I went to the doctor and he made me open my mouth and say *ahhh*. Then he reached in with a pair of teeny-tiny tweezers and pulled out the bone. I had to sit very still while he got it out.

Whoa! Like playing pick-up sticks!

That's exactly what the doctor said.

On the sidewalk, Roy and Ennio thanked her for their drinks.

You going down Ninth Street? Roy asked.

Yeah.

We'll walk with you for a bit, then.

At Fifth Avenue she stopped.

We're taking the R, said Ennio.

He pointed toward Fourth Avenue.

I'm gonna peel off here, Ellen said. Have a safe ride to Bay Ridge.

Ciao! said Ennio.

Ciao . . .

She turned left, walked a few yards, and glanced over her shoulder. Man and boy stood at a halt on the sidewalk. They waved at her, then pirouetted and took off, hand in hand.

Boom!

1

Approaching the top of Ninth Street the next morning, Ellen paused to extract a pebble from her shoe. Straightening up, she palmed the base of her bag to redistribute its weight.

What the hell was in there, a cinderblock? And that lottery ticket, where had it gone? It must be buried under the usual junk. No point searching now; it'd turn up eventually.

How crazy, though, actually buying it. Go on, indulge, cue a daydream . . . What could Win use? A new life, basically. Starting with an interview with a fancy-ass author who'd write a magazine profile on him. Everyone would be fascinated by this guy who'd been a composer for over twenty years, lost his girlfriend in the Madrid train-station bombings in 2003, then started drawing music instead of notating it in the usual way. Art galleries in Williamsburg would beg to represent him. He'd be a new *enfant terrible* with a second career as a visual artist. Everyone would applaud him for having jumpstarted a fresh conversation about musical-visual creativity. *Recomposition* would become a buzzword.

Or else he'd get bored by all that, and go back to regular notation. Whichever, it didn't matter, so long as he pulled himself out of his pit.

Phase two? A house for him somewhere in Brooklyn. Kensington, maybe? One of those nice mansions on a quiet side-street. With a housekeeper, of course. So he'd actually *eat*.

And he'd have a new wardrobe, too—all the cashmere sweaters and socks he'd ever want. And racks of shoes. Since Madrid he hadn't bought a single new pair, even though he'd always liked shoes.

Therapy as well. An hour-long daily session with a trauma-and-grief specialist, so he'd finally start reclaiming the person he'd been. Assuming that person still existed, and gave a rat's ass about self-reclamation. Or would ever get past the fact that his girlfriend had been drinking a *café con leche* at the station when the first bomb went off.

The problem with lottery-induced daydreams? Exposure of the winner's flaws of character.

Distractability, for instance. Flightiness. Sloth. Lack of self-trust.

One chapbook of prose poems published fifteen years ago, and right after the book's release, the publisher'd gone under, so the book flopped. And since then, what had she managed to put on paper? Perhaps a half-dozen poems. Three of which were published in a decent lit-mag a while back. But nothing new recently. Like, for the past seven or eight years.

Ridiculous the waste sad time. Thanks, T. S. Eliot, for that reminder.

Yet why *not* be a no-longer-writing poet? Was it such a bad thing to be a poet with an out-of-print chapbook, a has-been who read tons of poems and produced none?

Go to, you're a dry fool; I'll no more of you. And thanks to you too, Shakespeare.

2

The skateboarders were at it again, bouncing off the pedestal of Admiral Somebody's statue at the top of Ninth Street.

Well, at least they were *doing* it—playing the game, not just sitting on their hands in the dugout.

As for herself, were any other games being played at the moment? Not much since Paul. A few affairs, none torrid, with undemanding men, usually married. And always that sense of standing outside, detached . . . well, at least aloneness was real, not projected or imagined. Sometimes it felt awful, but pretty soon it went back to being normal again. And daily life was busy, the city a constant feast of distractions.

Of course there were constraints, as in feeling just barely solvent most of the time. In the money department, all the nearest-and-dearest had done well. Their mortgages were paid off, kids' college tuitions in hand, careers squared away or traded in for something fresh, like Anne's new acupuncture practice in Paris. Everyone was in fine budgetary fettle. Health-wise, too, they'd all been lucky; nobody had come down with any of the really bad stuff yet. Giselle had had thyroid cancer in addition to depression, but she was cancer-free now, and out of the woods emotionally. There'd been no heart attacks; nobody'd gone mad; nobody was addicted to pills; nobody alcoholic.

Except Win.

3

Prospect Park's Long Meadow: the fastest route to the museum. No traffic, just a bunch of undisciplined cyclists.

Edging the park's bandshell, she jogged along the path by the pond at the meadow's southern end. A few large trees near the pond swayed, leaves upturned, glinting . . . the sky pearl-gray now, emulsified. There'd be rain soon.

At a footbridge on the pond's far side, she slowed, out of breath. The path branched; one limb proceeded toward Grand Army Plaza, the other descended to the Ravine. Continuing northward, she entered a short tunnel beneath another footbridge, then scampered across the busy intersection at Grand Army Plaza and headed down Eastern Parkway. At the Botanic Garden's entrance, the sidewalk dipped abruptly toward the museum. There it sat, a kingly edifice with a glass-and-steel façade that jutted out at the front, taunting its critics.

The staff entrance was at the museum's rear. Several curators and a large crew of janitors stood in line; she joined the queue.

What'd be on the docket for the day? Updates for the employees' manual. A speech to edit for the museum director, some mumbo-jumbo for a consortium of nonprofits. Not poetry, any of it, though it did get her out of the apartment. At least she still had her hooks in the world. Unlike Win, that hoarder of misery.

Though not always . . . once upon a time there was Mel, who'd always been able to help him make light of things. She hadn't been in the least intimidated by his success. *If you compose during the day, doesn't that mean you decompose at night?* Wry, straight-talking Mel. She'd had a few nice friends, too, people Win actually enjoyed, though they had nothing to do with music. And a sibling as well, a sister she'd rarely been in touch with, whom she'd gone to visit in Madrid on an impulse. Win had wanted to give Mel a surprise birthday present when she returned. Even though he hated musicals, he'd bought advance tickets for a *My Fair Lady* concert to be held that August, at the Hollywood Bowl. That musical was one of her favorites. She used to sing *Wouldn't It Be Loverly* in her funny high voice.

She also sang "The Rain in Spain." And "Without You."

4

The queue inched forward. Someone in line was talking about the Coney Island boardwalk, how kitschy it'd become.

That boardwalk was where Win and Mel had met. Win had taken a bike ride out there, pedaled a few hundred yards along the boardwalk, and then *wham*, a flat tire. Out for a stroll, Mel had watched him try to fix the tire. She'd introduced herself, taken the pliers from him, and told him he was ruining a perfectly good rim. Then repaired the thing in a matter of minutes.

My metalworker, he'd called her after that. Which was true: she'd been the only female designer at the ironworks in Cobble Hill where she worked. There hadn't been much made of metal that she couldn't fix. She'd fixed Win, too. *Iron Man, your brother? More like Tin Man. Don't worry, if he falls apart I'll solder him back together.*

Win's best commissions had arrived while he was with Mel. The preludes, that chorale piece for the orchestra in Melbourne . . . he'd done a lot of arranging as well, and made decent money. Best of all, he'd stopped drinking so much. It used to piss Mel off, so he'd learned to settle for a bit of wine at dinner, no more vodka. After he got his shit together drinkwise, she'd left her studio in Cobble Hill to join him in Sunset Park.

Three years of it, they'd had. Happy madness, Win called it—like Joe Henderson playing that gorgeous tune on tenor, or Sinatra crooning the silly-sweet lyrics.

Then over, not with a whimper but a bang.

The queue came to a standstill as dark-gray clouds scudded overhead. A small group of janitors went through; one of them set off the metal detector. What was he carrying—dozens of keyrings?

Dropping her bag to her feet, Ellen laced her fingers together and cracked her knuckles.

Ever darker, the sky. *The rain in Spain . . .*

Skinny, Mel'd been, with long auburn hair. She always wore cool hoop earrings and bangles she created for herself. Her style was simple yet sexy: straight-legged black jeans, pointy-toed boots, loose white cotton shirts, long cabled wool pullovers in winter. No makeup.

How absurd, Win the composer falling for a woman named Melody. Like a poet hooking up with someone called Sonnet. Or a painter with a guy named Gesso. She'd called him Winsome; he'd liked that, and everything else about her. *Look at these fingernails*, he'd say, spreading her hands open. *What a screech on a blackboard* they'd *make . . .*

Crack of thunder. Any minute now, the skies would open.

Boom: the only word Win had been able to speak after the news came from Madrid—for days on end, just that one word. As if in his head he had to keep detonating the bomb over and over, so he'd believe it.

Meeting the coffin at JFK had been the hardest part. All those hours of paperwork, then standing around waiting for the plane to arrive. Mel's sister hadn't flown back to the States for the funeral; she couldn't handle any of it, didn't even want to talk on the phone. Win had to work out the logistics with her by email. She and Mel hadn't ever been close. Those few days in Madrid were the first they'd spent together in a long time.

According to the sister, Mel had liked the Atocha station. That was why they'd been having coffee there—so Mel could observe the ironwork, take photos, make sketches. Her camera'd been killed, too, so there were no visual clues as to what had made Mel happy that morning. Win was left hearing it in his head: *boom*, glass crashing, sirens.

5

A final janitor walked up to the metal detector. It let out a whistle. Fishing two keychains and a small St. Jude medal from his pocket, the janitor presented them to the guard, who waved him through.

Two curators remained in line. Closing her eyes, Ellen waited for them to proceed.

St. Jude: patron saint of hopeless cases.

After Madrid, Win had refused to answer his phone and shunned all visitors. She'd had to pound on his door every few days to make sure he was still alive. Finally he'd resumed talking a little, though never about himself, only about practicalities: filing paperwork, closing Mel's bank accounts, getting rid of her clothing. He'd sent her sister the information for Mel's life insurance company. The sister was the only remaining family member; both parents were dead. Mel's money went to her, not much, maybe forty grand.

When the bureaucratic work was behind him, Win got right back in the drunk's saddle.

The guard was waiting; she fumbled for her ID card.

Miss? You okay?

Yeah, I'm fine.

Her lips tasted salty; her eyes burned. Was she crying, for Christ's sake? Groping in her bag, she produced a handkerchief, wiped her eyes, and stuffed the handkerchief into her back pocket. Wait, what else was in there?

Her ID card.

Here, she said, handing it over.

All set, said the guard. Placing a hand on her forearm, he added: You take care now.

Raindrops falling hard, pelting now. And rumbles followed by flashes, a true thunder-and-lightning storm.

Holding her bag over her head, she skipped to the museum's entrance. Inside, she gave the bag a shake. Several coworkers dashed by, umbrellas splattering the hallway's marble floor.

Win would be slumped on the sofa in his apartment, listening to thunderclaps, imagining himself in Madrid. He'd be contemplating the absurdity of Mel's being in that city's train station on that morning, at that hour, having coffee. A knapsack left aboard an incoming train, and a clock, ticking.

All luck, good or bad, was absurd.

The ladies' room was down the hallway. Ducking into a stall, she locked the door, held a wad of toilet paper over her mouth, and wept.

Euphemisms

1

Blair stared at the subway map taped to her wall.

Prospect Park was a large blotch of green. A good place to hide.

Camus got it: every moral system started from the same incorrect notion that actions' consequences made the system right or wrong. The truth was that each person had to consider their actions' consequences without reference to any moral system. And had to be ready to pay up. That's how Camus put it. Pay up.

The night before, that boy in the park—she'd left a few scratches on his face. On his chest, too? Probably.

Annul the memory. Pay up.

That boy could've simply done to her what she was doing to him, fingering his ass. But he wouldn't stop there, kept wanting to fuck her instead. Kept wheedling, pushing. So the scratches were compensation. He hadn't realized how strong she was, much stronger than him. He'd whimpered but didn't really cry. And why would he ever speak of it—not even to other boys his own age, eleven, twelve at most? Of course he wouldn't talk about the scratches. Wouldn't recount how he'd begged her to quit using her fingernails. He'd want to appear tough in front of the others, a rooster who'd fucked his first chick in the park.

So he'd keep his mouth shut about what she'd done to him. And the chances of running into him again? Very low.

Best to avoid crap like that, though. Stay away from boys his age.

2

Which would be the right subway station?

Eastern Parkway wouldn't work. Its ceilings weren't good enough—too pockmarked. The surface area had to be smooth. Bergen, Carroll, and Smith-Ninth were too busy. Fourth Avenue was a dump, and its indoor space was too narrow.

The best station would be Seventh Avenue. It had little traffic in the early-morning hours, and no surveillance camera on its mezzanine level, where the MTA booth, fare-card dispensers, and turnstiles were located. The mezzanine's ceiling was coffered with seven steel beams in parallel rows. On each, she'd stencil a pattern identical to that of the Nethermead Arches—a repeating series of clover shapes. Within each clover she'd arrange her letter-magnets in bright colors. Glancing upward, viewers would experience something like one of those billboard series on a highway—*IF-YOU-LIVED-HERE-YOU'D-BE-HOME-BY-NOW.* The clovers, each filled with words, would read like a poem composed entirely of euphemisms:

> *extraordinary rendition*
> *to black sites*
> *where stress positions*
> *enhance the coercion*
> *of high-value targets*
> *neutralized*
> *under clear skies*

Not everyone would know what to make of those phrases. But perhaps a few dozen people would recognize what was being referred to: Clear Skies, the military program that managed US detention sites overseas. Men were extradited and held in soundproof rooms where interrogators got them to cough up—not just teeth or blood but something else, which the US government called confessions. Of course the men would say whatever their torturers wanted them to hear. They'd be broken, and they'd be lying.

By definition, said Camus, a government has no conscience. Words were fair game, and warmongers assigned them new meanings. *High-value targets* meant suspects jailed indefinitely without trial. *Black sites*: invisible torture chambers. *Enhanced coercion*: water dousing, waterboarding, stress positions, cramped confinement, insult slaps, facial holds, forced nudity, sleep deprivation during vertical shackling, dietary manipulation. After a while, not just the victims but the perpetrators, too, could get used to anything, Camus claimed. It was a matter of language.

At first, only a few people would notice her Euphemisms. Gradually, though, more and more subway riders would look up and realize they were staring at something like a coded message. And a few would start behaving differently. It wasn't important how many, or what they'd do—if they'd go out to vote for the first time, or take a nap at work, or give money to beggars, or have sex with a stranger. It truly didn't matter. Only that they'd perform some unexpected act of rebellion.

Leave a mark, a scar. Derange orbits. Otherwise art was pointless.

3

Subway personnel wore bright fluorescent vests. But the station cleaners didn't—they wore navy-blue uniforms and rubberized work-gloves.

Her MTA badge was a passable imitation of the real thing, and her trashcan was suitably scruffy. She'd scraped it with a rock to make it look beat-up.

Three in the morning, time to get to work. She took off the raincoat concealing her uniform, which she'd pieced together from a secondhand clothing shop. The coat went into the trashcan, from which she pulled a stepladder just tall enough to allow her to reach the first ceiling beam. Then the equipment: stencil, red spray paint.

Inside the station's main booth, an attendant with headphones sat reading a newspaper. She wasn't in his line of sight; she'd make no noise. He would notice nothing.

The stenciling took ten minutes, exactly as planned.

Blair paused to drink water from a bottle. Hearing footsteps, she quickly folded her stepladder and stuck it in the can. She was wielding her broom when the footsteps passed: a young couple, paying no attention.

She set up the ladder once more. The next part would take longer, about a half-hour. Each of the magnetic letters had to be put inside its clover-shaped space. She stretched one arm as far as it went; using the other for balance, she got all the letters in place. Stepping backward, she gazed up to check her work. Good: everything aligned.

Humping the trashcan upstairs, she deposited it on the curb alongside several others. There was a car-service office two blocks away. In the back seat of a sedan, she slumped and closed her eyes.

Improvisation meant waiting willingly, without impatience. Her job was to improvise—not to worry about Keith, not to give in to memory. Annul it.

The driver was playing a tape in Arabic, something religious. He intoned his prayers softly. Keith never used to pray; he said God was for people who couldn't handle being alone, and praying just an excuse to talk to yourself. Maybe he'd found a dog to keep him company. He wasn't showing up anywhere online. Perhaps he was working at an animal shelter.

He wouldn't take money from her, even if she had any to give him. He'd rather steal, especially from people who could afford to lose stuff. Take from the rich, give to the animals—Keith said that right before he stole the neighbor's car and burned it. The rich are animals too, she'd told him. Just a different kind of animal. You're right, he'd said. You're a smart pup, but watch your back. He'd taken hold of her earlobe and given it a quick twist, like when he needed to keep a stray cat in line—by flicking a fingernail at the spot right between its eyes, hard. Stunning it for a moment. Not to hurt it but to remind it.

4

Her seven lines got erased by MTA workers exactly seven days after she'd put them up.

Hundreds of riders must've seen the Euphemisms; now the words were expanding in their minds, generating unforeseen actions. Those actions would cause other people's minds to veer off course.

When the mind stayed stuck in the motionless world of its hopes, said Camus, nothing could happen. *But with its first move this world cracks and tumbles: an infinite number of shimmering fragments is offered to the understanding.*

Tumbling, shimmering fragments. Something to create—another project. But first the next one, which she'd already planned. Her paycheck wouldn't cover all the supplies she'd need to pull it off, and it'd be impossible to nick everything from her workplace. She'd have to hit up a couple of other stores. There'd be some physical danger, too, especially on a moonless night. But nothing like what people who lived in Baghdad experienced every day. When the floor supervisor at work took a coffee break, there'd be a few minutes to go to the stockroom and lift some red paint.

Why wouldn't Keith trust her enough to make contact? Or did he think he had to stay invisible to everyone—every single person, no exceptions, including herself?

Dead Ringer

1

The museum had closed to the public by the time Ellen headed upstairs to the front exit.

The plaza's fountain spurted, its plumes rising and falling unevenly. Several children stood near its low wall, giggling as they waited for ambush by water. For a minute or so the fountain danced, its geysers knee-high; then, without warning, the whole of it sprang to life, flinging water everywhere. The kids squealed.

Lovely, wasn't it, to be made curious rather than frightened by something unexpected. By the mess it made, for good or ill. Lucky kids—their curiosity still intact, stronger than fear.

She headed toward the park.

Two women were ferrying a picnic basket to the park's exit. One of them began singing "Can't Buy Me Love"; the other laughed, then joined in. At Ninth Street's intersection with Prospect Park West, Ellen paused. The women continued southward, snatches of song trailing them.

She gazed down Ninth Street. A half-mile away, the metal bridge spanning the Gowanus Canal winked as the setting sun struck it. Underground, the F lurched around the curve by the park. Steel whining on steel—how'd it go, that ballad about a train, those overwrought verses they'd been forced to memorize in fifth grade? Who wrote that poem, anyway? Robert Service, yes, one of those anthologized poets nobody'd ever heard of. *The treadless tracks, the gleamy rails . . .*

Gleamy, just the right word. Much better than gleaming or shiny. Now *there's* a word for metal, Mel would've said.

2

The two cats coiled round her ankles as she hung her coat by the door. Next to the coat rack were photos: Win with Mel, Walter in a tux at Tanglewood, Nola in the back yard with a watering can. *La mamma* used to do a bit of gardening. It got her outdoors, temporarily away from her gin.

Jesus—who could've imagined there'd be *two* women in America called Enola Gay, one of whom had a son who would name his B-46 bomber after her? Walter had transformed the other, Enola Gay from Cleveland, Ohio, into Nola Portinari. But the original name remained useful as a weapon. *My bombshell*, he'd needle her, *Hiroshima mon amour, what seems to be the problem?*

A talent for cruelty, he'd had. And Nola, for singing and for gardening while drunk. And Win for composing in his cage. And herself, erstwhile poet, for trying to equate doing nothing with feeling nothing, and failing at it.

The cats pranced to the kitchen. She fed them, then belly-flopped onto her bed. The cats followed, curling up at her feet. Within seconds they were asleep, exhaling raspy air-puffs.

She rolled onto her back, yawning. A quick pre-supper nap, why not?

3

Boy-Cat climbed onto her stomach.

Off, you oaf!

Was it too much to ask for—a brief respite, a bit of time with no thoughts at all about the future? A temporary silencing of the constant *what-to-do* refrain in her head? If no freelance work turned up soon, it wouldn't be pretty. And the museum gig was never destined to last.

Eyes open, closed, open, closed. The mind's theater, with eyelashes as the curtain. Picture it—if she were to win that Pick Seven game . . . *what-to-do*, indeed. A rat's-nest of *what-to-do*. Of course people who won the lottery had help, if you could call it that. They got advice, good and terrible;

in any case, they didn't just go it alone. Well, some of them tried to, and soon lost their shirts.

Picture it. A small cluster of men in dark suits would arrive each month for a meeting. They'd ring her bell, and when she opened the door they would stand in silence, staring at her, like a well-dressed hit-squad. The head honcho would greet her formally, then hand over a stack of checks and documents for her to sign.

Those new bonds you bought last month, he'd begin, were a smart buy.

I didn't buy them, she'd tell him. *You* bought them, using my money. I don't want to hear any details, remember? Just results.

Yes, of course, he'd murmur. We now have additional recommendations for you. We suggest that you invest in these new tech companies.

He'd offer her a set of brochures.

Don't show me that stuff, she'd say. I told you already—no details. I assume you're not screwing me over, or screwing things up. If you are, I'll fire you and hire one of your competitors. I've got more lawyers watching you and your lawyers, you know.

We are well aware of that, the man would respond with a pained smile.

Tell me about my bills, she'd say. All paid, yes?

Of course. Here's the printout of this month's spending. Apart from food and books, you spent more on shoes this month than last. Also on tickets for performances. But you have a very modest lifestyle. Exceedingly so, in our experience.

What about the house for my brother, in Kensington. Did you take care of that?

Yes, it's been bought outright, as you requested. No mortgage. Of course all his basic bills have been paid, too. And his new Steinway piano has been purchased. It'll be delivered in a few weeks.

What else?

Your co-op membership has been cancelled, per your request. We made your donation to the co-op anonymously, as you also requested. On a different note, our attorneys have nearly finished the work of setting up your private foundation. Have you made any further decisions about its mission? You'll need to start thinking in specifics, and considering who should serve on the board of directors.

I'm not ready, she'd say. Don't rush me.

Just a reminder, the man would say. There are consequences for delaying—tax-related . . .

I couldn't care less, she'd say.

All right, then. Oh—we are still interviewing for a personal assistant to help you organize your personal library. Are you enjoying the new handcrafted bookshelves? They're very nice. The artist who made them is happy with her commission; it was very generous.

Remember, she'd say, I need an assistant who actually reads poetry.

Finding such a person isn't quite in our wheelhouse, but we'll do our best, the head honcho would respond. And as you requested, we'll send someone to instruct you in the use of your new cellphone. It's got all the latest security features, which are crucial for you. These devices can be pretty challenging for a person who isn't well versed in—

—let's wind up this meeting, she'd interrupt. I have better things to do with my time. Like staring out the window. I do a lot of that, these days.

All right . . . We do hope you're enjoying your new financial security. We want our clients to *feel* happy, in addition to being happily situated. If there's anything else we can do to increase your personal satisfaction, do let us know.

At that, the team of advisors would stand up in unison, preparing to take their leave.

You're missing the point, she'd say to the head honcho. What you people don't understand is that suddenly becoming filthy rich is equal parts exhausting and terrifying. The word *fun* has nothing to do with this experience. It is *unnatural, absurd, ludicrous.* In my best moments I feel a panicky sense of freedom, as though I were riding a bike downhill with my feet off the pedals and only my forefingers touching the handlebars. In my worst moments, I find the whole experience just this side of grotesque.

In stricken silence, the men would file out.

So which was better: *that* scenario, or poverty?

Good lord.

The phone—was *that* the ringing sound in her ears? Yes . . . must be Dale, with news about the closing date for his apartment.

She reached for the receiver.

Sorry to bother you, El. You asleep?

Win? No, just dozing. What's up?

I've heard from Mel's sister.

What? She phoned you?

No, emailed. I happened to check my email this morning. She's coming to New York, arriving Wednesday.

When's the last time you spoke with her?

Not since we made the arrangements for . . . I didn't hear from her after that. She's been in Madrid all this time. Teaching ESL classes.

But she's coming back to New York? Like, for good?

Didn't say. I'll find out, I'm having dinner with her on Friday.

Look, don't get pulled into listening to stuff you don't want to hear . . . what's her name, anyway? I don't think you ever mentioned it.

It's Maria. Talk to you later.

4

Both cats perched at her side, ears upturned.

She tossed the phone to the foot of the bed.

What was this woman doing—contacting Win out of the blue like that, two years after the fact? Did she look like Mel, *sound* like her? What if she ordered a bottle of wine and started recounting every detail of that morning at the station? How messed-up would that be?

Well, at least he'd be drinking with a live girl, not a dead one.

Maybe this Maria would distract him. For sure she'd give him a chance to talk about Mel. Maybe for a few minutes he'd focus on the happy madness. Perhaps he'd be able to close his eyes and hear it, the music of it, of his love. Just that, nothing else. Maybe he'd realize he could write it down. Not draw it but notate it, so it could be played.

Boy-Cat and Girl-Cat hopped to the floor and looked up, inquiringly.

All right, *gatti*. Time to get up—it's *my* suppertime now.

Nothing to Report

1

You home, Ellen? I'm downstairs.

Dale—what was *he* doing on this side of the river at 7:00 a.m.?

You okay, bud?

Yeah, fine. I had a date last night and ended up here in the Slope, where she lives . . . you awake?

Up and dressed. Want a cup of coffee?

Buzz me in!

He looked tired. Not unhappy, just sleep-deprived. Sprawling on the sofa, he patted its cushions.

Hey, you cats, get up here next to me! What a night I've had . . .

I'm all ears, but I gotta leave at a quarter of, no later, okay? Oh, have you already closed on the apartment?

Nope, it's been rescheduled again. For next Tuesday. Anyway . . . I need to tell you about my date. So, I get to this woman's apartment after a really nice dinner with her. She's a printmaker, has a studio in Gowanus, does interesting work. We ate at that place you took me to once, remember? On Eleventh. Then we go back to her place, and we're talking and laughing and, um, preparing to do other stuff . . .

Really? First date?

Second, actually. Not my usual M.O., as you know. But in this case it felt like it wouldn't do either of us any harm and might actually do some good. So . . . things are starting to move in that direction, and then her cell phone rings. She glances at it to see who it is, and it's her ex, only I don't know that. But it soon becomes obvious, because she answers, and they have words—is that the right expression, do people still say that? Then she hangs up and tosses the cellphone across the room.

Throws it, you mean?

Yep. It doesn't break, though. Then she spends fifteen minutes telling me about the ex's unreliability, how he still has stuff of hers he hasn't returned, blah-blah, and I'm nodding and thinking, I'm outta here as soon as I can get a word in edgewise. But then she stops talking, starts laughing, and says, well, are you totally bored and irritated with me now? And I say to myself, why not tell her the truth? So I say yeah, actually, I am, pretty much. And she gives me this relieved look and says thanks, you're really great, I've been a total asshole, do forgive me, I don't know what got into me, I've been under a bit of stress, can we start over.

Huh.

Yeah. Kind of impressive, actually. And something in me says well, okay, why not. So . . . we do. And it's, um, it's quite nice. Like, really. And then, at around five in the morning, I wake up, and she's awake too. She turns and looks at me, and her look is . . . trusting, I'd call it. Calm and trusting. And then she goes, can I tell you about my brother?

Her *brother*?

Yeah. My reaction as well. She sees my puzzled face and goes, yeah, I know it's not the first thing you were expecting to hear, but I figure if you're the kind of man I take you for, you'll understand why I have to tell you. So I go, okay, tell me about him. She proceeds to tell me that when her mother died, she was sixteen and her brother was twelve. They were both home with their father when they got a call from the police saying the mother'd been killed driving home from work. Somebody'd hit her head-on.

Jesus.

Yeah. So Teresa—that's my date's name—she can't remember much about what happened after that phone call, except that the father kept walking around the room going *oh God, oh God*, but the brother said nothing. Just stood there staring into space. Then after a while the brother walked out the front door, without a word. No coat or anything. The father doesn't even notice at first, he's so distraught. But then he pulls himself together enough to realize not only is his wife dead, but his son is AWOL. So he and Teresa start calling around to the brother's friends' houses, but no one's heard from him. The cops tell the father to just wait, the kid will turn up. But the father insists on looking for him—the father's basically going nuts at this point—so he and Teresa get in the car.

Wait, where's all this taking place?

About fifteen miles from New London, Connecticut. You know, where the Navy has that submarine base? So anyway, Teresa and her father drive around a bunch of suburban neighborhoods, but they don't see the kid anywhere. Then they go to the base itself. It's a November night, cold, rainy. They go to the guardhouse and ask for help, saying the kid's missing, his mother's just died, et cetera. One of the guards gets a flashlight, and they start looking, and before long they find the kid. He's a couple hundred yards from the main entrance, and he's huddled with a guard dog. Lying on the ground with his arms around the dog—the dog having realized the kid's not a danger but is *in* danger. Both the kid and the dog are soaking wet.

Dale leaned back into the sofa, closing his eyes.

And then . . . ?

Sorry . . . I'm kind of wired and tired at once. Okay, so then Teresa stops talking, sits up in bed, and tells me she woke up just before I did, right in the middle of a dream in which I found the dog.

You what?

Uh-huh. She tells me that in her dream, *I* had the dog in *my* apartment. The very same dog, I mean. Only much older, of course—older but basically fine. And that's why we met, she says. It wasn't pure chance, and it wasn't because of Match.com. It's because I found the dog.

Hello? What?

Yeah, exactly how I reacted: what on earth are you talking about? So she goes, I forgot to tell you—the dog disappeared. Vanished.

In real life, you mean?

Yeah.

But how would *she* know that?

Again, my question. Teresa said she and her father drove the brother home that night, dried him off, warmed him up and—long story short, after a few months the kid seemed more or less okay. I mean, as okay as possible, given that the mother was dead. . . . Then one day about a year later, he said, let's go see the dog who helped me. That's how he put it: the dog who helped me. So they all drove to the sub base and stopped at the guard station and asked if they could see the dog. One of the guards recognized the three of them, and told them the dog hadn't been seen since that rainy night.

And?

Well, the brother got really upset when he heard this. Teresa said he's never really gotten over it; he's been in trouble ever since. Struggled through high school, flunked out of college, can't hold a job, can't stay in a relationship, et cetera. On top of which, Teresa's ex-boyfriend was supposedly a buddy to the brother, but after Teresa split up with him, the ex basically ditched the brother.

Dale put down his mug and rubbed his eyes.

I think Teresa's been feeling helpless all these years, he said. You know, watching her brother get fucked up. That image of the kid in the rain, lying there with his arms around a dog . . .

So what happened? Between you and Teresa, I mean.

Right before I left, she told me she would let her brother know the dog's okay. She said, I'm gonna tell him I've talked with someone who found out where the dog went. I'll tell him the dog lived til it was very old, with someone else who used to work at the base—an old officer. I'm sure my brother will believe me. I've never lied to him, but now that I've had this dream, I'll do it—I'll tell him. I think it'll help him.

Doesn't that sound kind of crazy to you, Dale? Why would Teresa's brother believe her story?

Because he's desperate. Teresa plans to tell him that after the dog disappeared, a buddy of this old officer saw the dog wandering around a nearby neighborhood, lost and thin. The buddy recognized the dog and decided to adopt him. A happy ending, get it?

It's awfully convoluted, Dale.

Yeah, but that's precisely why the brother will buy it. It sounds like real life. I think Teresa's right—she *should* tell her brother somebody found the dog. Maybe all he needs is to hear the dog's okay, and his life will turn around. Sometimes it just takes the smallest thing.

2

Why had Dale always been her favorite of the nearest-and-dearest? Because he believed in uncomplicated answers to complex questions.

Sure, he was the director of economic research at a big think tank. But in his personal dealings, Dale used simple emotional logic; he didn't like digging verbal trenches. Here he was, sympathizing with some woman he'd just met who had a messed-up brother, and was possibly delusional herself. But in Dale's world, what mattered was finding the dog.

Is there any more coffee? he asked.

Yeah, help yourself. But wait, I wanna see if I've got this right. The dog vanished—in real life, I mean—and then in Teresa's dream, *you* found the dog. That is, the dog showed up in your apartment. Yes?

Yes.

So what are you planning to do about it?

About what?

About the dog.

Hah. Yeah, the dog. What I'm planning to do is go home, take a long hot shower, and get to work.

Good idea. By the way, how'd you manage to extricate yourself this morning?

Not a problem. After Teresa told me all this stuff, she said she wasn't expecting me to respond. She was just glad I'd been willing to listen. But you know, she wasn't clingy at all. Seemed entirely normal, in fact.

Boy, you sure know how to pick 'em, Dale.

I knew you'd say that! Thing is, Teresa's not making any of this up, I'm sure. She didn't lay all this stuff on me for fun, or to mess with me. She's not crazy, I swear. She really *is* glad I found the dog. In the dream, anyway.

Doesn't make it any less wacky.

Depends how you look at things. Anyway, thanks for the coffee, I needed it!

I'll walk you to the station. We gotta mobilize, though.

Mais oui. I'm ready. When we both have more time, I'll ask how *you* are.

Still at the museum. Nothing more to report.

Oh yes there is, darling. There always is.

3

Entering the Slope Shop, Ellen bought coffee and a paper.

Is that your boyfriend, asked Mr. Reyes. That guy you just waved to.

Nah. A very dear friend. Known him since college.

Ah. Looks like a nice man.

He sure is.

As she put her hand on the door, preparing to exit, Mr. Reyes snapped
his fingers.

Oh, wait, he said. The numbers for the Pick Seven game, the jackpot
numbers . . . they were announced on TV, the night before last. And there's
been a winner, someone who bought a ticket in this neighborhood! Isn't
that great? I wrote down the winning numbers for you, but you didn't stop
by yesterday.

Ah yes. I forgot all about it.

You know, there are only four million or so people in Brooklyn, and
they don't all buy tickets in Park Slope. So if you've bought a ticket around
here, your chances are actually pretty good!

He pulled out his wallet, extracted a piece of paper, put on his glasses,
and recited seven numerals, slowly.

4

Onrush of vertigo, as when sitting up too quickly after giving blood. A
sizzle in the eardrums.

She pulled open the shop's door, stared at the half-full cup of coffee in her hand, and willed it to drop. The liquid splattered her jeans and pooled around her feet.

Oh, look what I've done, Mr. Reyes . . .

Don't worry, he called as he scurried to a sink at the back of the shop. In a moment he returned with a mop and a handful of paper towels.

Here, wipe off your pants! he ordered.

She took the towels and did as he instructed. He mopped the linoleum as she held the door open for him.

I'm so sorry . . .

Her stomach kited; she leaned against the doorsill, sweat breaking out everywhere—forehead, neck, armpits, chest.

No problem, Mr. Reyes said as he swabbed the threshold. Somebody drops their coffee here at least once week, I'm not kidding!

Mop aloft, he headed toward the back of the shop.

She gazed upward. Patterns in the shop's tin ceiling, shapely blossoms in rows . . .

What'd just happened—no, what *seemed* to have just happened—was a colossal error. A beyond-crazy mistake. Mr. Reyes could not have said those numbers. She'd heard him wrong.

She wiped her face with the back of her hand. Bye, Mr. Reyes, she called out. I'm late for work, gotta run!

On the sidewalk, she forced herself to move. Walking (or was this stag-gering, or reeling—would she pass out in the middle of the sidewalk?), she headed down Ninth Street.

Pick Seven, the game was called.

Six-three-eight-six-oh-three-three.

Trio, quartet.

Total Silence

1

Win was home. At this hour he'd have to be; he didn't make early-morning appointments. So why wasn't he answering the door?

A few more thumps produced him. The deadbolt slid sideways and he stood in the doorway, wearing a T-shirt and sweatpants, headphones slung around his neck.

El, what are you doing here? What time is it? Come in . . .

Jesus, I thought you'd never hear me! It's early, not yet ten.

He gave his head a quick shake.

You okay, Win?

I'm listening to my tinnitus, he said. Aren't you supposed to be at the museum, hanging out with the mummies?

I need to talk with you. Something's happened. I've just—I've won a whole bunch of money . . .

He frowned.

You what?

I won a lottery, Win. The man who sold me the ticket just told me the numbers, and I've won. It's this new game, you pick seven numbers—anyway, it's got an unbelievably huge jackpot.

Slow down. The man who sold you . . . ?

He's a guy who owns the bodega where I get my coffee. Near where I live. The day before yesterday, he talked me into buying a lottery ticket, and this morning he told me the winning numbers. When I heard them, I left without telling him I'd won. Nobody else knows. I came straight here.

Win began laughing softly.

Ellen, for God's sake, how d'you even know this guy got the numbers right?

I'm sure of it. Mr. Reyes takes this stuff very seriously.

Oh, come on . . . Did you look in the *Post*, or go online to check the numbers?

I came directly from Mr. Reyes to you. I'm totally freaked out.

Sitting on an arm of the sofa, Win shook his head, his smile partly a scowl.

You're acting like a kid, he said. Not your usual style.

Check the Lottery Commission's website for me. Please!

Can't, he said. My computer's in the shop for repairs. I threw it against the wall the other day.

You're kidding.

Nope. So, your lucky day, a pot of gold?

Win, please, come with me! Let's get the *Post*. I need you to tell me if this is really happening, I'm too agitated . . . I can't even take a full breath. I feel queasy.

He stood. Let's hope they've got extra copies of yesterday's paper, he said, or I'll really be wasting my time.

2

On the sidewalk, she took his elbow.

Listen to me, Win. We're just gonna get the newspaper and check the numbers. We can't let anyone around us know what's going on. Total silence, all right?

In the morning light his face looked sallow, the shadows under his eyes more pronounced than usual.

All right, he replied. But if you've won a couple hundred thousand bucks, you'll at least take me out to breakfast?

The jackpot's a whole lot bigger than a few hundred thousand. And if I've won, I'm gonna get right back on the subway and go home.

To do what? Consult with your cats, see if they approve?

I'm serious, Win. I'll need time.

He clucked his tongue. Like, til tomorrow?

Listen to me! If I've won, I'll need to figure out what to do. How to, you know, to live with it . . . I mean, it'll be the end of everything—of my life as it is . . .

They walked a few paces in silence.

You know, Win said quietly, I'm sure you haven't won. But do you realize you're making it sound like you've received a death warrant?

His smile was tight: he was angry.

I don't mean it that way, she said. It's just such a shock, so absurd!

It wouldn't be the end of your life. Why make it sound that way?

Look, I know . . . I'm just in a total tizzy.

You sure are. The newspaper kiosk is over there. Let's go check the numbers.

3

It couldn't be. Couldn't couldn't couldn't.

She checked herself in the small mirror by her apartment's front door. Glassy-eyed, and slick with sweat. The umpteenth hot flash of the morning.

Just sit the fuck down!

Was it only a couple of hours ago Dale had been here, talking about Teresa? *In my dream you found the dog.* What exactly had occurred since then? Dale had walked with her to Mr. Reyes' bodega. She'd purchased a coffee. Mr. Reyes read out the numbers, and she dropped the coffee. Somehow managed to get from Park Slope to Sunset Park . . . that part was a blur. She'd taken the R train, yes.

Then she and Win bought several newspapers. Then they went to an internet café, to double-check the numbers on the Lottery Commission's website. After which Win had called the Commission. He'd asked about the rules of the Pick Seven game. Inquired if there'd been a winner of the mega-jackpot.

Yes, the person on the phone confirmed, there was a winner. The Commission was waiting for that person to come forward. The jackpot totaled a hundred million dollars. The winning ticket had been purchased in Brooklyn. Did Win know who the ticket-holder was?

No, said Win, but thanks for the information.

Pulling the ticket from her wallet, she stared at it.

Seven numbers, black against a yellow background.

Another wave of dizziness.

Girl-Cat hopped up onto the table, nuzzling her wrists. Boy-Cat rubbed his cheeks calmly against her ankles.

She kept her eyes closed til the vertigo passed, then turned over the ticket.

The Pick Seven rules were written in plain English, exactly as Win had heard them over the phone. The winner had to notify the Commission within thirty days of the date on which the winning numbers were announced. The money wouldn't go back into the pot unless the winner forfeited the funds by not claiming them. The winner was under no legal obligation to reward the seller of the ticket. The Commission would provide the seller with one-half percent of the jackpot.

What did the calendar on the wall say? Twenty-eight days to go, since today was the second day since the announcement. By now, Mr. Reyes might've been informed that the winner had purchased the ticket at his store. He'd have no idea who the buyer was, or whether that buyer would actually check the numbers.

Not a good idea to return there. She couldn't lie to his face, if he asked.

This moment, this one, this moment only. The present, the only real time. Stay in it.

In my dream you found the dog.

The nearest-and-dearest—what on earth to tell them? *I've got news for you?* Oh Jesus fucking Christ.

She stood, filled a glass with water, drank it, sat down again.

At first they'd think she was joking. Then Sophie would kick into gear and insist she go to a lawyer—like, immediately. At which point Hank would start laughing maniacally, his way of being very nervous. Anne and

Dale would blabber *oh my God* over and over, paralyzed by astonishment. Giselle would babble in French—*mon Dieu mon Dieu mon Dieu* . . . but then they'd go silent, each of them. Because what more could they say? They'd be waiting for her to *do* something.

Had her friendships with them ever been put to a test like this, a preposterousness exam?

Say nothing, for now.

The ticket lay on the kitchen counter, a wee scrap of yellow and black. She held out her hands, palms up, watching them tremble.

Feeling, what was she *feeling*? An all-over numbness. How was it possible to be in possession of a lottery ticket worth a hundred million dollars and not *feel* a goddamn thing?

Because this wasn't real, hadn't actually occurred. Not truly. It lay in the future. The future was an abstraction.

So why not hand in the ticket right now, make this whole thing real?

O fuck.

More dizziness. Wasn't it trying to tell her something?

Her laptop lay open on her desk. She typed *haste* into the search-bar and clicked on a site of popular quotes.

Whoever is in a hurry shows that the thing he is about is too big for him, said Lord Chesterfield.

Make haste slowly, said Ben Franklin.

No profit grows where is no pleasure ta'en, said the Bard.

Okay, take a breather, then. Almost a whole month to go. The ticket would be safe.

Just wait.

TWO

Now What?

1

The Balcony was empty. In the nook at the far corner, the windows were wide open. That'd be the coolest spot.

Lying on the mat, Ellen closed her eyes.

It was nearly 2:00 p.m. by the time she finally made it to the museum. She'd called at 1:30, blaming her lateness on a delayed doctor's appointment. The head of the department was waiting by her cubicle when she arrived. Instead of barking at her, he'd asked if she could stay on as a free-lancer til they'd found the right full-timer to replace her, which might take six weeks. Oh, and was she feeling all right? She looked a bit flushed. Was the air conditioning working okay?

Yes, the AC was fine. And yes, she'd stay. Not for six weeks, though. Two weeks was possible.

On her back on the mat, eyes closed, she pictured a sugar dispenser, a squat glass jar with a metal pouring-chute. It sat on her kitchen counter, full of a rust-colored blend of sugar and cinnamon.

The ticket lay buried in what looked like dirty sand.

Sugar and spice, everything nice . . .

There *had* to be a hitch. Some sort of exclusion clause in the lottery rules. Yet she'd called the Commission herself and taken notes while on the phone. The computer program for the game altered the sequence of numerals every five seconds. To win, the numbers had to coincide with the sequence at the exact instant when the ticket vendor entered them into the system. If you won, you had to hand-deliver your ticket to the Commission by 5:00 p.m. not later than thirty days from the date on which the winning sequence was announced.

I'll think about it when I have time, Nola used to say. But now there was nothing to think about—the jackpot had been won, it was hers. Then how about this: *I'll* feel *about it when I have time.* Feeling's not your strong suit, Mel said once. Afraid of it, aren't you? Listen, Win's getting over his fear of it, so you can too. Practice!

If Mel knew about the ticket, she would burst out laughing. My God, she'd say. What a banana peel you just slipped on!

2

An old leather punching bag hung in one of the far nooks. Ellen gave it two whacks, one with each fist, then flicked each hand to make the pain go away.

Good lord, how stupid could a middle-aged woman look?

Don't hit the bag again. Just jog for now. Just run in slow circles.

Twenty minutes, then a cool-down.

She checked her watch. Five more minutes til the start of the class on the court below. A balance beam and tumbling session for junior high girls with Roy Lince as instructor, according to the signup sheet on the door.

She leaned over the railing. Several balance beams had already been set up. A dozen girls—seventh and eighth graders, dressed in bright leotards—entered the court. Peeling off sneakers and socks, they began stretching. A minute later, the door opened and a boy skipped in.

Ennio. In the same shorts but a different T-shirt.

He took off his shoes and socks and joined the girls, who greeted him by name. After a few minutes, three girls went over to a high beam and conferred in low voices, giggling. Then the tallest girl placed her hands on the beam and popped up, crouching unsteadily before standing.

Go! cried the other two girls.

The door to the court opened.

Roy, wearing a gray sweatshirt and black sweatpants. And a frown.

Get off there, he called loudly to the girl on the beam. You know better than that, Alma! Haven't I told all of you *never* to use the high beam when you're unsupervised?

I know, the tall girl said sheepishly. I was just—

—impatient? Roy cut in. He slipped off his sneakers and socks and tossed them to the side.

Get back on the beam, Alma, he said. But do a proper mount this time.

The girl mounted the beam. Ennio began touching his fingertips to his toes. After performing this stretch a few times, he lay back on the mat, his arms at his sides. He kicked his legs upward a few times, alternatingly, then dropped them to the floor. His upward-drifting gaze met Ellen's as she leaned over the Balcony's railing.

His mouth opened in surprise.

Shhh, she gestured with a forefinger at her lips.

After glancing in Roy's direction, Ennio grinned and flashed her a quick thumbs-up.

The girls did beam mounts and dismounts on the high beam, then practiced one-leg balancing, rolls, and lunges on the low beam.

For Alma (evidently the star talent), there was a lesson in hand-walking. To demonstrate, Roy leapt onto the high beam and inverted himself. Placing one hand at the beam's left edge and the other a few inches behind on the right edge, he took several hand-steps. Then he brought his legs down lightly, his feet echoing the placement of his hands.

Got it? he asked the girls. Now watch again!

He went through the moves once more, repeating his instructions. Watching, Ennio moved his hands in the air, mimicking Roy. As Roy's feet dropped onto the beam, Ennio hopped lightly in approval, then looked upward, checking. Spotting Ellen, he gave a little wave.

At that moment, Roy glanced at Ennio. His gaze shifted rapidly upward, then back down to the beam on which a girl was crouched, preparing for a forward roll.

Okay, Patty, he said, moving to the girl's side. Watch closely, everyone! Listen up! Remember, the power's in your thighs and knees. Round back, loose neck . . . don't take off too hard! Steady!

All eyes were on the beam. Which meant no one was watching Roy—who, while maintaining an unbroken visual focus on the girl-about-to-roll, lifted one hand slightly and waggled his fingers at Ellen.

3

Now what? said Ennio.

The class had ended, and they stood in an empty court. She'd been summoned from the Balcony by a giggling Ennio; Roy had feigned surprise, then given her a wink.

I dunno . . . are you hungry? he asked Ennio.

You bet! We didn't have time to eat before we got here, remember? Did *you*? Ennio added, turning to Ellen.

I think not, said Roy. Ellen has that lean and hungry look.

Good grief, I'm being compared to Cassius!

Well, do you scheme and plot? Do you have secret plans?

Her stomach pitched; she forced herself to smile.

Uh, no more than average.

Then how come that starved look of yours? How many miles did you jog up there, anyway?

Forget it . . . how come you're quoting *Julius Caesar*?

A tenth-grade class project. I actually liked that play.

Who's Cassius? asked Ennio.

A guy out to get another guy, Roy answered. In a play. The other guy was Caesar, the emperor of Rome. The two of them were having a fight.

Rome, like in Italy?

It's a long story, said Roy. Maybe Ellen can tell it to you over the dinner we're going to treat her to. Don't you think she looks like she's starving?

Yeah, said Ennio, she does!

Summarizing the plot of *Julius Caesar* for an eight-year-old wasn't easy.

He died *how*?

Which guy.

The one who killed Caesar.

Brutus? By impaling himself. Running onto his sword.

Whoah . . . that sounds hard to do!

Not much fun to think about, said Roy. Didn't I tell you the story was gory?

A gory story!

We're big on rhymes around here, Roy said to Ellen. And stuff like, what's it called, when the first letters are the same . . .

Alliteration.

Yeah. Pass the *hummus*, Ennio, you're *hogging* it.

They were eating Middle Eastern food at a small cafe on Third Avenue in Bay Ridge. To get there, they'd taken the R train.

Were the R's announcers as goofy as the F's? she'd asked Ennio en route.

I don't know, he'd replied. We never take the F, the R is the only train we can take to get here. It stays underground. When we finish eating, I'll show you where my mom and I live.

And, said Roy, we'll make Ellen some tea.

4

In the kitchen of Gina's apartment, a note for Roy lay on the table. His sister was at the movies with a friend and would be back by ten.

Roy prepared tea while Ennio showed Ellen his room: games, books, trading cards.

Hey guy, start winding it down, said Roy. You've stayed up later than usual. It's Ellen's fault.

Yeah, she said. And so I'd better—

—wait! said Ennio. Read me a story.

En, you're a little beyond that, aren't you, said Roy.

Just one!

Not a story, Ellen said. I'll recite a poem instead.

Recite?

Speak it aloud, from memory. Like reading, but without a book.

What poem will you recite?

Get your PJs on first, said Roy. And brush your teeth.

As Ennio went off to the bathroom, Roy lit the bedside lamp and pulled down the shades.

Thanks for bearing with him, said Roy. He likes you, I can tell.

He's a good kid.

In the room's low light, Roy's skin appeared darker than usual, his hair nearly black. Oddly familiar, this man, yet how could he be? She'd met him just the other day. Everything was strange, there was no familiar anymore. That category had been deleted.

Her stomach kited again; a hot flash commenced. She was somewhere in Bay Ridge, with roughly thirty bucks in her wallet and not more than ten times that sum in her checking account. Standing in a boy's bedroom talking with some guy she barely knew, a guy who'd deem her crazy if she were suddenly to announce *guess what, I've just learned something, I've got this ticket in a sugar dispenser and—*

Anybody home? asked Roy, waving a hand lightly before her eyes. You all right?

She returned his gaze.

Sorry . . . lost in space. I've really enjoyed myself this evening. I don't hang out with boys very often.

He let out a soft laugh. We're not *that* scarce, are we?

Young ones, I mean.

Ah. Well, it's good for Ennio to be with other adults. He's been leery of grownups since his father died. He can get sort of . . . testy.

He doesn't seem that way.

Tonight he was fine. But he sometimes behaves like a kid half his age. From day to day, you don't know which kid you're gonna get. And when he acts out, it's not pretty.

She sat at the foot of the boy's bed.

Ennio's father—what was he like?

Roy turned one hand palm upward, in search of a starting-point. Ennio reentered the room, flinging himself on his bed.

Come on, Ellen, the poem! Recite it!

How about *please*, said Roy. Say it in Italian if you want.

Per favore!

"*'Twas brillig*, Ellen began, *and the slithy toves . . .*"

After reciting the whole of "Jabberwocky," she explained that its author adored strange words and Cheshire cats. Her own cats grinned like Cheshires, but right now they were frowning, since dinner was late. Time for her to go home.

I'll walk you to Eighty-Sixth Street, said Roy. Gina'll be here in a few minutes. To bed, En!

<h2 style="text-align:center">5</h2>

They waited to leave the apartment until Roy's sister returned.

Gina bore no resemblance to her brother. Her body was stockier, her gestures rapid, her voice sharp-edged.

I'll call you tomorrow morning, she said to Roy as she sifted through the day's mail. Gotta make a few calls now. You're taking him to day-camp, right? Nice to meet you, she added, nodding at Ellen as she headed toward her bedroom.

After leaving Gina's, they passed in front of Roy's building, one block over.

He pointed to the second floor.

Those are my windows, he said.

It's good you're right around the corner, Ellen said. Must make things a lot easier for Gina.

For all three of us, actually.

Do Gina and Ennio have a good relationship?

He pondered the question.

Yeah, he answered, they do. They clash sometimes. Lately he's into telling her she doesn't listen to him.

That's normal at his age, isn't it?

Probably. With Ennio, you never know.

A few minutes of walking, without speaking.

Sugar and spice.

The jackpot couldn't be real. Yet it was—as real as this moment of dizziness. As real as the sound of Roy's boots on the sidewalk. As the hazy light of the streetlamps. She reached out and took Roy's arm for balance. He drew her to his side, his ribcage against her knuckles as their footsteps synchronized; then, after a few moments, he let go. Had he noticed the slight lurch in her step?

Ennio was a real mess after Renzo died, he said. You can't tell a four-year-old much about death, it doesn't compute. He didn't get how the train accident happened, kept asking what a derailment was. For a while, trains were the only thing he'd talk about. Sometimes when I tried changing the subject, he'd throw something at me—a toy, a book, things like that . . . once, a rock. He didn't have much of an arm back then, luckily. He's become a pretty good ballplayer.

Threw stuff at you?

Yeah. In anger, frustration . . . and then he has his silent spells, when he just won't talk.

That reminds me of Win, my brother. His girlfriend was killed two years ago, in Madrid. He's been in pretty bad shape since then.

Wow. Killed how?

In one of the bombings at the central train station.

He glanced at her, eyebrows raised.

Oh my god . . . your brother's girlfriend? What was she doing in Madrid?

Visiting her sister, who was living there at the time. I think I understand Ennio, because of my brother. The anger, the helplessness . . .

What's he like, what kind of guy?

Hard to describe. Win drinks way more than he should. He's a really talented composer, but he isn't working, isn't even composing anymore. Not in the usual way, at least.

How do you mean?

He claims he's still composing, but he doesn't notate. He *draws* what he hears. It's as if he's become a visual artist. Yet he still insists he's a composer.

That's kind of interesting, actually.

As a question of art, maybe. But in Win's case, the whole thing is a mess. He's still grieving for Mel, and this is how he's dealing with it—by refusing to notate his own music. He used to be well regarded as a composer, but he doesn't care about any of that anymore.

Does he get out much?

No. He can't handle public spaces. Not just aboveground train stations, like Ennio—I'm talking about any big gathering place. He's almost always at home, and he goes through a bottle of vodka a day. He's pretty much a hermit.

The station? Here it was, they'd reached it already. She steadied herself on the handrail. Sounds like your brother's had a rough time of it, said Roy.

Yeah, but Win's a grown man. It's different with Ennio. I can imagine your worries.

He nodded.

Listen, he said, thanks again for tonight.

Thank *you*. For dinner, for the evening.

You're welcome.

A few more beats of silence, then he added: You in the city often? For work?

Not too much, since most of my work happens in Brooklyn.

Mine, too. I'm teaching Phys Ed courses at Brooklyn College and LIU. Oh—and I have two dogs, and they're probably wondering where I am, like your cats are worried about you. So I should probably say 'bye.

She pulled out her farecard.

See you at the gym, she said.

He reached out and palmed the side of her neck, his fingers traveling lightly in her hair, his thumb tracing the underside of her ear.

Good, he said. Til soon, then.

Deferral

1

I thought you weren't going to be in touch.

Win's voice sounded a little gravelly. Was he sleeping? Taking at least minimal care of himself?

Just wanted to know how you're doing, Ellen said.

Come on, El, don't tell me you called to chat. Are you at work? What's that I hear in the background? Sounds like a sprinkler system. Is the museum drowning?

I'm on my lunch break outside, by the new fountain. You're right, I didn't call to chat. Just to find out how you are.

How *I* am? Well, I'm wondering how *you* are. Why haven't you quit, now that you're . . . what's the right adjective? Mega-rich?

I didn't call to talk about that, she said.

Well, I'm not sure I can talk about anything *but* that.

What do you mean?

I mean, Christ, you've gotta figure out what you're gonna *do*. It's been four days, right? As soon as the news is announced, your name will be tossed all over the place. You know that, don't you? Have you talked with anyone yet, a lawyer, an accountant?

The ticket doesn't have to be redeemed for three weeks, Win. I've still got plenty of time.

A group of young kids rushed toward the fountain's rising-and-falling plumes, shrieking as the fine spray hit them.

She stepped back. Why not squeal with the same happy hysteria? Why this mix of euphoria and dread? The seat of happiness—was *this* what it amounted to? And the vertigo, the hot flashes now every fifteen minutes instead of each hour, the swarming questions, when and where and how to find lawyers and accountants and computer security specialists and who knew who else, *what to do what to do what to do—*

Dale hadn't yet asked why she'd texted instead of calling to cancel their film date. But he surely would. Four days had gone by, and she hadn't answered emails from Anne and Sophie. They'd soon start wondering and worrying, too.

She'd had to talk briefly with a couple of people at the museum. Exchanged a few words with the lady at the dry cleaners. Spoke with the local pet store owner about four kittens, only a week old, each a tabby with green eyes. Did she know of someone looking for kitties? Could she help cover their upkeep in the meantime? If every customer contributed a dollar . . .

Wallet immediately emptied of thirty bucks. Which in that moment happened to be all she had.

There'd been a few conversations with Roy as well.

They'd talked on the gym's Balcony each evening before his class. Ennio had gotten into trouble on the playground. He was being kept at home after school, and wasn't riding the subway that week.

You all right? Roy asked at one point. You seem distracted.

Yeah, I'm fine, just a bit tired. Lots going on at the moment.

2

The fountain flung more spray. She covered her phone to protect it.

Don't kid yourself, said Win. Nobody's got plenty of time.

He hadn't hung up, though he'd gone silent for a bit. His tone was cooler now. But at least he was still there.

I know . . .

What's that noise, like rain?

I told you already, I'm outside the museum, by the fountain. Can't you tell me how *you* are?

I'm all right. You know what you might purchase for me when you finally cash in? I could use my own pianist. Someone like Tatiana Nikolaeva.

Who's that?

Dimitri Shostakovich's private pianist. He hired her to help him while he was on the road, so he could keep composing while traveling. They didn't get to work together for very long, though. She dropped dead after a few weeks. Heart attack.

A short, hard bark: his vodka-laugh.

Win, have you shown anyone what you've written so far? The preludes and fugues?

No. When I'm ready, I will. You fixing on becoming my manager?

Just wondering how you're doing.

Ah, *that* again. Well, if you mean, am I drinking myself into a stupor every night, the answer's no. Am I wallpapering my bedroom with photos of Mel, also no. Nor am I running personal ads in newspapers, or picking up whores. Does that answer your question?

A lot of nights you do drink yourself into a stupor, Win.

Nah! A *torpor*, maybe. There's a nice word . . . you should use it in a poem.

Ice plinking, then the crackling sound of liquid poured over it. Win's voice was clipped now.

Stop acting like all you've won is a plastic keyring, El.

For God's sake, I don't need to *do* anything right away! Not til the twenty-fourth of next month.

Lemme get this straight. You're planning on hiding out in your apartment til the day you've got to turn in the ticket?

I'm not hiding out, I'm working. There's no penalty if I wait, so I'm not rushing. By the way, why don't *you* line up an accountant? You'll need one, too.

More liquid, more tinkling, then a slurping sound.

I'm not hiring an accountant. I don't want any money from you. My music's all that matters to me. Either I make a go of it, or I'm not gonna be taken care of, by anybody—including you.

Shielding her phone, she took another step back as water splashed her feet. The fountain was dancing hard now.

For God's sake, Win, I'm not your keeper. I'm just going to buy you some time.

Uh-uh, he said. Time can't be bought. It has to be made. If you were still writing poems, you'd understand.

Why're you banging on *me*? I've barely got my head around this whole thing.

What whole thing? You mean, whether to take the money as a lump sum or in installments? Just do what your financial advisors tell you to do.

I really can't deal with this now . . .

He clucked scornfully.

Know what Mel told me once? She said, your sister's carburetor needs adjusting.

Look, if you're so het up about it, why not tell me what *you* think I should do with the money?

I've got nothing to say. It's none of my business.

But when you realized I'd won, you expected I'd offer you some cash, right, even if you'd already decided you wouldn't take any?

I don't want your money. As I've just said.

Whatever. But you do have ideas about how I should deal with it. It's not possible for you *not* to have ideas.

What I think is this, El: you need to hire some help and make decisions. Quit stalling.

What I think is this . . . could she herself utter those words, then finish the sentence?

I'm freaked out, Win. It's not stalling. I've got no idea what to do with the money. Or with myself. I mean, a ton of ideas and feelings come and go, but I can't *decide* anything. I need time to sort things out.

He snorted.

Take a couple of Xanax, he said. And now I gotta go.

Wait—did you have dinner with Maria yesterday? She's here, right?

Yeah, she's here, and yes, I did. Now go back to work. It's Friday, take it easy, go home early. Who cares if they fire you for it? We'll talk later. 'Bye.

3

So he'd seen Maria. And had probably subjected the poor woman to the third degree.

Like, had Mel been killed instantly? Had she spoken before dying? Tell me, he'd probably said after they'd gone through a bottle of wine. Tell me what the *air* sounded like when it happened.

And Maria had probably stared at him like he was crazy.

Then again, maybe he hadn't asked her a single thing about that day. Maybe he'd just asked about the best bars in Madrid. Maybe they'd simply hung out at his place and gotten drunk and yakked about how New York City had changed since Maria was last there. Maybe neither of them took note of the siren of a police car as it passed Win's building. Or the "if you see something, say something" sign by the entrance to the subway at Thirty-Sixth Street. Maybe they'd each decided not to talk about Mel, or even mention her name. Maybe they'd exchanged banalities for an hour, then parted.

Maybe Win wept himself to sleep after Maria left.

4

The Balcony was empty.

Eight o'clock on a Sunday morning, and scarcely a gym-rat in sight. Cardio area completely vacant. Only a few guys in the weight room.

Silence, such a gift.

Happy, was she happy to be a multi-millionaire?

Yes. No. Neither happy nor unhappy. Each word was way off the mark. Some sort of marvel was about to occur, and there were no marvels without mayhem, were there? A super-expensive haircut, her favorite perfume, a new pair of Armani flats, all that stuff was easy. Easy as well to imagine a vacation for all the nearest-and-dearest and herself—wherever they all felt like going, forget about the cost. And a housewarming present for Dale: his mortgage fully paid off, just like that.

As for Win, whatever it'd take to get him off the edge of the cliff.

But then what? Should she buy a bookstore, fund a poetry center, get every stray cat in the city neutered and fed? Should she come up with a bunch of projects—political, artistic—and spend her days meeting-and-greeting, consulting and being consulted? Or should she hire a bunch of go-getters—makers and doers—and step into the wings, not responsible in any way for *getting things done*, for *look at what all my money has wrought*, instead relying on others to come up with projects, plans, solutions? And in the wings, what should she do? Indulge her invisibility, sit around eating bonbons and reading poems? Accomplish zilch and be proud of it? And with whom should or could she spend her time? Why would anyone who knew her—very well, somewhat well, casually, not at all, whatever—want to spend time with her? To help or be helped by her? To give, take? Advise, consent? Could anyone ever feel at ease hanging out with a *nouveau riche* in a constant state of inner turmoil?

It all came down to one thing. What would the winner of the Pick Seven jackpot have to do to avoid launching a colossal farce—her new life?

At the Balcony's railing, she mimed the action of tearing a small piece of paper into pieces.

It'd feel great, it really would, to rip up the ticket. To destroy it right then and there in the Lottery Commission's offices. To walk in and say *okay, here I am, and here's the ticket—just let me sign the paperwork, so I can destroy the evidence.*

Tossing something overboard there, captain?

She wheeled around. Roy stood before her.

Good lord, you scared me!

Good lord, he repeated. Now *there's* an expression I haven't heard in ages. Smiling, he mimicked the movements of her fingers.

You fake-disposed of whatever it was very nicely, he said. Your fingers . . . Like a princess washing her fingertips.

She pointed at the court below. You teaching today?

Nope. I just like working out on Sundays. It's quiet.

Walking over to a nook, he sat cross-legged on a mat and pointed to the adjacent one.

Have a stretch, he said.

His arms rose over his head, fingers scrunching air.

I already stretched out, she said.

No you didn't.

I did!

Smiling, he shook his head.

People who're warmed up *look* it. I can tell you're not. Show me your routine—we'll make some adjustments.

The lesson bore no resemblance to childhood gym classes. No repetitive bobbing up and down or flailing of arms; instead, a half-dozen simple stretches.

Know what? she said. You're right, I really *wasn't* stretched out.

See? Now you know. And now you can do your run.

Yes boss, she said.

And when you're finished, go home and write a poem. Since your body will be loosened up, I'm sure you'll write more easily.

Aye-aye.

And while I'm giving orders: meet me tonight at seven, at the entrance to the Eighty-Sixth Street station in Bay Ridge, so I can take you to dinner. There's a nice little place . . . well, you'll see. Assuming you're available, that is.

Well . . . I am, in fact. But this time, *I* take *you* to dinner.

We'll argue over that later. Can I have your phone number, please, in case you get lost trekking from the Slope to the Ridge?

Ah, so you're one of those people who's never without his phone.

Only because of Ennio. Otherwise I'd toss the thing out the window.

5

Quarter to six. What to wear?

Not the usual uniform of jeans and linen shirt, for God's sake. Spiff it up at least a *little*. How about diamonds—just call Tiffany's, order something, have a messenger deliver it within the hour . . .

Vertigo.

A skirt, then. Nice sandals, the ones with the low heels and ankle-straps. And a linen shirt—okay, but it had to be new. That sleeveless, cream-colored blouse with the wood buttons and notched collar. Another great vintage-shop purchase, with the original tags from Bergdorf's, no less. Awaiting a special occasion.

She sat on the bed til the dizziness passed.

A special occasion. Also known as a date, this time with an unmarried man. Why not wear some jewelry? A necklace . . . the jade one with a gold clasp shaped like a bumblebee—the only item *la mamma* hadn't tossed out after Walter left. Purchased in Hong Kong for Nola's thirtieth birthday. That must've been before things started going totally downhill, sex- and drink-wise. Amazing that Nola hadn't pawned the necklace for gin.

Next to the jewelry box lay her mailbox key. Picking it up, she headed to the front door. Boy-Cat and Girl-Cat followed, nipping at her heels.

Easy, kittenettes, stay inside now, guard the fort. I'll be right back.

In the box downstairs were a lightweight blue envelope, an oversized BAM flyer, and the usual monthly bills: gas, electricity, phone.

Lightweight, blue? An old-fashioned airmail envelope.

Back upstairs, she sat at the kitchen table and stared at the envelope. It was postmarked Cremona, Italy, ten days earlier.

Her name and address had been typed on an old-fashioned manual typewriter. Inside were three sheets of paper: a photocopy of an official Italian document, its translation into English, and a neatly handwritten letter, also in English, on good-quality stationary.

The document was a death certificate, Walter's. Three weeks ago, in Cremona, of natural causes, age eighty-five, according to the translation. The letter, written in English, was from Bruno.

Dear Ellen,

I am hoping this reaches you. A friend with access to the internet helped me locate you; I do not own a computer.

As you can see, your father departed last Friday. In his sleep. An easy death, though unexpected. He was not in ill health, just a little tired. It seems his heart gave out—I believe that is that how it is said.

He was buried in the main cemetery in Cremona. I have not yet informed any English-language newspapers, but will do so shortly.

Italian bureaucracy requires effort to navigate, so I will go directly to the point. Your father has left you some money, and to receive it, you will need to come to Cremona as soon as possible. Not later than the middle of next month, when I leave the city for a month of rest in the mountains. You will have to sign several documents in person, and I must accompany you. Please bring, in addition to your passport, a phone number for someone at your bank in New York. You will have to pay a small fee for moving the money across the ocean.

I can be reached at this phone number: 0372.338.9491. Call me when you reach Cremona. I will be here, awaiting you. I am keen—is that right, in English?—to make your acquaintance.

Bruno

Slogans

1

Ninth Street, 2:00 a.m.: quiet, though of course more active than the park. Intermittent traffic. Mostly car-service vehicles and delivery vans.

Two people passed on the opposite side of the street. A truck, a minute later. Then silence.

Blair hopped onto a low wall at the back of a parking lot midway up Tenth Street. Her knapsack was cumbersome, but staying balanced wasn't difficult. Everything was a matter of not getting distracted.

A makeshift ladder led to the roof of one of the garages. Someone had already pushed aside the barbed wire blocking access to the ladder. She shimmied up another low wall sloping upward behind the garage. It led to the subway tunnel linking the elevated station at Fourth Avenue with the underground one at Seventh. On her belly, she snaked her way up til she reached a stretch of wire fence. It, too, had been breached; a lightweight patch covered the four-by-four hole.

Her wire cutters, lifted from Home Depot on a slow weekday morning, bit easily into the patch. Slicing it wide open, she climbed through the hole and pushed the torn pieces back together.

Over the apex of the tunnel was a concrete path.

Stay low. Standing or even crouching, she'd be spotted from the platform. On her belly again, she squirmed to the middle of the path. Thirty feet down, the Fourth Avenue platform began. It was lit, though not brightly. No one stood on the southbound side; on a bench near the end of the northbound side sat a man, elbows resting on his knees.

Half-asleep and exhausted. Not noticing a thing.

From her pack she pulled out a can of spray paint, then the stencils:

four rectangles, each framed in lightweight pine and measuring three feet square. Next she took out the pieces of balsa wood that would back each rectangle. They weighed little but required careful handling, as they'd splinter easily. The pine frames were sturdier. She'd had to disassemble them in the back of the store, then reassemble them at home so the hinges could be popped. That way she could carry the frames and then hook them up again. Both the frames and the hinges would be noted as missing, but the store manager would assume a customer had lifted them.

The X-Acto knife had been the trickiest theft. All the knives were kept behind a counter, and customers had to ask for the locked case to be opened. She didn't have access to the keys. She'd asked the cashier if he'd make a coffee run during a slow spell, offering to watch the register while he was gone. A minute was all it'd taken to get the key, open the case, and slip a knife into the pocket of her work-apron.

The sans-serif font she'd picked was easy to read, similar to what the MTA used.

After sizing each letter on paper, she'd mounted the paper mockups on her living room wall so she could see how the whole thing would look. Then came the task of incising the letters into the balsa wood. Once the frames were hinged together, each stencil had two words in each of its four rectangles: *You Suckers / You're Being / Taken For / A Ride.*

Color of the paint? Her trademark red, to keep things consistent.

2

She inched her shoulders and chest over the edge of the overpass wall.

Its surface felt crumbly and unstable. She pulled back a little, but that wouldn't work; to do the spraying, she'd need full range of movement. That meant maintaining her balance while levering her torso as far over the edge as possible.

She moved forward again, scanning below. Two sets of train-tracks entered the tunnel; a bright light illumined the entrance. The stretch of wall just below her ribcage—between the top of the overpass and the roof of the tunnel—was perhaps eight feet high. Its surface had been frequently tagged. The usual swirly bright shapes were outlined in white, the sort of graffiti found all over the city. A few days earlier, this stretch of wall had been repainted during the MTA's monthly cleanup. The surface was now a uniform light gray—a good backdrop. Against the gray, her red lettering would look just right.

A train was approaching from Seventh Avenue.

She felt the overpass shudder lightly as the train emerged from the tunnel, the tops of its cars almost touchable. The train whined to a halt at the platform. At the far end, the man seated on a bench stumbled to his feet and boarded the first car. It'd be twenty minutes til the next northbound train; the southbound would arrive in roughly two minutes. Late at night, the trains tended to run pretty much as planned.

Wiggling away from the edge of the wall, Blair got onto her knees and shook the can of paint, readying it.

Now for the measurements. Crouching, she fast-walked the length of the path: about forty feet. Then paced backward twenty feet, to the middle. Then leftward ten feet or so.

A southbound train was advancing, right on schedule.

She dropped flat, turning her head away so her face wouldn't be visible. The doors' chimes sounded; the train pulled away from the platform. A quick rumble and then it was gone. The platform below was empty.

Slipping on a face-mask made from an oversized ski cap, she inched forward again. Almost half her body was cantilevered over the edge of the overpass. She inhaled deeply, the can of paint in one hand and the first stencil in the other. Lowering the stencil carefully, she pressed it flat against the overpass.

Hold the can in front. Push its button firmly; not too much paint. Keep it steady, hold the button down hard.

The smell was noxious. She held her breath.

Now to the next frame. Then the next. Then the final. There: all eight words.

She pulled herself away from the wall's edge and sat up.

A little dizzy. No surprise, given the smell and the fact of having hung face-down for a while.

She took off her mask; a breeze cooled the sweat on her face. Her torso felt fiery, her back muscles tense. It'd taken a lot of effort to stay in place while spraying, but the job was done.

3

They were soft, but she heard the footsteps behind her as she was placing the stencils in her pack.

She put her mask back on, grabbed the can of paint, and spun around. A boy stood maybe five feet from her. Not too big or tall, maybe thirteen or fourteen years old. A round, stupid-looking face. Arms too long for his body.

She pointed the can of paint at him and shook it before speaking.

Come any closer and I'll spray this shit right in your eyes.

He gazed at her, smiling a little.

What are you doin', he said.

None of your fucking business.

A girl taggin' . . .

Beat it, she said. Go away.

Hey, the kid said. Lots of us come up here. But no girls.

I told you—get lost.

Listen up, he snarled. You think you can—

She made a move toward him. He turned just before the spray hit him; it reddened the entire side of his body.

Bitch! he yelped. Stupid cunt!

He looked as if someone had shot him. She could hear him swearing softly as he went down the incline.

She finished packing up and made the descent. Nobody else was around; it was almost 4:00 a.m., very quiet. Back on Tenth Street, she trotted down-hill to Fourth Avenue and entered the station, jumping the turnstile. Ascending the steps to the Manhattan-bound side, she walked several yards down the platform and turned to gaze up at her work.

Each letter was spaced right; the spacing was exact, too. Just as planned, even though she'd had to execute the whole thing upside-down. The train engineers and the passengers riding in the front car with the window, along with everybody on the platform during daylight hours, would have a clear view of what she'd done. Glancing toward the tunnel, they'd surely notice what was just above it. At first they'd be struck by how neat the whole thing was, the strong red color of the lettering. Then they'd start puzzling over the opening pair of words—*you suckers*—and the disturbing cliché that followed: *you're being taken for a ride.*

They'd wonder. Nobody likes to be made a fool. Was this just about the subway?

Ripples, implications.

Keith would praise her. You were like a snake up there, he'd say. Slithering right to the edge.

He'd want her to keep going. What you're doing is good, he'd tell her, but it's not enough.

4

The boy emerged from the shadows just as she walked out of the station. His hands were still stained red from the paint.

You, he said, grabbing one of her shoulders and twisting her sideways. You little bitch.

He must've waited for her. Before she could squirm away, he pulled her arms behind her. She bucked, trying to throw him off. His breath smelled rancid. He shoved her into the wall of the station. Keep still, he said, or I'll bash your fucking head.

One side of her face was pressed flat against the wall. She couldn't see him, only smell the funk of his sweat. His breath foul as an old dog's.

Who d'you think you are, he said. I got red all over me! My clothes all ruined. Bitch!

He shook her; her cheekbone scraped against the wall.

I'm gonna make you bleed, the kid said. Make *you* turn all red.

He pushed into her with all his weight, jamming her against the wall and rubbing her face against the rough cement.

Fuck! she called out.

Shut up, he said, pulling her face away and clamping a hand over her mouth.

She bit into one of his fingers. He screeched, then stepped away and backhanded her across the face. A passing car slowed, pausing as she yelled and waved her arms at the driver. The kid took off down the street. The car stopped; the driver opened his door and stepped out.

You okay? he called.

She turned and reentered the station.

Waiting was the only thing to do.

She stood in the station a half-hour before exiting. It'd be better to run on the street than in the station.

The coast was clear. She inhaled deeply, fatigue invading her whole body. She shook her head back and forth to clear it, then headed home.

5

Back in her apartment, she winced while washing her face.

Several big scrapes covered her right cheek and temple. There was blood and some bruising where the boy had hit her. She'd invent a story: a slip on the subway steps. No one at her workplace would care. Her face would heal before long.

That kid should've been able to tell she wasn't actually a girl but a short tough boy, with a boy's strong hands and feet. A boy who didn't want to have sex with boys as much as with girls but would do it with either, as long as nobody got on top. A boy for whom sex was merely something the body occasionally required, like water for thirst. You quenched it, but you could go without it.

She slathered antibacterial cream on her cheek and taped a bandage across the messier part of it.

Black coffee, rye bread and butter, a banana for the potassium. A glass of water.

Six in the morning. She'd need to leave for work in two hours.

Her sketchbook lay open on her table. She scribbled a fast portrait of the boy, then scratched it with her pencil til his face disappeared. Tearing the page from the book, she lit it with a match and flushed the ashes down the toilet.

There could be only one reason for Keith's silence: it was better that way, better for him.

He was okay, wherever he was. Not in trouble. Of course it would be easier if he hadn't gone silent. But Keith knew what he was doing, and he'd expect her to know what she was doing, too. His silence was his way of saying he trusted her. His pup.

He'd always known who she was.

That boy tonight, though, with his stinking breath . . . Next time she crossed paths with a boy like that, a boy who refused to recognize who she was—he'd pay for it.

Diamond Doves

1

Inside the modest trattoria, the air held scents of rosemary, garlic, and lemon. A waiter led them through the interior and out to a walled garden, lighting a candle on their table.

Too warm for you out here? Roy asked.

No, it's fine. I smell roasted chicken . . .

They do it really well here, said Roy. With balsamic vinegar drizzled over it. You hungry?

Hungry, was she hungry? Was it appropriate to be hungry? How would Walter answer that question? He'd say, *Eat*.

Yes, I am. Let's have the chicken and some salad—the arugula one sounds nice.

It does. And wine?

You choose, please.

He scanned the wine list, then gave their order to the waiter.

Do you eat out a lot? she asked as a bottle of Vermentino was brought to the table, along with crusty rolls and a dish of olives.

More than I should, he answered. I'm not much of a cook; neither is Gina. Renzo was the chef in the family. We all like Italian food, needless to say.

She spooned some olives onto her plate. Is Ennio a good eater?

Roy smiled as he poured the wine.

You bet! Remember how he hogged the hummus? He takes after his father. Well, and after me, too. Cheers, he said, clinking his glass against hers.

They drank; the waiter filled their water glasses.

My father . . . he liked to eat, too.

How long's it been since you last saw him? Roy asked.

She took a roll from the basket, sipped some water, fanned herself with her napkin.

It *is* warm, she said.

You all right? Want to go inside? It's air-conditioned.

No, I'm fine. Just . . . adjusting. Wow, these olives are good. My father . . . he left when I was eight years old. I've seen nothing of him since.

Ah. What's he do for a living?

He's—he used to be a professional singer. A baritone. He toured all over the States and Europe.

Roy took a roll, broke off a piece, ate it.

That's impressive. And you have a brother who's a composer? Plenty of music in your family. You see your brother recently?

We mostly talk on the phone. What about your parents?

My mother died when I was a toddler. Leukemia.

Ah . . .

And my father lives in an assisted living community in New Jersey. It's a good thing he's there, since he's gotten pretty senile. He can't do any cooking or anything like that for himself. I don't see him often; he doesn't want any visitors, isn't fun to be around. He was always a crabby guy, but it's worse now.

I grew up in New Jersey. Maybe he's crabby because he lives there.

He smiled. Nothing to do with that. How'd you end up in Brooklyn if you're a Jersey girl?

I went to NYU and decided to stay in the city. I moved to Brooklyn quite a while ago. Much nicer than Manhattan.

I agree. Especially for kids.

2

The chicken arrived; Roy poured more wine.

Buon appetito, he said. So tell me about your father. I can't imagine having a dad who sings. What's it like hearing his voice when you haven't actually seen him in decades? I assume you've listened to his recordings?

She broke a roll into pieces, pushing them into a little pile on the table-cloth before speaking.

Some of them, yes. He's . . . Walter used to have a very good voice. He sang opera, lieder, some choral music. He left my mother for a man, an Italian who makes stringed instruments. Violins and violas, mostly.

Roy's mouth pursed in surprise.

Where'd they meet?

At a music festival in Tuscany.

How'd your mother deal with that?

I'm sure she knew he'd had affairs with men. She never talked about him after he left to be with Bruno. He just kind of vanished.

Roy frowned.

Wait a minute. Your father's name is Walter, and he's with someone called Bruno . . . Wasn't there a famous musician named Bruno Walter? I seem to remember that name from my music-history class in high school.

Bruno Walter, yeah. He was a conductor.

That's pretty weird. The names, I mean—your dad and his partner.

A moment to salt the potatoes on her plate. Another to sip some wine and try for composure.

Yeah, it is. But when it comes to names, that's not the only odd coincidence in my family. My mother's first name was Enola, and her last name was Gay.

Roy frowned. Lemme think . . .

Remember the plane that dropped the bomb on Hiroshima?

He leaned back in his chair. Oh shit, that's right—the Enola Gay. My God, your poor mother. Her parents didn't have any idea when they named her, did they?

Nope.

Wow. After your father left, did your mother remarry?

No. She lived by herself, didn't want anything to do with family. Or any other relationships. When she died, I hadn't seen her for several years. Neither had my brother.

Not even for birthdays or holidays?

I used to go to friends' houses for holidays. My mother was usually drunk. If it weren't for my father's alimony payments, she'd have been on the street. She couldn't hold a job.

Where'd she live?

In a studio apartment in Morristown, New Jersey, where I grew up. She sold the family home and got the apartment; it was easier for her. She and I communicated by phone. She never picked up, so we traded messages.

That's kind of intense . . .

I got used to it. Sometimes she'd recite bits of songs or poems in her messages. Walt Whitman, Emily Dickinson . . . song lyrics and poems were the only things we had in common. She'd leave a few lines of a song on my answering machine, and I'd recite a poem on hers.

Your own poems?

Oh God, no. She never knew how to react to my poetry, or to Win's music.

Well, if she was drunk most of the time . . . but after your father left, didn't you live with her?

Yeah, for a few years. But then Win left for college, and when I went off to NYU, my mother moved into the apartment. The proceeds of the house sale kept her afloat, thankfully.

How'd you afford NYU? If you don't mind my asking . . .

My father paid for it. After he left, he set up a fund for my brother's and my college educations. He arranged it so my mother had to spend the money on tuition.

And then she passed away while you were in college?

I'd been out of school for a year or so. Living on my own by then.

That was thirty years ago, you said? Hmm . . . I figured you weren't much over forty.

Ah, you're a good liar. I'm fifty-two.

He shook his head, smiling.

You don't look your age, he said. Which makes *you* the deceptive one.

3

The waiter removed their plates, replacing them with smaller ones. He brought a bowl of greens to the table, dressed the salad, and served it.

Tell me something, said Roy. Are you a good poet?

Why do you ask?

I'm interested in how people arrange their lives. Like, if a person believes she's good at doing something, can she put that thing first?

Uh, do you have a particular *she* in mind?

Not you; someone else. A woman who was my closest friend for many years. Her name was Nadine. She was my age—I'm forty-seven—and she had a couple of heart attacks, two years ago. The first was so mild it almost went undiagnosed, but a few months later she had a second one, and it killed her.

How terrible . . .

Turned out she had serious heart disease. A fluke, since she'd always been in perfect health. She was a painter. She painted money.

Money?

Yeah. Bills, not coins. She made the same kind of painting over and over, an image of a bill—money, I mean. Usually a ten or a twenty. In the center of each painting, she put a bird instead of the usual presidential portrait. All different kinds of birds. And she came up with new wording for each bill, tweaking the legal language. Like, "to God we're dust" instead of "in God we trust."

He paused.

I liked her work very much, he added. There was something haunting about it. I wish she'd had time to do more.

D'you remember that hundred-dollar bill we saw painted on the sidewalk the other day? Was your friend's work anything like that?

No. Nadine's paintings were more . . . fanciful, I guess is the word. A bit out of focus, dreamlike. She never did any street art. It wasn't her thing.

Did she show her work anywhere?

No. Not because she lacked talent, but because she didn't believe in herself. She hung her paintings on the walls of her apartment. She and her husband had a place in Sunset Park. That's where your brother lives, right? I used to love walking into her place and seeing her work. It always cheered me up.

The waiter cleared their salad plates.

Dessert? Roy asked.

No thanks, I'm full.

Me too. Let's just sit, then. Finish our wine.

It's peaceful here.

That's why I wanted to bring you to this place. It's one of the few restaurants in Bay Ridge with a nice garden. Sometimes I fantasize about buying it.

A wave of dizziness; she covered her eyes with one hand, willing it to recede, then pushed herself to speak.

So, I'm trying to picture your friend's work in my mind. Did she think of her paintings as a series?

Yeah. They all had great titles, taken from songs that deal with money in some way. One was called *The Eagle Flies on Friday*; it had an eagle at its center, of course. *The Price Is Getting Steeper* was from a Van Morrison song, and *Take the Money I Make* was from Ani DiFranco. Then there was *I'll Get You Anything*—that one had a woodpecker in it.

What about the Beatles? I can think of one song . . .

He nodded.

I own that painting, in fact. Nadine called it *Buy Me Love*. It's the only one left.

The other paintings were sold?

No. Her husband threw them out.

You're kidding.

Nope. After her first heart attack, Nadine told him if she were to die, he could toss her paintings because they weren't worth keeping. So when she passed, he took her on her word.

Wow.

They had a complicated marriage. Neither of them behaved like a saint.

He was a very successful sculptor, and he considered her, what's the word for it? Not an amateur—oh, it's right on the tip of my tongue . . .

A dilettante?

Yeah. A somewhat talented dilettante, but without the will or force to be a quote-unquote real artist. And I think his attitude wore off on Nadine. Not that it was all his fault. She never had faith in herself as a painter, even though she was a good one. That's what got me interested in the question of priorities. So: do you think you're a good poet?

She spun her glass by its stem.

Your question makes me wince.

Why?

Because I haven't been writing for a while.

Can I ask if you've published anything?

Yes. A chapbook of prose-poems, a while back, and some poems in literary magazines. Nothing recent, though. You can't make a living as a poet, in case you're wondering. I write and edit all the time for my freelance jobs. But not poems.

I haven't read much poetry, I confess. Not that I don't enjoy it, at least sometimes. But I find it kind of intimidating.

Lots of people do. In school you're told to look for meanings. What matters first is sound, though. The poem's music.

I can't even imagine how you'd actually write one . . .

Well, I can't imagine doing a backflip.

Ah, that's not so hard. I think you should get back to writing—poems, I mean, not whatever it is you do for money. You come from an artistic family, why waste your genes? I bet your father's wondered what you're up to. Like, whether you became some sort of artist, too. Don't you think?

She patted her forehead with her napkin. *Full fathom five thy father lies.* Had anyone but Bruno been there for the lowering of Walter's coffin? Anyone read a poem or sung a song?

Honestly, Roy, I have no idea.

4

The waiter approached and lay the check on the table. Roy was gazing at her.

Hope I didn't seem pushy about the poetry, he said.

No, you're right to ask if I'm doing it. I should ask myself more often.

She reached for the check. Please, let me get this. I'd never have found such a nice place on my own. It's been a treat for me.

All right, he said. This time.

You got the last one, don't forget.

And I'll get the next.

He pushed back his chair. Time for a little air, don't you think? A stroll? Then some tea at my place?

His apartment was small and tidy. Two compact Australian sheepdogs awaited them at the door.

Kay and Nine, meet Ellen, said Roy.

Kay and Nine? Like, canine?

Uh-huh. Pretty lame, I know.

She pet each dog, scratching their chins.

I got 'em when they were pups, he said. They're siblings, and I knew I'd be calling them dozens of times a day, so I decided their names ought to be entertaining.

They're great, actually.

We nonpoets do our best . . .

In the kitchen he put the kettle on, then plucked sprigs of mint from a plant on the fire escape. Cups in hand, they walked back to the living room, which was furnished with a sofa, an armchair, and an old leather-and-brass trunk serving as an end table. Two lamps softly illuminated the blue-gray walls.

She pointed at a painting.

Yep, he said, taking a seat beside her on the sofa. That's *Buy Me Love*.

The canvas was perhaps thirty inches wide and half that high. It depicted a ten-dollar bill in mottled shades of green. Across the bottom of the bill, *a diamond ring* was scrawled in yellow. In the central oval of the bill was a bird with a long, white-tipped tail and a creamy belly. Its gray wings were flecked with white.

I'm going to loan the painting to a gallery in Park Slope, he said. A friend from the gym told me about it. They're looking for local work for a show they're doing, so I sent them a photo and told them they couldn't sell the painting, but if they wanted to display it, okay. It's my way of helping Nadine after the fact. I'd like to imagine her getting past her . . . what's the word for it? Modesty?

Reticence?

Or just plain insecurity. I still don't know which.

What sort of bird is that?

A diamond dove. See the sparkly bits on the wings? When they're paired, diamond doves peck each other around the neck while they fluffle their wings. Nadine and I watched a video about them.

Fluffle?

You know—they shake out their wings . . .

He mimed the movement, shoulders undulating. Then he pried off his boots and removed his socks.

Make yourself comfortable, he said.

5

She took off her sandals. He tapped her bare ankle a few times with the side of his foot.

Humans fluffle, too, he said.

She made herself return his gaze.

I imagine they do, she said. In their own way.

His gaze held.

I figure at some point you did something along those lines yourself? Some fluffling, here and there?

A while back, she answered. Then I went into hibernation.

Silly—birds don't hibernate, they roost! Didn't you learn the correct use of verbs in poetry class?

Taking one of her hands, he spread it open and, using a forefinger, traced the number three on her palm.

Three words, he commanded softly. Give me three for who you are.

Who I am?

Yeah. Describe yourself in three words.

Closing her eyes, she saw the sugar jar on her kitchen counter, a pale-blue envelope lying next to it.

Rich, rich, rich.

Uh . . . wary, she said.

And? Two more words.

She shook her head. That's the only one I can come up with right now, she said. But don't take it personally—it's just that I'm not used to describing myself. I feel . . . kind of rusty.

Wary and rusty. That's two. I figure there's got to be a more positive word for your third . . . but I'll give you time to think of it.

He turned and put his arms around her. His heartbeat steady, unrushed.

Then he stood, pulling her to her feet, and led the way to his bed. Lay his hands on her shoulders and pushed her very gently downward til she sat. Rolled her onto her side. Lay on his side, facing her, then rolled her onto her back. Carefully removed her shirt, skirt, underwear. Gazed at her body. Turned her slowly onto her stomach and straddled her. Spent time (how much?—she'd lost track) expertly massaging her back, pressing and kneading.

Then took off his own clothing, unhurriedly. Knelt naked at her feet, sliding a hand beneath each of her knees. Pulled them apart very slowly, his gaze never breaking from hers. Saying nothing. Then went on his stomach, inched downward, and put his face between her thighs, slowly tonguing forth an orgasm, then another. Then entered her mouth with his cock and moved there languidly, hips rocking lightly. And came at last with what sounded like a little gasp of disbelief.

Throughout, not a word exchanged.

6

Dawn, pale-gray and velvety. His hand squeezing hers.

Awake? he asked softly.

Awake, she answered.

Sleep okay?

Mmm, yes . . . the bed's very comfy. So're you.

You, too.

He turned on his side to face her.

May I ask you something? she said.

Sure. Ah—but if it's about sexual health, I'm clean and tested. As I assume you are. Else we'd have spoken about it.

No, it's not that—I figured the same thing. But there's something else, and I'd just like to understand . . . Gina's not your girlfriend, is she?

He threw a startled glance but didn't pull his hand away.

No, Gina's my sister. My half-sister, actually. What makes you ask?

Something's not adding up for me. I know that must sound absurdly suspicious. And I'm not normally like this, not that you'd have any reason to believe me . . .

It's okay.

He rolled onto his back for a moment, then returned to his side, facing her once more.

I've known Gina since I was a kid, he said. Our families lived on the same street, not far from here. My mother died when I was two, and Gina's father died in a work accident—he did construction jobs—when she was three. My father began dating Gina's mother when I was in junior high; he married her when I was eighteen. She died four years later, when Gina was fourteen and I'd just finished college. She got cancer, like my mom.

Whoa. That's a lot of deaths.

Our families have had bad luck.

Was there no one else to help raise you after your mother died?

Before my dad started dating Gina's mom, he hired babysitters for me.

And my grandmother—my mother's mom—used to take care of me too, sometimes, but she died when I was ten. Then Gina's mom became my stepmother. She wasn't the most stable person, she popped a lot of pills, but at least she was there for Gina. And for me, too, for a few years. She meant well. But I didn't spend much time at home; I was into sports in high school, so I often stayed over at my friends' houses after practice or games. Anyway, that's how Gina and I know each other. She's my half-sister.

And Ennio is your boy now?

I'm his uncle.

Yeah, but you feel he's yours now . . .

Roy said nothing.

I'm sorry, I must be picking up on something that's not there.

No, it's all right. Let's just say the situation's complicated . . . it has to do with Renzo.

Nine hopped up on the bed and moved to Roy's side, flopping against him. Sitting up, Roy thumped the dog's ribcage lightly with the flat of his hand.

You want the whole story? he asked.

Sure.

Okay. So Renzo and Gina were involved a long time ago, in high school. They were in the same class, seven years behind me. Gina broke up with him when they went to college, and by the time he showed up again, she'd ended her first marriage, which was short and not happy. So she started seeing Renzo again.

Where were you at that time?

I'd finished college, got my master's in phys ed, then returned to Bay Ridge. I managed to buy this apartment cheap, with some help from my father. And I was involved with a woman who Renzo had also been with, several years earlier, only I didn't know that. Neither of them ever mentioned to me that they knew each other.

Speaking of coincidences, you're swimming in them!

Yeah, I know. But we're all from the same neighborhood and school district, and Bay Ridge isn't that big.

So what happened?

Well, Renzo wanted a kid, and Gina did, too. So they got married, but Gina wasn't completely on board. She knew Renzo's track record—I mean, he'd had a fair number of women over the years. She had reason to be suspicious, because after a while Renzo started hooking up with my girlfriend.

How'd you find out?

I sensed something was up, so I confronted her. She admitted she was seeing somebody, and when I pressed her, she told me it was Renzo.

Did Gina know?

Not from me. She definitely suspected Renzo was cheating on her, but I didn't want to be the one to tell her what was going on. I don't know if she ever figured it out; we've never discussed it. Gina's not much of a talker. She takes after my father that way.

7

Kay climbed onto the bed and began licking their legs.

Stop that, Kay, Roy ordered. My legs, all right, but not Ellen's!

It's fine, I don't mind. I really do like dogs, almost as much as cats.

And I like cats almost as much as dogs, so we're even. But Kay, no, you can't stay here—get down!

Back to your tale . . .

Okay. So, after discovering what was going on, I broke up with my girlfriend. Right around that time, Gina found out she was pregnant. Renzo was thrilled, but for Gina, the pregnancy pretty much uncorked everything. She was constantly angry with Renzo. I think she'd guessed what had happened, and felt trapped.

How did Renzo react?

Roy shrugged.

He didn't fight with her, didn't get nasty, never said anything. Maybe he just wanted the whole situation to go away.

So you and he never spoke about it?

God, no. There wasn't any point. My relationship with my girlfriend was over; I wasn't trying to get her back. There was nothing to salvage.

She'd always been a loner, no friends to speak of. There was a sister, but they were rarely in contact.

How long were you with her?

About two years. She was . . . I guess I'd say she was someone with no way of expressing herself except sexually. At the beginning, I didn't mind her silence. It was seductive for a while.

What about Renzo, was she in love with him?

I still can't figure out her deal with Renzo. Dunno if she felt strongly about him, or if it was purely physical.

And Renzo, any idea how he felt?

Well, after Ennio was born, Renzo spent as much time as possible with Gina and the kid, even though he was often on the road for his job. Renzo was a good father, actually. Whatever his other faults, he was great with Ennio.

He paused to stroke Kay's muzzle.

In any case, he added, something was busted in my sister's marriage. That's how things were, when Renzo died.

He closed his eyes for a moment.

So you can imagine how floored I was when I found out Renzo and my ex-girlfriend were together at the time of his death.

Wait—you're kidding.

I know, the whole thing sounds like a dumb melodrama. But it's true. After Renzo's death, I handled all the legal and financial paperwork for Gina. I got a copy of the bill from the hotel in London where Renzo'd been staying; it'd been sent to his office, which forwarded it to me. My ex-girlfriend's name was on the invoice, along with his, of course. She'd been with him in London, and stayed there while he took the train to Manchester to attend a trade show for a few days. I guess they planned it so he'd get his business done, then return to London to be with her. If he'd been on a different train, or if he hadn't been planning to spend time with her . . .

My God. And where's she now?

No idea. A while back, I heard she'd moved abroad. For all I know she's still in London.

He rolled up to a sitting position, then levered himself to his feet.

It was a big mess, he said. And then it ended, though not for Ennio. Like I said, the situation's complicated.

He stood and reached out a hand.

Okay, up you go. Now you know the whole back-story. Change of subject: want some breakfast?

Sure.

In the kitchen, the dogs danced expectantly as Roy picked up their leashes.

Hey, how about taking a quick spin with the canines before we all eat?

If I had a tail, I'd be wagging it.

8

A brisk walk, then a shower, then toast and tea. Shortly before eight, they headed for the subway.

Near the Eighty-Sixth Street entrance was a deli; in its window hung a bright poster: *Play Mega-Millions Here!* Ellen wiped her forehead. A week—had it really been just a week since she'd found out?

Lemme get us each a bottle of water, said Roy, gesturing at the deli. Today's gonna be a scorcher.

He returned with two cold bottles. She rolled hers along the insides of her forearms and across her forehead, eyes closed.

Smart, he said. Never thought of that!

She drank, then nodded at the poster in the deli's window.

Here's a question for you. What would you do if you won?

The jackpot? Of that lottery?

Yeah. Let's say you won . . . a hundred million bucks.

He shrugged. Never thought about it, he said. Of course I'd be totally shocked.

Do you know what you'd do with all that money?

Give a lot of it away.

To whom?

At this he turned to stare at her, smiling a little.

Why're you asking me all these questions?

Just curious.

She reached into her bag and made a play of searching for something, then pulled out a tube of lipstick.

May I? Roy asked.

He uncapped the lipstick and stroked it across her lips. Nice, he said. Normally I don't care for this stuff, but on you it looks great. Anyway, to answer your question, I think lotteries are a waste.

But people do hit the jackpot sometimes.

Yeah, but how often? The system's made for losers.

I know. But just pretend you've won, big-time. Say, a hundred million bucks. What would you change?

Change?

In your life. I mean, shouldn't winning that much money be a chance to change something? I don't mean your apartment or car. Like, you know, how you actually live.

My guess is, you'd be in no position to change much of anything.

Why not?

Because that kind of money would change *you.*

They were approaching the stairs to the subway.

But you'd redeem the ticket and claim the money, right? she asked.

Well, of course.

Would it maybe be more . . . interesting, to give the ticket to someone else? Let that person make all the decisions about how to deal with it?

Give the ticket to someone in your family, you mean? Or a friend?

Not a friend, exactly. A trusted person.

Like, a financial manager?

Not necessarily. It could be an acquaintance, someone you may not even know very well but sense you can trust. You give the money to him or her, and keep whatever amount you'd need to live on, and let the other person handle the rest.

Scaredy-cat—you afraid of managing a fortune on your own? Have *you* ever played a lottery?

Yeah . . . only once.

Same with me. Last year, Ennio bugged me to buy a ticket, so I said I'd get us each one, and if I was a winner he could have whatever I won. But we'd have to use *his* money to pay for the tickets. We lost, of course. At which point Ennio decided there were better ways to spend his allowance.

Placing a hand on her hip, he shook it lightly.

Speaking of Ennio, I gotta get him now. It's my turn to walk him to day camp. So, thanks—for our, our . . .

Searching her face now, smiling.

Give me a word, poet. Or is it poetess?

How about . . . our tryst?

Yeah! I'd never have thought of that. We'll see each other soon, okay?

A light warm kiss, then he turned and walked off.

9

A packed R train wheezed into the station. The only way to get to the pole in the middle of the car was to crab-walk.

Ellen joined several other passengers clinging to the pole as the train lurched forward. They all gyrated a little before regaining balance.

She closed her eyes. *Only here, only now.* There was nothing to conclude or decide; not about Roy, not about the news from Cremona, not about Win, not even about the jackpot. Nothing more to do than hang on to a pole.

Stepping off the train onto the platform at Ninth Street, she inhaled the usual scent of urine and ammonia. A forlorn pigeon flitted by. If that pigeon were handed a hundred million dollars, would it make a nest with the banknotes and seek a mate? Or would it flap around in such bewilderment that all the hundred-dollar bills would swirl out the end of the tunnel?

The cats . . . they'd be truly nervous by now. She'd been away much longer than they were used to. Food bowl empty, full, empty, full: to them, that was all that mattered. The beauty of repetition, of knowing what would happen next.

Everything in her apartment seemed exactly the same.

The usual midmorning light fell on the bookshelves. The three volumes of Shakespeare on the lower shelves were as sun-faded as ever; the spine of Kafka's *The Castle* was still yellowed; next to it sat the essays of James Baldwin. And *Leaves of Grass*. And a volume of Borges stories, cracked by wear-and-tear.

How'd it go, that Leonard Cohen song? Something about the light getting in through the cracks?

For now, the ticket was simply a piece of paper with seven numbers printed on it.

Was it real, truly madly deeply *real*?

Of course it was. Of course it wasn't.

Boy-Cat circled hungrily; Girl-Cat wanted to be stroked.

The beauty of repetition.

For God's sake, little oafs, stop whining and tell me to *do*!

The message light was blinking on her landline phone.

Ellen dear, do please call your friend Dale one of these days. Remember him—Dale whom you've known for, oh, forever? I am fine, thanks, not that you've been wondering. Did you get my message on your cell phone, about rescheduling? Are you checking your messages once in a blue moon?

She examined her kitchen calendar. Still three weeks to go. First things first: make a reservation for a flight to Milan. Then call Dale. What to tell him? Say that in a few days everything would be clear, but right now life was . . . sort of a mess. Yes, she was fine, not to worry. Just too much to recount on the phone. Everything going okay with the apartment? And what about Teresa? Glad to hear it. See you soon.

Shortness of breath. Sweat all over, in every crease and hollow. More than a hot-flash, this—her solar plexus felt locked.

She lay on the floor and slapped her diaphragm with both palms, gulping air. What the fuck did she *want*? How could she not *know* what she wanted? What sort of person came into a hundred million bucks and had *zero* idea where the goddamn seat of happiness was?

Rolling onto her stomach, she pounded her fists on the floor.

Balcony

1

Was it possible, the Balcony completely deserted on a Friday night?

Must be the late hour, nine-thirty. Closing time a little over an hour from now, which meant everyone had already left. Gone home, or out on the town. *The eagle flies on Friday* . . . well, solitude was even more pleasurable when it wasn't supposed to be available. Like, at the gym on a Friday evening.

Where'd this past week fled to? At the museum there'd been three new brochures to edit, which left little time for browsing the websites of wealth-management firms. The sites boasted pictures of pine forests in Switzerland, yachts off the coast of Sardinia, women in pearls and handsome silver-haired men (everybody white, of course). And the language, so opaque—*optimal individualized tax-favored investment strategies with intensive analyses of risk profiles*—with some pseudo-reassuring stuff thrown in for good measure: *absolute trust, full transparency, utter dedication, total confidentiality.*

Midweek, there'd been a problem with Girl-Cat, an infected tooth. Boy-Cat was skittish with his sister overnight at the vet's. And then there'd been a three-hour shift to do at the food co-op on Thursday. Hence no gym workout til now. No sight or sound of Roy, either.

The nook nearest the door had the most room. She lay on her back on the mat, eyes closed, knees drawn up to her chest.

A lovely sensation, that release in the lower back. Pull each knee to the chest, left then right—forehead touching knee. Now onto the stomach for a cobra stretch. Always that stiffness in the lower back. Tightness in the chest, too. The body on guard, its radar picking up distress signals even when the mind said no problem, everything hunky-dory, you're a multi-millionaire-to-be.

The mind a liar, the body honest.

How come her willingness to open up with Roy, to have dinner with him, talk with him, sleep with him? How come it'd all felt right? It wasn't a question of sexual touch, skillful as Roy's had been. It was his tone and gaze: with those he'd kept things calm enough, relaxed enough, for her to respond.

How long had it been since their tryst? Five days.

Full fathom five thy father lies.

On her back now, the space around her spinning a little, the overhead lights kaleidoscoping—did all multimillionaires have daily bouts of vertigo? In any case, another encounter with Roy wouldn't happen soon. The next evening she'd be on a plane to Milan, then a train to Cremona. Then another train back to Milan, and a plane home. Forty-eight hours of travel, like the troupe in *Kiss Me, Kate* doing a whistle-stop tour of Italy, from Venice to Verona to Cremona . . .

For a few hours, she'd walk the streets of the city where Walter'd spent the past forty-odd years.

2

Rolling onto her stomach, she dozed for a few minutes, face turned toward the wall.

A slight pressure on her lower back. A foot, was it?—bearing gently down.

Rise 'n shine, sleepyhead . . .

The foot jiggling her now.

Naptime's over. Up, girl!

Now a hand, warm, midback. As he crouched at her side, she could hear his steady breathing.

Hey, Roy, a male voice called from the door. Almost closing time. Make sure the Balcony's cleared out, okay? Don't forget the lights.

Sure, I'll take care of things.

Do I need to leave now? Ellen murmured.

Nope. They're closing the exercise rooms, but we can stay here. *I* can, that is. *You*, on the other hand, are supposed to go home. But you can stay, if you're quiet and behave yourself. Think you can do that?

Maybe.

Good answer.

One hand still on her back, he slid the other beneath her stomach.

Now, on a count of three, I'm gonna flip you over. Actually, you're gonna flip yourself over. Ready?

At *three* she rolled a half-turn, not away from but toward him, pinning his hand and forearm beneath her side. Her eyes still closed.

Now what, she said.

Hm. Some people just don't like to follow orders, do they?

Stiffening his forearm under her ribs, he began levering her upward. A quick shove of his shoulder rocked him backward; he toppled, laughing as he fell. She sat up and shoved his shoulders with both hands; still laughing, he clamped her elbows at her sides, using his weight to put her on her back once more.

Chest to chest now. His mouth on her neck, tongue tracing circles there. Hands still holding her elbows tight.

She tilted her head sideways; he licked the length of her neck.

Hold on, he murmured. Ready?

Rolling off her, he pulled her back on top of him, gripping her waist.

Okay, wrap your arms around me and shut your eyes. Hang on—we're gonna do a roll now. Key words here are *fast* and *light*. All set?

Grasping her, he put his head next to hers so they were ear to ear.

Go!

He pulled sideways, rolling back onto her. Then off, quickly. Then, still rolling, back on then off, on, off—fast, light, as if down a snow-padded hill.

3

Tired? he said.

They'd halted at the edge of the nook, side by side.

No, but I'm panting—I mean, I thought you'd squish me to death . . .

Nah. It's safe if you go fast. Bet you haven't done *that* before!

Nope.

One time, with a kid in my seventh-grade class, we rolled like that down the steep bank near the Tennis House, in the park. You know that hill where kids go sledding in winter? It was rockier than we realized. We got pretty bruised . . .

She poked at her side. This part here right here took a bit of a hit, she said.

He walked his fingers lightly up the steps of her ribs.

I predict a speedy recovery, he said. But I should assess the situation more carefully . . . wait a sec.

Propping himself on one elbow, he scanned the Balcony.

Nobody'll come here til the final check, he said. All the trainers have left, so it's just the janitors and the guy at the front desk. The janitors are cleaning downstairs, so we're basically on our own for the next forty-five minutes.

An overhead light hummed tinnily.

Too bright, she said, waving a hand upward.

Still on his elbow, he gazed down at her, smiling.

We'll have to act fast if the game's interrupted.

It might be tricky. Depends what inning we're in.

We'll take a rain check if the game's cancelled.

Inclement weather?

He slid a hand under her T-shirt, palming her belly. Hand on her breast now, fingertips teasing its nipple.

I really hadn't pictured this, she said.

Me neither. I mean, not here, for sure . . . But I *was* hoping you'd show up tonight. You've been AWOL all week.

He got up and turned off the lights; the Balcony went dark.

It's a moonless night. Wish I could see you more clearly, he said as he lay beside her. It was broad daylight that first time, I can still remember the sweatpants you were wearing . . .

Actually, it was Ennio who found me.

Now it's just us. Which make me even more glad.

His hands traveling the length of each arm, then reversing direction at her fingertips. Ascending again, knuckles grazing the undersides. Then his warm palms on her ribcage, moving upward to cup each breast.

You've been on my mind a lot ... I keep getting distracted while teaching. One of these days I'm gonna fall off the beam because I'm thinking about you. I tell the kids to stay alert, the beam's dangerous, yet there I am, daydreaming. And if *I* fall off, how'm I gonna explain it?

The kids will be, like, what's up with Roy today?

Yeah. There, touch me there, yes ...

Somewhere outside, a car horn. Roy's fingers wandering over her collarbones. Silence, peaceful. A knee gently roving, now on her inner thigh. A light, happy-making pressure.

She closed her eyes and opened her legs.

4

Stay quiet, dove, he whispered. Don't make a peep.

Okay ...

The guy at the front desk knows me, but he won't like seeing a gym member on site at this hour. So you gotta stay invisible, okay?

At the door of the main staircase, he put one hand on the doorknob and the other on her hip.

I'll go down first, he whispered. I'll tell the guy I was working on some routines, and I need him to help me adjust the balance beam in the main studio. That'll use up a minute or so. When you hear the studio door slam, you take off, okay? Go down the back stairs. Just don't bang the front door as you leave. Let it close softly behind you.

Okay. But wait, I meant to tell you something ... I'll be away for a bit. You won't see me here for the next few days.

What're you up to?

A short work trip—I'll be back by Tuesday night.

Travel safe, then. While you're gone, I'll go to the Balcony and lie down on our mat, and have the most excellent fantasies.

He gave her hip a little shake, then leaned in and sucked softly on her lower lip.

Let's go, she said. Because if we keep doing this . . .

Yeah, we can't stay here all night! Ready? On your mark, get set—

He pushed open the door and descended. She went to the stairwell and heard his voice, then another man's. When the studio door slammed, she slipped downstairs and out the front of the building.

If we keep doing this . . .

The cats were at the door as she entered, chiming in unison. They followed her to the kitchen.

If we keep doing this . . . long-short-short, long-short-short: dactylic. IF we keep DO-ing this, I might be HAP-py and ROY might be TOO.

That's just doggerel.

Happy, as in full of hap. Chance, it meant. Any kind of luck, good or bad. Hap was random.

Boy-Cat yawned, tail in air, front paws extending languidly. Sliding alongside him, Girl-Cat leaned in and nipped his ear. Boy bit the tip of her tail, then both cats tore down the hall and vanished, who knew where? Whatever they'd be getting up to, a hundred million bucks wouldn't affect it in the least.

Not for Sale

1

On a bench on the platform of the F train, a flyer for a new gallery in the Slope: Zero Kilometer Art. Local work only. Support your neighborhood art-making community. Come to our latest exhibit.

Inked in: *Closing reception 5:00 p.m. today!*

Blair checked her watch: half past six. The gallery was around the corner from the station. It'd probably be near-empty, maybe even shut by now.

She climbed the stairs to the street.

Viewed from outside, the gallery was well lit. Good track lighting, well angled, not too bright.

Perhaps a half-dozen people were still inside, drinking wine, talking. And the work on the walls? Hard to tell from outside. Some of it looked obviously amateurish, though there seemed to be a decent litho in the far corner. Abstract, not garish. A bit derivative but well executed.

She stepped inside and moved toward one wall, avoiding eye contact. Most of one side of the room was boring—three inept sketches of horses, a weird collage involving snails. Was this an animal show of some kind?

As she moved to the opposite wall, someone handed her a glass of wine—a woman in her thirties. Dressed in the usual black. The gallery manager, presumably.

Thanks, Blair murmured.

If you have any questions, the woman said brightly, just come find me, okay?

2

On the far wall was a composition of wood and feathers, quite ugly. Then a photo, retouched, of an old cargo plane from World War Two. Three airmen stood under one of its wings; their heads had been replaced by hand-drawn soccer balls with anti-war slogans scribbled on them.

Heavy-handed. Tedious.

Next to it, a piece called *Buy Me Love.* Familiar . . . she'd seen it someplace. She peered at the lower right corner of the canvas. Nadine somebody, the last name an illegible scrawl.

Interesting, isn't it, said the woman in black, now at her side. We were lucky to get this for the show. The owner lent it to us; it's not for sale.

Owner?

Yeah. The artist herself died a few years ago. Had a heart attack out of the blue, right in the middle of the day. She wasn't even fifty, isn't that sad? There were other paintings, but something happened to them—the owner wouldn't say. All gone. A mystery . . .

Do you know what the rest of the work was like?

I've no idea. The owner said something about a series having to do with money. He mentioned there were birds in each one. All I know is the bird in the center of this painting is a diamond dove.

The gallery would close soon. Its manager was saying goodbye to the last few guests.

Sorry to interrupt, said Blair. Do you have any written information on the painting called *Buy Me Love*?

Oh, yeah, hang on . . .

The woman pulled a piece of paper from a drawer and handed it over.

Have a look at this, then leave it on the table, okay?

She returned to her guests.

Blair scanned the descriptive information. At the bottom, *Return to Owner* and an address in Bay Ridge was scribbled in pencil. Certain numbers weren't hard to recall, especially if they came in clusters. Three-four-five Eighty-Sixth Street was easy—almost a straight sequence, with a little twist. And the apartment number? Seven, the numeral that wasn't part of the sequence.

She lay the paper on the desk and left.

Cremona

1

Bruno had turned out to be easy to find.

In some tucked-away *vicolo*, or so she'd imagined—a charming alley, unnoted on the city map in her hotel room. The apartment he and Walter had shared for decades would be bright, serene. Several of Bruno's stringed instruments would be lying around; there'd be CDs on a shelf, mostly Walter's recordings. Books and paintings and old ceramics.

Wouldn't it be great to simply run into Bruno in some public place, recognize his face, and greet him as if by chance?

Which was how it happened, in fact. Though not where expected.

The journey was uneventful but long: an eight-hour flight to Milan, then another hour-plus on a train to Cremona. A taxi to a hotel.

Midmorning on Monday, she'd walked to the Piazza del Duomo. The space was dominated by a tall medieval campanile. She'd stood for a while, listening. A pigeon cooed. The piazza was tranquil, lovely, tourist-free. What might Win have heard if he'd come with her, what music within the silence?

Walking toward a café beneath the Palazzo's portico, she'd tensed at the sight of an elderly man seated alone, reading a newspaper. No, not Bruno, though it might've been—brushed-back hair, aquiline nose . . . Drawing closer, she'd seen no scar anywhere on the man's face. Bruno had a noticeable one along his left jaw, from a riding accident. Walter had pointed it out on the back of a photo that had arrived in time for her eighth birthday, in an envelope with no return address. *This is my friend Bruno,* he'd written. *He makes violins here in Cremona, and he likes horses. He fell off a horse once. See the scar? Maybe someday you'll meet him.*

The photo had been mailed along with a birthday card. Nola'd seen the card with its bland greeting—*have a special day*—but not the photo. The envelope had arrived while she was out on an errand; Win had opened it and insisted on hiding the photo, leaving only the card. Over the next several months, Walter had continued sending postcards from Italy, Germany, and France, none with a return address, each bearing the same banal sign-off: *Hope all goes well.* After a year or so, the cards ceased. Paternal duty fulfilled, over and done with.

Taking a table next to the pale man in the khaki jacket, she'd ordered an espresso and a brioche. The man was reading the *Guardian*. Noticing her, he gave a short smile, his teeth nicotine-stained.

Would you like a section, he asked, holding out the paper.

His accent was British.

No thanks, she said. You've figured me for a tourist. I didn't think I stood out.

His smile grew imperious.

Easy to spot, he said, though I wasn't sure if you were British or American. The Duomo here is impressive, but do go see San Sigismondo. The Campi frescoes there are marvelous, and the church itself is more congenial. It has remarkable light. Take the number two bus down there at the corner. The ride's short. Here's a couple of extra *biglietti*, I don't need them.

He handed her two tickets.

2

Bruno had been sitting in the empty church. In a pew, by himself.

Brought there by what—a need to pray? Inconceivable that Walter had lived for decades with a religious man. Once, after the death of a neighborhood cat, he'd scoffed at the mere mention of heaven. *When it's your turn, you'll suddenly be dead and not even know it. You don't go anywhere but into the ground.*

As it turned out, Bruno lived just down the road from San Sigismondo, in a tiny hamlet on the eastern side of the city. He'd walked to the church that afternoon as he did on most others, to be alone for an hour or so, and to sing.

She'd heard his singing as she approached. The great wooden front doors of the church were open wide, and a voice—tenor, not baritone—emanated from within. The light inside was as the Englishman had described; buttery yellow rays coated the stone floor. She'd walked a few paces down the central aisle. The singing had continued softly, then ceased. Her footsteps made the only sound. Partway down the aisle, she saw the singer on the right, a few seats in. His face was in profile, but there was no mistaking him; a scar ran along his left jaw.

Still handsome at eighty-something.

He'd been singing the love duet in Act Two of *Tristan*. In that moment, she hadn't recognized it. Slipping into the pew, she'd sidled toward him. When he noticed her presence, he'd frowned and stopping singing, then stared.

Dio mio. You are Ellen, he said. It's you, isn't it? Walter's daughter.

Yes.

You look very like your father. I am Bruno, as you have no doubt guessed.

His English was accented but clear.

Yes, she repeated.

He stared some more before speaking again.

I have lived in this city my whole life, he said. Even so, only Walter knows—knew—who I really am. I'm known in Cremona as a violin maker, but in most other respects I have often felt invisible. Yet you, his daughter, found me here, of all places . . . I'm not surprised. Coincidences happen all the time, they're as common as salt, sprinkled—is that the verb?—sprinkled all over our lives. It was pure coincidence that I met your father in Firenze, you know. Walter wasn't supposed to be at that festival. He decided to go at the last minute.

He stood.

Come, he said. I'll show you where your father's been all these years.

3

They'd walked in silence to the apartment, a suite of graceful rooms in a building dating from the nineteenth century.

This apartment, said Bruno, has been in my family's possession for well over a hundred years. I was born here. But these rooms became your father's home, too. After the first six months, he said he felt as if he'd always lived here.

It's lovely.

Your father liked to eat. As you may remember.

Yes. That much I recall.

Bruno led her through the living room. Books and journals sat in neat stacks; a cashmere sweater lay folded on the back of a chair. He proceeded to the kitchen, a well-lit space with an old trestle table against one wall. There was a marble-topped island in the center; a ceramic jar full of wooden spoons sat next to the stove. Copper pots and pans hung from an iron bar near the stove.

She sat at the table and stared at the spoons.

Your father, said Bruno, did all the cooking here. But I shall make us a little lunch.

He poured some *prosecco*, then put out a plate of olives, cheese, salami, and bread. They ate and drank, saying little—a few words about the violins in the Stradivarius Museum, a few about San Sigismondo. Then Bruno began to speak about Walter.

For two decades, your father performed all around Europe and Asia.

She nodded.

But eventually it started to fatigue him—the hotels and airports, the strain on his voice . . . so when he turned sixty-five, he decided to retire.

To do what?

To help me manage my studio. Walter had a good business sense. He encouraged me to train two young Japanese apprentices; they run the studio now. I'm sure my clients will continue to patronize the studio after I leave it in my assistants' hands.

When will that be?

I plan to retire in a few months.

Why?

He shrugged.

My fingers are no longer agile. And now that Walter's gone . . . here, take one of my cards. A little souvenir.

He handed her a cream-colored business card embossed with his name and the studio's address.

Your father knew how I like my coffee. And which columns in *Corriere della Sera* I read first. What music I admire most, which artists, which books . . . and what makes me melancholy. All the details. Not to mention the names of every man I'd slept with.

He looked away.

Since his death, he added, I walk around the streets of my city like a . . . what is the word for a ghost who returns?

A revenant.

Yes. That is what I am now. A ghost returning to his home as though it were someplace he'd never seen.

4

She pushed away her glass.

Bruno, are you aware that my father walked out on my brother and me?

His gaze was perplexed.

You're mistaken, he said. Walter walked out on your *mother*.

He poured himself some water.

Your father married an alcoholic, my dear. He was living with a woman in love with gin, and then he fell in love with me. What choice did he have but to leave your mother?

Now his gaze was trained steadily on her.

Ellen, he said. A nice name. Walter chose it, did you know that?

No. And I'm not sure I believe you.

He nodded calmly. No matter, he said. I can see you are tired. And dehydrated. Your father would always return from his travels and immediately drink a liter of water. Can I get you anything else? A coffee? Your journey has surely exhausted you.

Thanks, she said. I'm all right. I'll be going back to my hotel shortly.

A pause, then he said: I would like to know something. Have you ever been taken?

Taken?

Perhaps I am using the wrong word. Taken, as in captured. By another human being, I mean. Or perhaps the word I am looking for is captivated?

She shook her head; he smiled.

You are skeptical, I see. Like your father. In this regard I can say that I changed him. Walter's skepticism diminished over the years. He began to see it as a waste of energy. Truly strong emotions are not defeated by skepticism.

His hands on the table were age-spotted but wiry, an artisan's hands. He flexed his fingers lightly before resuming.

Please understand, I am not merely going through the motions, my dear. I would like to know the truth about you. Have you ever experienced ardor?

Ardor? The word puts me off. It's for sentimental songs.

Bruno smiled a little.

Perhaps you confuse it with passion, he said. That is not what I am referring to. Passion is fueled by sex—sex and its demands on one's dignity. One imagines oneself capable of endless physical desire. Then fatigue and boredom do their jobs, and eventually it all grows . . . tame, I think that's the word. The body begins to withdraw. This is natural.

He rolled his neck briefly; she could hear its clicking.

In the end, he continued, passion makes a person disloyal. Not to the love-object but to himself. It gives rise to jealousy, anger, mistrust. Your father was loyal, to himself and to me. This I call ardor.

5

She finished off her water and took her glass to the sink.

We all have our definitions, she said, rinsing her glass. I'm not the most receptive audience for this, Bruno. I'm not the person to talk with about Walter's loyalty.

I don't expect you to be. From your perspective, your father was perhaps a selfish man. But one must learn to walk all the way around whatever one is looking at, don't you agree? Like looking at a sculpture. You must see it from all sides. I do not think you have understood your father.

I'd say the failure of understanding was mutual.

Bruno stood.

Let us go to the living room, he said. The light is best there at this time of day.

He led her to a comfortable-looking leather armchair next to a window. Its view was of the rear of San Sigismondo, its plaster walls burnished by the sun.

Beautiful, he said, pointing at the church's facade. Even the back side, which so few people see. Have a seat. That was your father's chair. I want you to know something: your mother wasn't a passive victim, Ellen. Perhaps you are unaware that your father wrote to you and your brother repeatedly after he left?

I received a few postcards from him, she said, while he was traveling. For about a year. Win didn't get anything.

Walter sent you *letters*, my dear. In addition to the postcards. One each week, in fact, starting right after his arrival here. I walked with him to the post office to mail the letters, so I am sure of their frequency. But you didn't receive any of this mail, because your mother intercepted it.

Why should I believe that?

He stood.

Would you like to read the letter from your mother in which she announced that your father should cease writing? I have that letter in my desk. Your mother said she was destroying all communications from Walter before you could read them. She wrote him three times after he left. Once to tell him not to write you again; once to ask for more money, which he gave her; and once to say that she intended to drink herself to death, which she did. Would you like to see this correspondence?

No. Let's be clear, Bruno. My father could've gotten in touch with me—and with Win, too—if he'd wanted to. Nobody was stopping him.

Bruno clucked his tongue.

You are forgetting the times, my dear. In the sixties, a man who left his family in order to be with another man, especially a foreigner, was not likely to be permitted access to the children. Your father had no desire to turn your life into a *tiro alla fune*, a tug-of-war . . . on her side your mother had all the power, legal and social. Your father had none. He felt it would be better for you if he didn't try to pull you away from your mother. My daughter will always land on her feet, he told me. My daughter's a cat.

At that she stood, pulling her bag onto her shoulder.

I think I'd better go, Bruno. You're right, I'm tired. We should make a plan for tomorrow morning. Where are we meeting—at Walter's bank?

Bruno was silent for a moment.

Yes. At the corner of the Piazza Roma, he said finally. You can walk there from your hotel. I will be there at ten.

I need to be at the station for a noon train to Milan. I'll be flying out from Malpensa in the late afternoon.

A very short visit, Bruno said.

I haven't time for anything longer. I need to get back to New York.

Let me call you a taxi, he said. It will be here in a few minutes.

6

They'd walked to the front door, which he opened for her. As they stepped outside, she'd paused.

Can you tell me how much money my father has left me?

Yes, of course. Twenty thousand dollars.

You're sure? Twenty thousand?

Of course I'm sure. Our lawyer drafted Walter's will; I have had a copy for several years. The bank will give you a copy as well.

Was anything left to my brother?

Bruno's brows rose.

Of course not, he said.

With that, the dialogue commenced its descent.

What do you mean, she asked.

I refer to the fact that your brother ruined your father's career as a composer.

What? Are you talking about the score my brother lost? That's ridiculous—Win didn't ruin anything.

You are very mistaken. What your father wanted most of all was to compose. To be known not just as a wonderful singer but as a composer, a brilliant one. Over the years, this goal became more important to him than anything else. But your brother made it impossible.

That's absurd, Bruno. Did Walter tell you what actually happened? Win took Walter's score to school to make a photocopy, without asking Walter's permission. He was a ten-year-old kid trying to teach himself to notate, and Walter never bothered to instruct him. So Win took the score from Walter's study and made a copy of it, but he forgot to take the original out of the photocopier. Another kid found it there. The kid didn't like Win, so he threw out the score. Later that day, Win left the photocopy on a bench at the school-bus stop—he was that kind of kid, distracted, forgetful . . . When he went back to the bus stop the next morning, the copy was gone.

I know the facts, said Bruno. Walter recounted them to me as you just did.

Then it should be obvious to you that Win didn't do anything on purpose. It's crazy that Walter would hold a grudge against his son for this.

Bruno clucked his tongue.

You haven't understood. What your brother destroyed was a commissioned work. When Walter couldn't produce the score, the orchestra canceled the commission. He'd already been given an extension because of his busy performance schedule. Your brother's actions ruined Walter's reputation as a composer.

Bruno, we're talking about a *kid*. A boy who made a mistake, and should've been forgiven for it.

He shook his head.

We are going in circles, he said quietly. After he came here to live with me, your father did want to see you again. But your mother prevented any contact. When you were older, Walter thought it best not to complicate your life by asking to meet you. He knew what your mother would have told you: everything was his fault. It seemed to us both that if you wanted to see him, you would communicate this desire to him.

Are you kidding? As far as my brother and I were concerned, our father had already renounced us. Why would *we* take the initiative—and how exactly were we supposed to communicate with him, in any case? We didn't even know where he lived! For all we knew, he'd left *you*, too.

My dear, to find out where he lived, you could have contacted his agent any time. Your father was always willing to see his daughter, but you decided against it. That was your choice. And as for your brother, since he'd ruined his father's prospects as a composer, why would Walter make any effort in his direction?

7

The next thing she'd said had not seemed to take Bruno aback. Perhaps he'd even been expecting it.

Bruno, do you think my father actually wanted to have children, or was he tricked into it by my mother?

He smiled.

Nobody could trick your father, my dear. Initially, he thought he and your mother could maintain an amicable, mutually useful partnership. He wasn't in love with her. He was young and ambitious, and he didn't want to be deeply involved with anyone. He wanted to be a great performer, and he didn't want any rumors about not being . . . fully heterosexual. Your mother was young but not stupid. Walter offered her a clear proposal: all she had to do was take care of the practicalities, and he would pay for everything. Being in the closet, as you say in English, was burdensome for him, and marrying a woman who didn't require him to be at home all the time made sense. He felt, however, that Nola would need a couple of children.

Why?

To prevent her from becoming too solitary while he was traveling. And to be useful to her as she aged. As you are surely aware, your mother was not a woman who enjoyed the company of others. Your father never asked her to change; he accepted her as he found her, a reasonably intelligent woman who appreciated his musical talent. But her drinking became a problem he did not expect. In any case, he fulfilled his role in the partnership.

Which was . . . ?

To demonstrate how to be an adult. When he was at home, your father had no difficulty instructing two young children how to behave. But he insisted on freedom for himself—doing as he liked, going where he liked, enjoying sexual as well as artistic liberty. All this he made clear to your mother before they married: she was not to interfere in his musical or private life. Everything went fine until your mother became an alcoholic. And then the commissioned score was destroyed—which was your mother's fault as well as the boy's, since she failed to keep Walter's study locked. The situation was obviously falling apart. By then, Walter had met me, and once again he demonstrated how to be an adult, true to one's own nature. He was ready at last for a deep involvement. The partnership with your mother was over.

My mother had no idea he'd leave her, Bruno.

Oh, your mother merely pretended to be shocked, my dear. She claimed she didn't want Walter involved any longer in raising you or your brother, but she'd always known about her husband's sexual desires. Her reaction was pure hypocrisy. The truth was that she could not imagine Walter actually wanted to *live* with me. That was the problem for her. By that time, you were old enough to know who Walter was—how important an artist . . . Must you still claim that his wife was a good mother, or are you willing to admit she was simply a drunk?

The taxi approached; Bruno signaled to it, then continued speaking.

Remember, *cara*, that your father sustained both his children up to adulthood. He paid for your college educations, and he sent your mother a monthly stipend until her death. She was never in danger of starving. The fact that she preferred drinking to eating—well, there was nothing Walter could do about that. As for your brother, it was better to let it go, as you say in English.

He paused, then picked up her suitcase and walked to the taxi. Spry, he was. The weight of the bag no problem, his balance still good.

So there you have it, he said as he opened the taxi's door. Your family was a failure, yes, but not your father's failure. I will see you tomorrow at the bank, *cara*. I hope you are able to rest this evening.

He closed the door and turned away.

The next morning, the bank made the transfer swiftly.

As Bruno chatted with an acquaintance in the foyer, an English-speaking manager took her into his office and helped her fill out the forms. For this transaction, he explained, her physical presence had not actually been required; she could have simply faxed him the necessary notarized documents. She'd been told otherwise? Ah well, in any case she'd had a chance to visit Cremona, a lovely city, *non*? So the visit was worth it. Signor Portinari was a client of the bank for many years. *Condoglianze, signora*, we are all sorry for your loss.

Bruno accompanied her to the station. On the platform he handed her a fountain pen, the one he'd lent her to sign the documents. It'd been Walter's, he said, and she should keep it. A gold-capped Parker, difficult to find on the collector's market.

She put it in her bag. Checking into a hotel in Milan, she used the pen to sign the register, then gave it to the receptionist.

All yours, she said.

Really?

Yes.

Bellissimo, he replied, smiling. *Grazie!*

Sell it if you like, she said. It's worth real money.

Bewilderment

1

Sitting at her kitchen table, Ellen stared at the sugar dispenser. No need to check: the ticket was buried there. Invisible, safe.

She wrapped her fingers around the glass jar. Warm, was it warm? Cold, tepid? Could she *feel* it, her fortune?

On the counter lay a stack of mail: flyers, two literary magazines, a few bills, some insurance paperwork. A renewal form for her driver's license. The food co-op's newsletter. Jetlag was a bitch . . . what time was it? Ten o'clock, her cellphone said, though it was 4:00 p.m. in Italy, and her body thought she was still there. Good lord. Had the trip to Cremona really happened?

She pulled the bank receipt from her wallet. Here was proof: twenty grand in her account. As for the rest of Walter's money, where'd it all gone? Impossible to guess what *il baritono* had had up his sleeve when he wrote his will. Bruno had no offspring, nor any need of money. Maybe Walter'd simply dumped his sacks of euros in the Po River.

Finito. All in the past.

The story Bruno had told was Walter's, hence not a story but the truth— for Bruno. A brilliant musical artist with a drunken wife leaves his family for a fresh start, after his son ruins his chances as a composer. Because what else could a real artist do?

But one thing went unexplained in Bruno's retelling. Walter must've felt some sort of physical desire for Nola, at least initially. And he'd funded a four-person family for over ten years. That was a fairly long time to play charades. Of course *il baritono* had sought to avoid the stigma of being gay, but even in the Fifties, that fact wasn't likely to damage a career as major as his. So why'd he stuck around for as long as he did?

Habit, probably. He'd been performing constantly in those days, always on the road. The family was a predictable backdrop. The house in Morristown had been Walter's green-room, the place where he could wipe off his stage makeup, cook a decent meal, shut the door of his studio, sing, compose, be alone. Not with his family but with himself. The family could always be pushed aside.

Then Walter met Bruno, and no longer wanted to be solely unto himself.

A strange word, ardor. And its opposite? Indifference, frigidity?

Fear, maybe.

Pushing the sugar jar to the side, she lay her head on her arms, awaiting the mercy of a nap.

2

Awakened by Girl-Cat leaping onto her lap, she reached for her cellphone.

What time was it? Eleven in the morning. She'd napped an hour. And it was Wednesday. There were calls to make. First Win, then Dale.

The call to the bro would be short. At this point he'd be totally unaware of Walter's death. But Bruno had told her there'd soon be an obituary in the *Times*. Was that worrisome? Not very, since Win never read the obits; he barely glanced at the front-page headlines. Might somebody email him about Walter's death? Doubtful. His former friends would be skittish about offering him condolences. Anyhow, he'd basically dumped everyone he used to know.

Dale might actually notice the obit. More likely, though, he was wondering what cliff she'd driven off. When *was* the last time they'd talked? Sometime before Cremona . . . yes, she'd called him to cancel their get-together. The first purposeful lie she'd ever told Dale. And she'd said nothing about Walter's death.

For his part, Dale had sounded upbeat. Work was fine, things were good with Teresa—they were spending several nights a week together. He'd asked about the guy from the gym. There was stuff to report, she'd replied, but it'd have to wait. How about if they talked in a week or so, would that be okay?

Sure, he'd answered. Keep me posted.

His tone could've passed for distracted, but wasn't. He'd known something was up. It wasn't possible to get a fastball past Dale.

3

What are you doing here, El?

Closing the door, Win leaned against it. Tired, he looked. Tired and pasty-faced.

I'm giving you some money.

What?

Not much. Eighteen thousand. I need your bank account information.

He scowled.

Christ, Ellen, I already told you. I don't want any of your money.

It's not from the jackpot. I've done pretty well on some recent gigs, including one for an Italian marketing firm—

—forget it.

Walking to the piano bench, he picked up a near-empty glass and gave its ice a shake, then tilted it in her direction.

Something to drink?

No, thanks.

He went to the kitchen, returning with a refilled glass.

Cheers, he said, raising his drink. You wanna start giving away money? Find some real charities.

You're not a charity.

Give it to Maria, then.

Mel's sister?

Yeah. She's moving back to New York for good, and she's looking for a studio apartment to rent. I told her it's cheaper out here, so she's looking in Sunset Park. She'll need cash for a deposit.

Does she have a job?

She teaches ESL, so she should be able to get work pretty soon. She says ESL teachers are in demand. She'll stay with me til she finds an apartment.

But you don't have a spare room.

She can sleep on the couch.

How much did she ask for?

Two thousand. She'll pay me—you—back. Maybe not for a couple of months, but she will.

Two thousand's not a small amount.

He knocked back his drink and wiped his mouth with the back of his hand.

That's pretty vulgar of you.

Vulgar?

You're acting like a loan officer.

Oh, come on. I don't know if she's trustworthy.

You already sound like a cheap millionaire.

You know what, Win? That stuff you're drinking's not water.

No kidding.

Where did he *go* when he drank like this? Into what dark?

Look, I'll send a check to Maria at your address. She's got the same last name as Mel, right?

Yep.

Will I be able to meet her sometime?

Do you want to?

Of course. And I want to lend her the money.

Practice.

What do you mean?

You gotta practice giving away your money. Why don't you hand her the check in person, instead of mailing it? How about Friday?

Does she have a bank account here?

She's gonna open one. I'll let her know.

Friday, then. Six o'clock?

Wait, isn't Friday the day . . . ?

The deadline's *Monday*. Not this coming Monday, though—the next. You haven't mentioned the ticket to anyone, have you?

Moving to the window, he stood with his back to her.

No, he said. But I'd have told Mel.

I know. Please don't tell Maria, though.

I won't.

You're looking kind of pale. You feel okay?

My tinnitus is noisier than usual. The highest registers are tough. There's a constant needling that makes it hard for me to sleep.

I'm sorry.

He shrugged.

I'm using it, he said. I'm making new work based on the tinnitus. Drawing lots of squiggly lines.

Picking up her bag, she went to the door.

You'll let me know if you need anything, right? Promise?

See you Friday.

His cheek as she kissed it was stubbly; he hadn't shaved in days.

Take care of yourself, bro.

Stop hiding, El. Get your show on the road. Take the ticket in.

5

Back in her kitchen, she picked up the sugar jar and gave it a shake.

Half an edge of the ticket poked out of its cinnamon-sugar sand.

She tossed some dry food into the cats' bowls, then made a salad and ate it while skimming the newspaper. More awful news from Iraq. Christ, how many civilians were dead now, and how many Americans totally clueless . . . Letting themselves be gulled by a president who lied through his teeth. Young American soldiers killing and getting killed for a ridiculous falsehood. What was that thing she'd seen, riding the subway—a phrase painted across the overpass to the tunnel at Fourth Avenue? *Suckers, you're being taken for a ride.* Now wasn't that the truth.

She shook the jar again; the ticket vanished beneath its white-and-brown sand. The line in that poem by Cesare Pavese, how did it go? She'd bought a bilingual edition of Pavese's poems at the airport in Milan—had she left it in the cab? No, there it was, in the laundry basket with her dirty clothes.

She riffled the pages. Yes, there: *The only joy in the world was to begin.*

Written by a poet who ended up killing himself.

Still, one way or another, a person had to begin.

The check could be picked up—so the rules stated—at the Lottery Commission's offices, a few days after the ticket was surrendered.

It'd be a fake check, of course. An oversized souvenir mounted on posterboard. Something for the winner to frame and hang on a wall. The money would be direct-deposited; there'd be no paper check to hand to a bank teller.

How much would a hundred million bucks amount to, after taxes? Roughly forty million. It could be taken all at once or in installments—a million a month for forty months. All of it taxable, of course. If taken as a lump sum, the funds would have to be deposited in multiple accounts. Winners weren't allowed to stuff that much money in one mattress.

Stop hiding, Win had said. He'd meant herself, not the ticket. *Take the ticket in*: that sounded like bringing in a fugitive.

What he hadn't said was that Mel would be appalled by her dithering. C'mon, she'd order, get a frickin' move on!

Robin Hood

1

You're here . . .

Roy's smile was quick and warm. A thumb and forefinger on her earlobe, like that first time when they'd stood by the entrance to the R train.

Did you have a decent work trip, dove?

Yes, fine. Mission accomplished.

You look well.

I'm a bit tuckered out. But basically fine—glad to be back.

Good! Listen, can we go somewhere to talk? I'd rather not have a conversation here.

She nodded.

Am I being pushy if I suggest we go to your place, since getting to mine
means taking the subway?

Say *yes*. It was high time he saw where she lived. Her nest, soon to be very
nicely feathered.

Sure. My apartment's not far, and you can meet my housemates.

Housemates?

Girl-Cat and Boy-Cat.

Ah, the felines! Finally I'll have something to tell Kay and Nine. They've
been asking me why you have such a nice undoggy smell.

2

First the cats, who took to him right away, rubbing their cheeks on his
knuckles.

Then her books. Then the music stand in the corner of the living room.

Then the bedroom and its large, east-facing window. The family photos in the hall. Then back to the cats.

His attention restless, absorbing all the details.

Have a seat, she said, pointing at the sofa as they reentered the living room. Tour's over, you've seen the whole castle . . .

I like it here, he said.

There's not much in the way of visual art. No paintings, like in some people's apartments.

Yeah, but plenty of books. Man, you read a ton of poetry! Did that music stand over there belong to your father?

Yep. The cats like to jump on it and knock it over.

Dropping onto the sofa, he pulled her down next to him.

Talk to me, he said quietly, keeping her hand in his. Tell me what's up. Because *something* is.

I'm not sure where to start.

Doesn't really matter, does it?

Right. So, okay . . . I can't seem to shake two feelings. The first is that you're totally trustworthy. And the second is that you're hiding something, but I don't know what it is.

Funny, I have those same two feelings about you.

Should we . . . show our hands, then? You know, show or fold—isn't that what card players say?

He spread his palms open.

I don't want to fold, he said. I think we should show.

3

Extending his legs in front of him, he summoned the cats by patting his knees.

C'mon, guys. I'm gonna talk to Ellen, and I want you to listen, too.

Boy-Cat scooted up Roy's shins and thighs, settling on his stomach. After a moment Girl-Cat followed, nestling at his side.

Okay, he said, stroking the cats' heads. So here's what I haven't told you: I'm Ennio's guardian.

Guardian? In what sense?

I'm his steward—that's the old-fashioned word for it. He has no idea about any of this, by the way. To him, I'm just Roy, his uncle. And that's the way I want it, at least til he's eighteen. Legally, though, I'm his father.

Father?

Yeah. I adopted him after Renzo died. Hadn't planned on it, but then Gina asked me to do it. At first I didn't see any reason for it; I'd already told her I'd help out however I could, for as long as she needed. I didn't see the point of adoption, didn't want to try being Ennio's father. Ennio already had a father. I mean, Renzo was dead, but he was—is—still the kid's dad.

Back up a bit, Roy. Gina herself wanted Ennio, right? I mean, her pregnancy wasn't an accident?

No. She was ambivalent about Renzo, not about having a child. But after Renzo died and Ennio started having big-time behavioral problems, Gina got pretty stressed. One boy in kindergarten broke a wrist when Ennio pushed him down the stairs; another kid, a girl, got bitten by him . . . there were other incidents. Ennio just couldn't make sense of what'd happened to Renzo. It's still an issue for him, like I've said. In fact, he had a little blow-up at day camp the other day. Sometimes his confusion turns into anger.

Toward his classmates?

Not only. One morning he and Gina and I were in Gina's kitchen, and he hurled a jar at Gina.

A jar?

Yeah, the kind with a metal pouring spout. About this big, sort of squat. Like what you'd use for sugar, you know?

He traced its shape in the air.

Sugar and spice and now a hot flash, *whoosh* . . .

Yeah, I know that type of jar. What made Ennio throw it at his mother?

I'm not sure. Ennio kept asking Gina why the train engineer wasn't able to stop the train before it derailed. The kid had been asking stuff like this for weeks; he wouldn't let up. When Gina finally said she didn't want to talk about it any more, he picked up the jar and tossed it at her. It hit her in the middle of her head at the back, and blood went everywhere . . . It was a superficial wound, not serious, but we had to take her to the emergency room, and the kid was terrified. I'm sure he thought he'd killed her. Gina was pretty freaked out, too.

Roy stopped, closing his eyes for a moment.

That's when I realized that adopting Ennio might stabilize the situation for Gina. Plus, if anything were to happen to her—

—you mean, if Ennio were to really—

—no, I mean in case Gina had a car accident or something. Or got very sick. She was really worried about not having anyone else to count on. So I went ahead and did it.

But what if Gina were to meet someone and get involved with him?

We talked about that. She said she didn't think it was a good idea to assume there'd be another guy in her life, someone who'd be willing to act as Ennio's legal guardian. And if somebody were to show up eventually, he'd just have to accept the situation, see it as a legal formality. So I said okay. The thing is, to Ennio I'm what I've always been: his uncle.

When he turns eighteen, what then?

Gina and I will tell him what the legal situation is. We won't conceal it from him forever, but until he's older and needs to know, there's no reason to confuse him.

How come you didn't tell me all this before now?

At first, because I was worried you might say something to Ennio by mistake. But that's an excuse, I realize. You wouldn't have done that. Mainly I was worried . . . about what if you started getting closer to me. And me to you.

I to you. Wrong pronoun.

Right. *I* to you. In which case, I was worried you'd . . . shy away, once you found out I had a kid. Take a step back.

But I already knew you had one. It's obvious, your attachment to him.

You're right. I could tell you understood right away what Ennio means to me. That's why I'm sharing the whole thing now—because I figured you'd have already backed away, if the fact that I've got a kid to take care of were a problem for you. But I don't know if my being Ennio's legal guardian will make a difference to you. A negative difference, I mean.

He nudged Boy-Cat gently off his stomach.

Hey dove, any reactions? You've gone quiet on me.

I'm just sort of . . . letting the facts settle.

That's fine, I'm not pushing you to react right this instant. Just hoping you'll talk to me. Don't clam up, okay?

It's all very . . . startling. I don't know any other uncle-father helping his half-sister raise her kid.

It's not a choice I ever thought I'd face, that's for sure.

And here we are.

4

Boy-Cat hopped back onto Roy's stomach.

Uh-uh, said Roy. I evicted you, guy. Off you go! Your turn, Girl-Cat. Actually, it's your owner's turn.

Hah. I don't own either of these cats, they own *me*. Wait, you haven't finished. Tell me what went on the other day, at Ennio's day-camp.

Ah, that. Well, Ennio hit another boy, Robbie, in the forehead.

With his fist?

No, with a wooden hammer.

Wow.

Yeah. It's been a while since something like that happened. Gina and I both thought the worst was behind us. Ennio's teachers called Gina; I met up with her, and we took the subway out to Bay Ridge. We both needed to be there.

What made Ennio hit the kid?

Something Robbie said about how trains were better than cars. Apparently Robbie didn't believe Ennio when he said his father was in a train wreck. Whatever Robbie said, it pushed Ennio over the edge.

Have you tried a therapist?

Not yet. I'm a part-timer at each place where I work, so I don't get healthcare benefits. I have really crappy, minimal health insurance. I set aside some of what I earn each month, but it's not enough to pay for therapy for Ennio, and Gina's health plan covers only short-term therapy. We spoke with two doctors on her insurance company's list, but they weren't trained for something like this. Basically, we've been hoping time will be on the kid's side. This is the kind of thing that makes me think I'm not a very good father, by the way. At my age, I ought to have real health insurance.

Yeah, well, join the club—you and a whole lot of other people . . . I've got a doctor in an HMO through my freelancers' union, but my coverage sucks.

Taking her hand, he spread it open, planting a fingertip on each of hers.

So have I answered your questions?

For the most part, yes.

Good. Wanna hear mine now?

Yeah, I do. Actually, first I want to tell you about something that just happened to me. Maybe it'll be like your telling me about adopting Ennio—maybe it'll make things clearer.

Okay. But don't you think we need a little . . . intermission, first?

5

One leg draped over hers. Hand on her breast.

Dove, he murmured. What great fluffling.

She threaded her fingers through his. His kissing gentle now, no longer urgent.

Roy, tell me why you've been alone for a while. It's not just because of Ennio, is it?

He exhaled slowly.

Not just that. But he's been the major reason.

The other reasons?

I've been working a lot, since I need to do more than just make my own ends meet—I've got a kid to help support. Between my jobs and the time

I spend with Ennio, there's not much energy left. And then, oh, I don't know . . . I've tried with a couple of women over the past few years, but it hasn't worked. I got bored.

Do you miss your ex-girlfriend?

Nope. She was bad for me and for everyone in my family. And you, do you miss your old boyfriend?

What old boyfriend?

He took her chin and shook it gently.

Talk to me, why don't you?

Tell him. Go on.

Jesus Christ. Tell him *what*? That she'd never figured out how to couple, save in the physical sense? That she hadn't thought about Paul for more than five minutes in as many years? That there'd been no steady relationship before Paul, and none after?

Stupid trying to explain any of that. Better to talk about money instead, but keep it vague. Say there'd soon be a large up-tick in her bank account balance. Call it an unexpected influx—some very generous funding from a source she wasn't at liberty to disclose. Cash arriving out of the blue. Say it as if the whole thing were just a lark.

Then say she planned to share the funds with friends in need. Say Ennio sounded like a good candidate for therapy. Say she'd gladly pay for it.

6

This isn't at all what I was expecting, said Roy once she'd finished talking.

How do you mean?

You know, you asked me about my past, and I told you about it. So I was thinking you'd tell me how come you've been alone for a while, too. I definitely wasn't expecting you to talk about money. Or offer me any.

Look, Roy, my romantic history—there's really very little to say . . . I was a loner in my twenties, then I was with a guy for about ten years. The marriage ended when I was forty-one. I'd reached a point where I couldn't imagine being with him any longer. I'd published a book of poems, and hoped to keep writing and publishing. But he was always busy with work, and he wanted a family, and I didn't . . . It just wasn't there, the urge to have a kid. It never was. So he and I disappointed each other, and the disappointment ended up being bigger than the love. After we broke up, I pretty much lost my appetite for the whole thing.

What whole thing?

Being in a couple. I just got used to being alone. It didn't feel impossible or awful. It became normal—*is* normal, for me. I was never someone who longed to be in a relationship or had to be a mother. And I've never feared solitude.

So you had no sex or companionship during all this time? Like, a decade?

No, I've had a few affairs. It's not that I don't enjoy being with other people, or having sex. But I haven't been actively looking for a partner. I've got a few close friends; that's been enough for me.

He rubbed his thumb across the palm of her hand.

There's something you're not saying, he said. I can feel it. Something that's got nothing to do with romance.

You're right . . . it's Win, my brother. I'm really worried about him.

How come?

I can't count on him to take care of himself. He's in debt, he's a mess, he drinks constantly. I'm going to give him some money, but it won't fix anything. He'll just give the money away and keep drinking. He's on a downhill slide, and it's excruciating to watch.

Sounds like you think of yourself as your brother's steward. Not in a legal sense, but still, you feel like you're his guardian, don't you?

I guess so.

You know, if I were in his shoes, I doubt I'd want someone else thinking they had to take care of me. I mean . . . it's weird for me to feel indebted to Gina.

Financially?

No. I'm in debt to her for something I didn't even realize I wanted: my relationship with Ennio. That isn't Gina's doing; it's just what happened—

to her, to Ennio, to me . . . I realize I don't actually owe her for anything. But it's weird anyway.

That makes sense.

And I'm uneasy about being in *your* debt as well. Because if I start taking money from you . . . I dunno, the whole thing makes me uneasy.

I understand, Roy. But I'm not making you a loan, so you're not in my debt at all. There's nothing you'll have to pay back. And we're just talking about money here. It's not like with you and Gina and Ennio—that's a totally different situation. Look, just pretend there's cash lying on the street, and I just happened to spot it and point it out to you, so you can pick it up. That's all.

He shook his head.

Sounds nice. But the thing is, suppose you give it to me and then realize you need it yourself? And I've already spent it?

Don't worry about that. And none of this has anything to do with . . . whatever is going on here, between us. It's just a matter of redistributing resources. It's like I'm Robin Hood, and I'm giving away money.

At that, he smiled.

Didn't Robin Hood steal from the rich to give to the poor?

I haven't stolen anything from anybody! It's just . . . call it luck of the draw.

Awfully mysterious. Is it legal?

Perfectly. Sorry I can't say more; not yet, anyway.

Reaching for his clothes, he began to dress.

Let me think about your offer, dove. It's extremely kind.

Ah, don't put it that way. Don't sound so formal, please.

I'll need to speak to Gina before I can give you an answer.

Gina?

Yeah. I can't just go find an expensive therapist and expect Gina not to wonder how the bill's gonna be paid. If I tell her a friend's giving me funds for it, she'll worry the money-source might dry up, and then what'll we do?

Tell her I promise to cover the cost for as long as Ennio needs the therapy.

Look, Gina's still gonna wonder. I mean, be honest—it *is* pretty weird to have someone you haven't known for very long offer to pay for your kid's therapy. It's like pulling a prize out of a Cracker Jack box or something.

God, do they still make that stuff?

They do! It gives Ennio a stomachache when he eats too much of it, which is good, else he'd be totally addicted. C'mon, get up—let's have a glass of wine or a cup of tea . . . oh, wait, shit, what time is it? I didn't realize it was this late. Gina's going out tonight, and I'm taking care of Ennio, and now I've totally lost track of time . . . I'm sorry, I have to get home.

Hey, it's good to lose track.

Yeah . . . but I'm still sorry. When can I see you again?

Lemme think, what am I doing this week . . . tomorrow I need to go to Sunset Park. Want to come with me?

To your brother's?

Yes. Someone else will be there—the sister of his girlfriend, actually. She's been in Madrid since the bombings, and now she intends to move back to New York. Win has asked me to give her a bit of money, to help her get back on her feet.

Okay, I'll go with you. I'd like to meet your brother.

Can you get there at six? We'll stay a half-hour, not longer, I promise.

Sure. Then I'll take you to dinner afterward. And we'll spend the rest of the night together.

Yes . . .

His tongue tracing circles on her throat.

Go now! Ennio needs you. The canines do too.

Text me Win's address, okay?

7

A hum in the silence. Roy's absence palpable, like a scent. Absence, redolence—there was a poem in those words, if she'd not skitter off before trying to write it.

What *was* the last thing she'd written? The last actual poem?

Going to her desk, she pulled a notebook from a drawer. There: four years ago, at the end of December 2001. A half-dozen lines. Four fucking years. And Walter dead now for four weeks, Walter who left Morristown almost forty years ago. When he left, Win kept asking *where's Walter* and Nola kept not answering. She'd been focused on some tragedy in Peru, a volcano that had recently avalanched. Nine miles in seven minutes, she kept saying, the avalanche had traveled nine miles in seven minutes . . . Win had snapped nine beats with his left hand and seven with the right. Making music of it. As for herself, she'd carried Clef the cat upstairs, murmuring a couplet to him: *Walter isn't coming back, Walter's gone away for good . . .*

Had she really made a poem of it—Walter's abandonment of the family? Yep, a couplet, written in simple, clear kid-speak. *Away for good.*

Ennio was a kid who liked poems. Liked "Jabberwocky," at any rate. What else might appeal to him?

She pulled a couple of books off the shelves.

Something with lively rhymes. Poe, yes; Stevie Smith, yes; maybe even Tennyson. *Ring out the false, ring in the true.* Those bells Tennyson heard ringing wildly all by themselves, during a storm—Ennio would like the sounds and images.

And look, a copy of Tennyson's play "Becket" tucked in with the poems. Where'd *that* come from? On the flyleaf was Anne's name. Inside were a few scattered underscores and two sentences highlighted in sparkly light-blue magic marker—Anne's trademark. She'd always kept one of those markers in the back pocket of her jeans.

Gold spoils all. Love is the only gold.

Which brought to mind Nola in the living room, singing "Speak Low" so quietly as the day ended.

8

The phone ringing. Wasn't it the middle of the night?

Win, are you okay?

It's not Win, it's me. I'm downstairs at your building's front door.

Roy—are *you* okay?

Yeah, fine! Just get up and buzz me in.

What time is it?

Not too late, only 2:00 a.m. We've got hours!

Panting slightly from the trot upstairs, he radiated heat as he held his arms open for her.

Hi, featherweight . . . even in your robe you're light as a sparrow.

I'm not a dove anymore?

Sparrows are even lighter! Yeah, you're still a dove. But no fluffling now, okay? Let's just sleep. Good thing I didn't have to wait more than a minute for a train. I got here fast.

Lucky man. Lucky me.

Seven-thirty. Roy's breath like the cats', a light reassuring rasp.

They'd both fallen asleep within minutes. And she hadn't woken up once, nor felt the slightest concern that he'd shown up in the middle of the night. But now a hot flash—her entire body heating, scalp, forehead, neck, chest, arms, stomach, crotch, thighs.

Good morning, furnace!

Yeah, well, there's no thermostat. I can't regulate it.

I like it, actually.

His fingers gently wiping away the slick across her face and neck. Now his tongue between her breasts, licking.

If *you* caught fire ten times a day, Roy, you'd like it not so much.

I can imagine. Still, I like it when you get warm like this. Selfish of me, I know . . . okay, rise 'n shine, let's get you cooled down.

Black tea, sliced apples, buttered toast. The cats nuzzling Roy's ankles, one on either side.

Ellen, these cats are like dogs! Ah, it's eight-fifteen, I gotta go walk the canines.

What's on your docket today?

A couple of classes in Bed-Stuy. Did I mention I'm working at a new community center? The pay's decent, but getting there from Bay Ridge is a drag. Don't you have to go to the museum today?

His hands on her shoulders, thumbs kneading tight muscles.

Yeah, but I don't need to rush. Ah, there, you've found it, that spot where it's always tense . . .

I can feel it. Ennio likes it when I rub this exact same spot. Okay, that's enough! See you tonight at your brother's, okay?

Boy-Cat and Girl-Cat both moved to the door, blocking his exit.

Move, cat-pals! 'Bye, dove. I'm glad you let me in.

Me, too. Hey you two, come over here . . .

She pinned both cats to the floor as Roy let himself out.

Could someone with a kid always tell if someone else really wasn't into the kid?

Yes. Hence Roy must believe she was into his kid. Did that mean she was? Did he know what she wasn't yet sure she knew? Or was afraid to know: was that it?

Ennio: a wounded boy-bird.

If it was because of Ennio that Roy hadn't had a girlfriend since the one who'd slept with Ennio's father, and if the boy himself was of mixed minds about his uncle's new woman, and if his mother was ambivalent as well, and if the new woman turned out to be not Robin Hood but a jackpot winner, *then* what would Roy think—no, feel?

Impervious and Stubborn

1

How to raise the stakes?

Blair stared into the canal. The water lay stagnant below the Third-Street bridge. It smelled bad. But there were trees on either side of the Gowanus, and no one else around.

Always go too far, Camus said, because that's the only place you'll find the truth.

Going too far wasn't a question of raw force or power, though. You could knock out the global stock market if you were a good enough hacker. Yet even if you came up with all the right algorithms to mess things up, you wouldn't necessarily be making anything *new* happen. For that, you had to derange mental orbits.

Babysitting that six-year-old kid during high school, she'd learned how derangement worked.

The kid she was babysitting had invited his cousin, a five-year-old boy, to play. The kid found an empty cardboard box, put it on the low arm of a sofa next to a glass-fronted bookcase, and told the cousin to climb into the box. It'd be a boat, he said. They'd sail it on the sea.

The kid held the box so the cousin could climb in. Watching, she'd figured the kid would slide and tip the box over onto the sofa cushions. The kid told his cousin that the cushions were waves in the water, and the sofa was the sea. But he didn't slide the box onto the cushions; instead, he gave it a push in the other direction, and it tipped over and went right into the bookcase. The glass doors shattered, and the five-year-old got a gash on his elbow. She'd had to put both kids in a cab to an emergency clinic. The injured boy had needed a bunch of stitches.

What was that about, she'd asked the kid as they waited for his hurt cousin's parents to arrive. What the hell were you doing?

The boy wasn't fazed. The books were the rocks, he'd answered.

Rocks?

The boat smashed into the rocks. That's how it was supposed to happen. I made it happen that way.

She hadn't forgotten those words. The kid had done what he did because he knew it was supposed to happen. It happened just as he imagined it. That kid was managing perception.

2

The biggest challenge was money. Her job paid shit, but asking for a raise would draw attention.

No borrowing, though. No owing anyone anything. No one on top.

The problem would need to be solved in a different way. There were plenty of rich people in the city, people who wouldn't miss a hundred bucks any more than she'd miss a dime. It wouldn't be hard to pick the right person. Simply a matter of the right occasion.

The words she'd stenciled over the tunnel had lasted for a week.

Those seven words painted across a train trestle were enough to make some minds veer off track.

Camus liked the story of Sisyphus. Whenever Sisyphus returns to his rock and starts readying to push it up the mountain again, said Camus, *in that slight pivoting he contemplates that series of unrelated actions which becomes his fate, created by him.* A slight pivoting, the simple act of turning to push the rock, and suddenly Sisyphus understands that his seemingly unrelated actions have become his self-created fate. *Each atom, each mineral flake of that night-filled mountain, in itself forms a world.* A world that Sisyphus sees in a new light, each time he pushes.

3

For the next thing she'd do, she'd need to be in good shape. Leg muscles, especially.

One of the guys in the stockroom at work belonged to a gym in Park Slope; he'd given her a couple of guest passes. A few hours on the leg machines would be useful. She'd need to round up supplies, too: a couple of hardened-steel chains, cable bike locks, and high-end padlocks. The police had bolt cutters, but a combination of bike locks and a padlocked chain would be hard to deal with.

She'd get two metal plates made. Each would be roughly three feet square, and not so heavy that they couldn't be carried easily. There was an ironworks company over in Cobble Hill that could make the plates. She'd have holes drilled in the top of each for the bike-lock cables. The chains could be carried up, too.

The details could be figured out. The important thing for now was staying under the radar. Her new work would be for Keith and people like him: misfits, loners, people who didn't care what others thought or did. And who paid for not caring.

There's a desert in everyone, claimed Camus. No one can survive in that desert without being impervious and stubborn—those were the adjectives he used.

Keith knew how to survive in his desert; he'd figured it out. So she had to, as well. There was no other choice. He'd want her to.

4

How long had it been since she'd had a conversation?

Since that evening at the art gallery in the Slope. Before that, several weeks of silence.

Talking was a waste of energy. During sex, especially. Males tended to stay quiet. Females were talkier, though also better sexually most of the time. Sometimes they were hesitant, mistaking her for a girl. That's when conversations became traps. Explanations were tedious, useless. Labels meant nothing.

No one but Keith had ever gotten it about her being a boy. Or an artist. As for other street artists, they just wanted to be "discovered," or to play silly hide-and-seek games. And most art critics considered street art a thing mainly for amateurs, in any case. Not a money-maker. The money they'd all make—the artists, critics, gallery owners, investors—was what they were interested in.

She would sidestep all that, not get trapped by anyone's wallet.

The only useful dialogues were wordless, like those between artworks and their viewers. Actually, some visual art made sounds, though not many people could hear them. When the Russian composer Mussorgsky saw an exhibit of sketches by a dead friend of his, he insisted the sketches made music, and he said he could score them. Everyone thought that was ridiculous. His scores of the sketches weren't published til after his death. That's what happened to misfits.

Keith had to be in hiding somewhere rural, without a cellphone or computer. In a cabin near the Canadian border, maybe? Doing odd jobs to stay afloat, and taking care of stray animals. He could write a letter, though. But maybe he was worried it'd get intercepted.

The only thing to do was wait for him to make contact.

When he disappeared after he got released from jail, the parents said it was time to move on. They kept repeating *get closure*. By that point, they'd made up their minds: Keith had brought all of it on himself. Their need for closure was his fault, too—that was how they wanted it, that was the story they told, so they could claim Keith was gone and their friends would feel sorry for them. Nobody would have to think about him again. He could be written off like a lousy investment.

He'd gone to ground, as an animal would. But he wasn't truly gone. *They* were—the parents. Dead to the world. Lost in fakeness.

Keith would come back. He had to; his pup needed him to come back.

We have art, said Camus, in order not to die of life.

Queste Cose Mi Rendono Felice

1

Odd to be walking up Tenth Street instead of Ninth, her usual route. But Ninth was risky: Mr. Reyes might be outside his shop. Or might notice her outside his window.

The phone, ringing. The museum, maybe? She was late for work, but so what? Today was her last day there.

Ah, Dale, we speak at last! You okay, bud?

I'm fine, fine.

Don't tell me there's been another hitch with the closing . . .

Nope, everything's good. It's been postponed to a week from Monday, but it'll happen.

The twenty-fourth?

Yeah. I've made a reservation at Bouley afterward, for lunch. Since you've put up with me throughout this ordeal, we both deserve a great meal, don't you think?

For sure. I'll be busy that Monday morning, but don't worry, I'll be at Bouley at the appointed hour.

Busy, ten days from now? With what, or should I say with whom? You've been so secretive lately!

No, just lots going on. I'll be doing an errand that morning. Some paperwork.

Paperwork? Never touch the stuff. Okay, see you at Bouley.

At the museum, a quick scroll through the *Times*'s headlines.

Ongoing mess in the Middle East and Central Asia. The death toll for civilian protesters killed last summer in Uzbekistan was estimated at one thousand five hundred. And a year after a collision of three express trains in Pakistan, victims' families were still struggling to put their lives back together.

Boom.

Jesus, the emails were stacking up. One from Sophie and Hank asking if she'd gotten their recent messages. And from Anne saying she'd put off her departure date, since Giselle's thyroid numbers weren't where they ought to be.

Oh shit. Poor Giselle.

And now an email from her supervisor: the museum would pay for a car service to take her home. And a PS: thanks for everything, you've been great, we'll be glad to provide a letter of recommendation.

Into a cardboard box went a dozen books of poems, a shawl, and an umbrella. Right before the car arrived to take her home, a second brief email from Anne offered better news: Giselle now appeared not to be in any danger. A second test had been done, it was okay.

Heading upstairs for the final time, Ellen glanced at the Egyptian Room.

Goodbye, mummies! Goodbye, old life.

2

Can you stick around til my tumbling class is over?

Roy's shoulder propped open the door to the Balcony as he spoke.

It's a forty-minute class, right?

Yeah. Can you wait that long? I can't remember what you told me this morning . . . do you have errands to run now? Sorry, I'm a little tuckered out from last night—in a good way, I mean. A really good way.

Yeah, me too . . . we didn't get enough sleep, did we? Anyhow, yeah, I can stick around. I'll do more stretching, it can't hurt. Wait, doesn't this class usually have another instructor?

Yes, but she's sick, so she asked if I could handle it. See you in a bit.

Down below on the court, a quick slap of bodies landing on rubber mats as the girls practiced forward rolls.

In the farthest nook of the Balcony, Ellen lay on her back and pulled her knees to her chest. Pull, stretch, again, again. Closing her eyes, she replayed the scene from the evening before. She'd arrived at Win's and met Maria, who looked somewhat like Mel. Nose and cheekbones almost the same, hair a bit darker. Stylishly dressed in a skirt and sandals with heels. Sultry, was that the right word? Not lean, like Mel. A bit shorter, her shoulders rounder; attractive, yes, though her smile seemed tight. Maybe she was exhausted. Or hadn't wanted to be at Win's. Maybe he'd pushed her to stay there til she found her own place, and she'd agreed, reluctantly.

Though it hadn't seemed like that, given the way her hand brushed his shoulder as she walked past him, asking *do you want another* as she reached for his glass. Maria was a drinker, too, but not on the same order as Win. She seemed like the kind of drinker who'd make sure his glass was topped off while not overdoing it herself.

They'd talked for a few minutes. Maria spoke of Madrid with what sounded like affection, yet she was moving back to New York for financial reasons, she said. Too much bureaucracy in Spain. And the salaries were low.

Then the doorbell rang and Roy entered, introducing himself to Win. He took in the scene in the living room, including the woman on the sofa, her legs crossed, one sandaled foot nestled against the other. He stared at Maria for a moment. Like a cat, he was—motionless, tense. Then he inhaled and moved toward her, extending his hand.

Hi, I'm Roy.

Maria. Nice to meet you.

Have a seat, said Win. Can I get you both a drink?

I'll pass, thanks, Roy said as he sat on the bench. A glass of water would be good, though.

How about you, Ellen?

Me too.

Right, coming up. And you, Maria?

Still working on mine, she said, tilting her near-full glass in Win's direction.

They'd sat in silence til Win returned to the room, highball glass in one hand and a pair of half-filled water glasses in the other. He handed them off, then turned to Roy.

So, what's your line of work?

I teach phys ed classes at a couple of places, including a gym in Park Slope. That's where I met your sister.

I have no idea how to work out, said Maria. I walk a lot, that's my exercise.

I drink a lot, said Win, that's mine.

And your work? asked Roy.

I'm a composer. I draw music.

Don't composers usually write?

Had that been it, the moment when something shifted? Before that, there'd been a chance for a conversation, but with Roy's question that chance had gone up in smoke.

Most composers, Win answered. I don't notate, I draw. I make sketches, black-and-white line drawings that capture my music.

Can you sell your sketches, asked Roy. Like, as art?

I doubt it, Win answered. In any case, what I'm doing isn't for money. It's for me, for my music. Ask my sister—she'll explain it to you. Or not.

At that, she'd stood and pulled two envelopes from her bag.

Listen, Roy and I need to get going. We've got dinner plans. One of these envelopes is for you, Maria—this one, with your name on it. I wish you luck finding an apartment and a job. Hope you enjoy living here in New York. And Win, the other envelope . . . it's cash, not a check.

She put Win's envelope on the end table by the sofa. He said nothing, turning toward the door.

Thank you very much, said Maria, putting her envelope in her bag. I'll pay you back as soon as I can.

No worries. Nice to meet you, Maria.

Yes, nice to meet you both, said Roy.

Win held the door open in silence.

On the sidewalk outside Win's building, Roy'd taken her hand.

You always that rough on your brother?

It's how we deal. Win doesn't respond to nuance—he drinks too much for it.

That was a little . . . unnerving.

Yeah, I know. You got a good look at how it is. My brother's living in la-la land. Those drawings of his—I mean, he can barely make rent . . .

And Maria?

What about her?

Is she staying at his place?

Dunno. For now, maybe.

You know, I was kind of startled when I first saw her. She reminded me of my ex.

In what way?

Physically, for starters. But also her way of holding back, stepping to one side.

Seemed to me she was just watching.

Perhaps. I have a funny feeling about her, though.

Hey, let's go eat. I'm tired of worrying about my brother. And I've been looking forward to this evening with you.

Me too. How about back to Bay Ridge?

Yeah—to the Italian place. I'd like to eat there again.

Good. It's our place now.

3

Roy's skin was slick with sweat as he opened the Balcony door.

Man, it's hot in there, he said as he toweled off his face.

Drink some water, said Ellen. You look pretty dehydrated.

You're right, I am. Thanks, dove.

He squeezed her elbow, his thumb caressing it for a moment. Let's go up the street, he said. I need to talk to you.

In the park they sat beneath a tree. At the base of the grassy slope, a boy Ennio's age was playing with a terrier. His parents stood nearby, smiling.

I want to talk about last night, said Roy. At Win's, I mean. The rest of it was great.

Okay, but first I have a question for you. You said when you saw Maria at Win's, you thought of your ex-girlfriend?

Actually, that's what I wanted to talk about.

You haven't seen your ex in something like five years, right?

Longer than that. But when I saw Maria, it was as if she and my ex were the same person. There *was* some sort of resemblance; it was a little bit physical, but even more in their energy . . . it hit a nerve. Remember how you asked me once if I knew where my ex was living? And I told you I'd heard she went abroad?

Yes.

I've no idea where she ended up. She never said anything to me about going to Madrid. It doesn't matter, in any case. The thing is, when I first walked into your brother's apartment, I felt like I was being confronted with Renzo's killer. I know that's crazy; Maria isn't Gina, and it wasn't Gina's fault that Renzo died.

Gina?

Yeah, that's my ex's name. Same as my sister's. Her real name's Virginia, but she was called Gina. Still is, I imagine.

Good lord. Two Gina's. Remind me how you met her?

She grew up near me. Went to the same high school as my sister and me—and Renzo too, of course. After college, she came back to the 'hood; that's where I met her. She was doing some dog walking to make money. We got to talking because of Kay and Nine. Anyway . . . your brother, how do you think he reacted to our visit?

Win was focused on Maria. Having her there is like being with Mel again. That's what I'm worried about.

He'll have to adjust. It'll take time.

Time's one thing he's got plenty of. And booze. But no money.

4

The dog ran around the boy, barking at the stick held out of reach.

Happy frustration, said Roy, pointing.

Yeah.

Look, the dog just got his stick back. Now let's see how the boy feels about it . . . that dog's not gonna surrender easily! You know, the idea of Maria with your money, it's like she's taking advantage of you . . .

I don't care about the money. Maria can do what she likes with it. I care about my brother—about what he might be getting himself into.

Did he and Mel hang out with her before she moved abroad?

Win never met her while he was with Mel—Maria was already in Madrid by then. The two sisters had been out of touch for a while. They used to talk by phone now and then, but that was it. For Mel, the trip to Spain was a whim. She was working on a design for a wrought-iron gate and wanted some visual inspiration. So she figured, why not go there?

So Win met Maria after Mel's death?

Nope—Maria didn't come back for the funeral.

Ah. What about the parents?

Mel's and Maria's? They died a while ago. In a car accident, when Mel was twenty or so.

You know anything else about Maria?

Only that she teaches ESL. I gather she's been doing it for a while. She's lived abroad for at least a decade. She's ten years older than Mel—around forty-five.

So for Win, she's basically a stranger?

Yeah. And I hope things stay that way.

5

Late-day sunlight, angled low. The playing fields were empty now.

Man, your hair's a mess, Roy! Here . . .

As she raked his hair, he caught her hand, spread its palm, kissed it.

Your plate is full, dove. With your brother, I mean. I didn't enjoy seeing the tension between the two of you. Your reactions to him seemed a bit harsh, but I'm starting to get why. I mean, it's like you had to push back because he's sabotaging himself.

That's just the right word for it. Thanks for putting up with what happened last night. And for talking about it now. Every time I visit my brother, I feel like hurling every bottle of vodka in his apartment out the window. It strangles my heart to watch Win drink like he does.

It's pretty intense. Though he does hold his liquor well . . . he's not one of those falling-down drunks.

No. But in a way, his type is worse. I'll tell you what, though—I sure won't be taking any other friends to meet Win and Maria. Way too much drama.

Just for the record, I don't have any other "friends" like you.

Not sure what word to use . . .

How about lover, or is that too old-fashioned?

No, it's good, I like it.

Glad you, uh, concur—is *that* the right word? Hanging around with a poet, I gotta be careful.

Dusk was settling in. The dog and boy had already headed off; a few stragglers ambled toward the park's exit. Sitting cross-legged, Roy placed his hands at the back of his head and swiveled from side to side.

You're so flexible, Roy. I envy you.

You could be too, lazybones.

Not like you. I bet your body's always been that way.

That's the good part of my work, it keeps me loose. Your work keeps your tongue loose, right?

Hah. Sometimes I'm afraid I'll turn into a parrot and just spout whatever crap I'm writing or editing.

You're no parrot. You're a dove.

I wonder . . . a while ago I did a freelance project for a big client, a manufacturer of tiles for bathrooms. After several months, it felt like all I could talk about was grout—you know, that cement stuff between tiles. I became totally fluent in grout.

Why didn't you write a grout poem?

Same reason I don't write any other kind of poem, I guess. Too caught up in other people's words.

There's more to it than that.

I've lacked . . . belief, I guess you could say.

In poetry? Or yourself?

Poetry's not the problem, I've always had faith in poems. Reading them has pretty much kept me alive. My own poems, though . . . that's another story.

What happened to your book?

The publisher folded right after it came out, and it basically fell through the cracks. Since then I haven't written much.

But you read poetry all the time. So you must be thinking about poems constantly, even if you're not writing them, right? You know, I'd really like to read something of yours.

I could give you a heap of pages about grout.

Seriously. Will you give me a copy of your book?

Sometime.

Sometime very soon, okay? Ah, this hour in the park, dusk . . . it's calmer now. I like it. This is Ennio's favorite time of day. He says dusk is when things get quiet and he can hear his father's voice in his head. There's a streetlamp that starts humming outside his bedroom window at dusk, and Ennio hates it. He says it's like a sword attacking his father's voice.

Wow. Quite an image.

Yeah. He even drew a picture of the sword. I've tried to get the city to fix that streetlamp, but no luck.

Drawing a sword because it makes a sound—that reminds me of what my brother's doing . . .

6

Roy rose to his feet and extended a hand.

C'mon, let's get something to eat. But we gotta do a quick stretch first.

Oof, I'm so stiff!

That's only because you don't stretch every day. Here, lie on my back for a minute.

He stooped, hands on knees.

Go ahead—turn around, lean backward and lie on me. Yeah, that's right—back to back. Let your feet leave the ground. I've got you, you won't fall off. Now I'm gonna jiggle you a little . . . feels nice, doesn't it? Like a standing massage. Okay, down you go. Now stand up nice and straight. Ah, a bit of skin's showing, what a great belly you have . . . you should always wear shirts that are slightly too short.

Great as in great, or great as in large?

What sort of poet are you, that you'd have to ask?

They descended Ninth Street.

Hey, said Roy. There's another of those hundred-dollar bills on the sidewalk. Or is that the one we saw the other day, with Ennio?

Same one, I think. Yeah, by the entrance to the F.

Sometimes I think New York's all about repetition. How often have you been on the subway and bumped into someone you haven't laid eyes on forever, and then you see that same person a few days later? Ennio loves that kind of thing. Coincidences—he's a magnet for them. We get on the train and there's his old babysitter, or some kid's mom he hasn't seen in ages. Or he sees a kid wearing the same T-shirt he's wearing. Or someone's whistling one of his favorite songs. Whenever that kind of stuff happens, Ennio says *queste cose mi rendono felice*.

My Italian's rusty. Does that mean the people he runs into make him happy?

No, it means the coincidences themselves make him happy. I hope he can hold onto that feeling. After all, positive coincidences happen a lot. Even if we don't always register them.

Yeah. But sometimes it can be hard to know what to make of something good that happens by chance.

Usually we don't have to make anything of it. Just be glad it's happened.

They crossed Eighth Avenue.

I have an idea about Maria, he said. Why not tell her she's got to leave Win's apartment and find her own place?

Well, I can't just flat-out *order* her to go.

Okay, but you could tell her she's welcome to your money if she moves out soon, but otherwise, you'd like your money back.

Sounds bossy. Win won't like it. He'll say I'm interfering.

Well, since you're providing the money . . . speaking of which, I talked with Gina, and we'd like to take you up on your offer to cover Ennio's therapy. But not for more than six months. Is that okay by you?

Of course. Whatever you'd like. Is five hundred okay for starters? I'll withdraw it tomorrow.

Ellen . . .

Halting on the sidewalk, he pulled her to him.

This help you're giving us—I want you to understand how grateful I am. Gina is grateful, too. And I'm trusting you mean it when you say it's not a problem.

Absolutely. I just hope you can find the right therapist for Ennio.

We've already got two appointments scheduled.

Have you said anything to him about it?

Just that the three of us are going to talk to a doctor who knows about what happened to Renzo.

That sounds right. Not that I know anything about how to handle kids in such circumstances

Who does? I'm crossing my fingers.

They paused at the corner of Seventh Avenue.

Any decent food around here? Roy asked.

Let's keep going, Fifth Avenue's got more restaurants. D'you like sushi?

He ran his thumb along her lower lip.

Yes, I like sushi. Dove, please come back to Bay Ridge with me tonight . . . we'll have to get up early, is that okay? Ennio's coming with me to my Sunday morning class in Queens; I'll need to pick him up first, at his mother's. We'll have to be out the door at seven. Can you deal?

No problem. I've gotta feed the cats tomorrow morning, in any case.

The dogs will be thrilled to see you again.

Ah, the canines . . . oh, here, this place has good sushi. Dinner's on me, okay?

He hesitated, then put a hand on the small of her back, fingertips tap-dancing lightly.

Accepted, he said.

Needling

1

Not Win but Maria answering the door. Wearing a loose, pale-blue linen shift, her hair tousled, feet bare. Looking like the relaxed woman of the house.

Come in, she said.

Do you know where Win is? I need to speak with him.

He stepped out for a moment. To the store.

The liquor store, you mean? On a Sunday?

There's one that stays open til noon.

I didn't call, so Win's not expecting me. I'll wait for him. How are you, have you found an apartment?

Not yet. Have a seat.

She moved to the spot she'd occupied the last time, in the corner of the sofa. Her own place, already claimed.

Are you looking around this neighborhood for a place to live?

Yes, and elsewhere in Brooklyn as well.

Know anyone in the city, other than Win?

Maria draped an arm over the back of the sofa. Her expression was unreadable, her body quiet but not stiff. She waited a few beats before answering.

I've got a few contacts. And I've already lined up several job interviews for next week.

That's good. What about friends, do you have any?

Not really, not anymore, I've been away a long time . . . but I'm not worried about that.

Silence; then Maria stood.

Would you like anything to eat or drink?

Is there anything to drink besides booze? Or to eat?

A pause.

Yes, there's fresh food. I've been cooking.

My brother isn't well, Maria. As you may have noticed—or maybe not. So I'm telling you: he isn't well. It's not a good idea for you to stay here. You really should get your own place.

You needn't worry.

Well, I do worry. About my brother.

Maria shrugged.

Win seems all right to me, she said. He drinks more than he should, but otherwise he seems okay.

You don't know what he used to be like.

True. But he's shown me some of his new work. He's into it, and it's good.

New work?

Yeah, new drawings—based on his tinnitus.

Raising the lid of the piano bench, Maria extracted some paper.

Here, she said, carrying a half-dozen sheets to the table and spreading them out. Take a look.

Wiggling penciled lines, thick and thin, pushing and tugging at one another. Coiled like snakes or skeins of rope.

I can hear what it sounds like, said Maria.

You think so? You're hearing what you want to hear. That's what my brother doesn't understand: no one can play this. It's not a musical score—a composer can't hand this to musicians.

Maria shook her head.

I disagree, she said. If you just look at it for a while, you can tell—

—whatever. Win needs to realize if he keeps doing these drawings, he's no longer a working composer. My brother hasn't put a single note on paper in over two years, did you know that? He's had no commissions for his music. He used to write advertising jingles on the side, too, to earn some money. But he's stopped that as well. It's very troubling.

Maria gave a half-smile.

He's doing what he wants, she said. He says music isn't dots and lines, he's not writing code. He's composing. Notating, too, in his own way.

The point is, Maria, he's totally broke. On a different subject . . . do you miss your sister?

Maria shrugged.

I didn't know her well. As kids we weren't close, and once I left for college, we fell out of touch. There wasn't much for me to miss.

Why were you out of touch?

Mutual lack of interest, I suppose. We didn't have a falling-out or anything. As I said, we weren't ever close. Just very different people.

Can I ask what you and Mel did when she was with you in Madrid?

I was working, so she went on her own to the Prado and a few other museums. I think she enjoyed herself. She filled a notebook with sketches; I've given it to Win. He said the sketches will help him with his own compositions.

Your parents died in a car crash, right? Mel mentioned it once.

Yes. Quite a while ago.

How'd it happen?

They were driving to a marriage counseling session. The therapy was pointless, the marriage was over, but that's another matter. The guy who hit them was stoned; he died, too.

Have you talked about it with Win?

At that, Maria stared for several moments before responding.

You know, my parents—my family—it's none of your business.

You're right. I shouldn't be asking questions like this. But there's something you need to understand: Win shouldn't have to deal with stuff that's not *his* business. He's had a very rough time of it since Mel's death. So think hard before you start using him as a sounding board. Don't talk with him about stuff that'll bring him down. Especially what happened in Madrid.

Maria gathered up Win's drawings and replaced them in the piano bench.

You've got it backwards, Ellen. *I'm* the one doing the listening. Win needs someone to talk to, so I listen. It's not my job to straighten him out. If he wants to talk with me about Mel or anything else, that's fine.

My brother hasn't been *working* since Mel's death. It's a really bad situation.

Doesn't seem to bother him. Maybe it's only a problem for you.

Look, I've given you the money you need. I have to say, it seems to me you're freeloading.

Maria gave a short laugh.

Are you kidding? Did you know I'm buying the food here? And cooking it. I'm actually getting Win to eat real food, not just cereal and sandwiches. Yeah, I've had some of your brother's vodka. So? I don't see anybody else bothering to sit down and listen to him.

The door opened.

El, said Win. What brings you here?

He placed a bag on the table; its contents clinked.

Some news I need to share with you. Can we step out for a walk?

No, said Maria, you two stay here, I'll go. I have some errands to run.

Win frowned. Maria, you don't have to—

—it's fine, really. I'll be back in an hour or so.

They looked at each other for a moment.

Okay, Win said quietly. See you then.

2

The kitchen was tidier than normal. A clean wok sat on the range, cloves of garlic on the counter, fresh bread on the table. Maria hadn't lied: none of this could possibly have been Win's doing.

Lemme make a drink, he said. Then you can tell me your news.

He pulled two quarts of vodka from the bag and twisted the cap off one of the bottles.

So what's up? Did you land another hundred million bucks?

No. It's about Walter. He died a few weeks ago.

Opening the freezer door, Win pulled out an ice-tray and cracked several cubes into a glass.

I assume you don't want any, he said, tilting the bottle of vodka in her direction.

No thanks.

He poured a drink and raised his glass in a toast.

Cheers, he said. So the old man's dead. Long live the old man's Deutsche Grammophon recordings.

He drank, then topped off his glass.

How'd you find out, anyway? Internet?

No. Bruno wrote to me.

Win's brows rose slightly.

Bruno? You two been in touch?

First time in my life I've heard from him. Apparently a friend of his helped him find my email address . . . Bruno said Walter died in his sleep, exactly one month ago today. I thought you should know.

I don't need to mark the date, thanks. Did you write Bruno back and tell him he ought to visit New York, maybe sell a few fiddles here?

I didn't write him, no.

He gave a low chuckle.

Ah, Walter . . . you know, it was Mel who got me to stop wasting my energy. She said, either get in touch with your father or quit thinking about him. Make him real, or recognize he doesn't exist for you.

He dragged his fingertips across his eyes, pressing for a moment on his eyeballs.

So I stopped thinking about him. And you know what? It worked—Walter stopped existing for me. Hate to be rude, El, but I'd like to get back to work now.

All right, I'm leaving. By the way, Maria showed me a few of your sketches.

The ones in the piano bench?

Yeah. She said they were based on your tinnitus.

They're new.

Can you tell me something about them?

He took his drink to the sofa.

There's a drummer in Queens who hooks up musicians to an electronic stethoscope. He's got this computer program that analyzes the sound-patterns of their hearts. Every person's heart makes sounds. Not just the usual thumping, but other sound-patterns, too, with different pitches and rhythms. It depends on the walls of the chambers. If the heart's in good shape, the walls bend; if the heart's unhealthy, they don't. Stiffer walls produce higher-pitched tones, flexible walls make lower pitches. Anyway, when this drummer heard his own heartbeat for the first time, he said it sounded like free jazz, with rhythms he'd heard only in Cuban and Nigerian music. Slower, but the same rhythmic patterns.

He drank, then rattled the ice.

I didn't want to bother with a stethoscope, he added. So I'm listening to my tinnitus.

I thought you said you can hear just one sound. You said it was super-high and sharp.

One part of it, yeah. But there are other sounds. The high needling is the obvious overtone. Then there are bass undertones. A kind of underwater whoosh.

Like when your blood pumps in your ears?

Sometimes, yeah. Other times it's more like an engine room. And the whole thing, all the sounds together—it follows a rhythmic scheme that keeps changing. Like there's an orchestra improvising in my head.

3

At least he was talking. Conducting an actual conversation.

Those drawings of yours . . . they're intense, Win. It must take a fair bit of energy to make them. I hope Maria finds an apartment soon, because you need your space for yourself. You need silence, privacy.

He sat his glass of vodka on the coffee-table before speaking.

Maria can stay here as long as she needs to. There's no reason for her to leave.

Look, I gave her money so she could find a place of her own. Not so she can camp out with you.

Either give Maria the money with no strings, or don't give it at all.

I could have given it to somebody else in need. I haven't forgotten the fact that Maria inherited forty thousand dollars when Mel died.

So?

So I have the right to ask if Maria's spending the money I've given her on an apartment, or on other stuff. It isn't my intention to pay for her food or clothes. Besides, doesn't it complicate things for you, her staying here?

I want Maria to stay as long as she needs to. She looks at my work and listens. And she helps me hear what it sounded like.

What *what* sounded like?

Mel's death.

Oh, Christ, Win.

He was gazing into space now.

I don't want to talk about this anymore, he said at last. Leave Maria out of it, and don't mention money to me again. By the way, I gave away the cash you left here the other day. It was two grand, right?

Gave it away?

I didn't give it to Maria, in case you're wondering. Or to my local liquor store, in case you're worried. I sent it to a nonprofit group that provides medical care for children injured in wartime bombings.

You're kidding.

No. I told you, I don't want your money. I'll send you the information so you can write off the donation on your taxes.

Jesus, Win.

You're about to enter your own private fairy-tale, El. Don't try to drag me along for the ride. Go now, please, I'd like to get back to work.

Gym Rat

1

The weight room at the gym was full. A few women were on the upper-body machines, but the leg machines were monopolized by guys. A few of them glanced at Blair as she walked in.

One guy finished his workout and left the room. Blair reset the weights of the leg-press he'd vacated, then adjusted the height of its seat. Another guy entered the room and dropped his sweat-jacket next to hers, on a ledge by the door.

Mind if I work in with you, he said as he sauntered over. I'll set the weights for you when I'm done.

He put his hand on the machine, keeping it there. Like he owned the machine. Had a right to go first.

You probably don't even weigh what I leg-press, he added, smirking. What're you doing, thirty pounds or so?

I'm on this machine now. Use that one over there—work in with that guy. Not with me.

His brows rose. Yes ma'am, he said, giving a mock-salute. Whatever the little lady says.

Up yours, gym rat.

Whoa. You a member of this gym, sweetheart? I don't recall seeing you here before.

He waved a trainer over. Hey Jeff, is this girl a member? I don't think so. She's clogging up the works.

I have a pass, she said. And I'm using this machine now.

The trainer frowned. Look, he began, you two gotta work this out . . .

There'd be other machines somewhere else. In another room, or another gym. Waste of time to get into it with this asshole.

She turned away and walked to the door, then paused. The guy had already jumped on the machine and was doing leg-presses, his back toward her. The trainer was nowhere to be seen.

She picked up her sweatshirt on the ledge by the door. Then reached into the pocket of the guy's sweat-jacket.

A couple of bills, folded in half.

Slipping her closed fist into the pouch of her sweatshirt, she left the weight-room.

2

In an adjacent workout space, the hum of a dozen treadmills drowned out all voices.

She scanned the room, then headed toward the back. A short staircase led to a landing and another door, which gave onto a jogging track. The track was strange—suspended along the perimeter of the basketball court below, like a deck on a boat. And nobody was using it.

Opening her fist, she inspected the money: two C-notes. As far as that guy in the weight-room was concerned, she didn't exist. He'd figure some guy had ripped him off—someone he'd recognize as male. To him she'd be invisible.

A gym class was happening on the court below. Bunch of junior high girls. In any case, the running track was empty. Some leg stretches and a half-hour jog would be enough.

And then? A subway ride to Bay Ridge.

She lay on a mat and pulled her knees to her chest.

If the owner of *Buy Me Love* were home, how to explain showing up there? Just say the art gallery had provided the address. Ask if it was okay to take a couple of quick photos of the canvas.

The painting had stayed in mind. As had the initial meeting with the artist in the park. And of course the hour or so in her apartment. Most of all that moment when the sensations turned weird, the woman on top motionless and silent, a literal dead weight. All of it had resisted erasure from memory. And now there seemed to be a reason why.

The painting would launch a new project, "Intervention." Its context: an unknown artist makes a series of paintings, then dies unexpectedly during sex with a stranger. After the artist's death, all but one of the paintings disappear. The stranger with whom the artist had sex creates the next work in the series. Not another painting, though; something else, connected to the series yet altering it.

The absurd creator—that was Camus's designation for a person such as this stranger. A particular sort of interventionist. An artist whose job, Camus stated, is to project himself as deeply as possible into lives that are not his own.

One of the girls on the court down below let out a yelp; the others clapped.

On the mat, Blair rolled onto her stomach and raised herself up on her elbows, listening. The instructor called out a name. *You're next, kiddo, step lively* . . . The girls whooped and yelled. *C'mon—go go go!—you can do it!* The stomping of their feet echoed around the track. They sounded happy.

Had Keith ever been happy? How to be a boy like him, a perpetual outsider. How to be such a boy, and be happy? The word seemed inert, meaningless.

A noise: the door to the track was opening. Someone entered, pulling the door shut.

Blair sat up.

Nonetheless

1

No workplace. No necessary tasks. Nothing that *had* to be done, or else. And *this* moment, right now? In this instant, the cats were batting a toy mouse across the kitchen floor while she sat and watched, fingertips tapping her kneecaps. She stopped and slid her hands, palms up, under her thighs. Christ, was she now literally sitting on her hands? While a hundred million dollars flashed in front of her like a strobe light at some surreal discotheque, the brightest of warning signals?

Eyes closed, she felt it coursing through her: something like a hot flash, though it wasn't.

Fear. Not of the fortune but what it would expose. No dodging the fact of failure: despite a few good endorsements, her chapbook of poems had come and gone, mostly unnoticed. After which she'd used a chronic lack of money as an excuse for staying in a rut. Sure, there'd always been freelance work to be searched for, the constant pressure of earning. But so what? She could've pushed herself to keep writing poems; there'd always been some time left over, even after freelancing took its share. Maybe not a lot, yet shouldn't she have treated each extra minute like the gold it was?

Failure of the chapbook, failure in its aftermath.

No reimbursement for remorse. No paying oneself back for lost time.

2

An email from Dale topped her inbox, a one-liner with none of his usual *xxoo*'s at the end. *Hope you're up to something interesting, my dear.*

Irked by her silence, evidently. And Dale wasn't alone; the inbox held messages from Anne and from Sophie as well.

The night before, in Roy's bed: languid sex, sucking each other into arrival. Roy waiting, entering only when she was ready. Even then she'd winced, her body making her pay for pleasure, fiery with pain. It's just the goddamn menopause, she'd said. I'm hurting you, Roy'd said, I'm so sorry, let's stop . . . there's always plenty else we can do. I don't want any of this to hurt you.

He'd withdrawn, but only physically. Then they'd played—a little of this and that, fingers and mouths, then more til they each came, eagerly. Afterward his breath on her shoulder was a wave lapping her, gently. When her usual 4:00 a.m. flop-sweat woke her, he'd woken too, pushing the top sheet aside and sliding a hand between her breasts, wiping off the slick. Then he'd brought his fingertips to rest on her earlobes, massaging them softly. They'd fallen back asleep til his alarm went off. In the shower, he'd kissed her as though they had all the time in the world, which they didn't— Roy had to teach all day. To earn his daily bread.

And you, dove, he'd asked. What's on your schedule?

I've just lined up something, not sure how it'll pan out . . . we'll see.

Where is it?

Nowhere in particular. I mean, I'll do it from home.

Well, that's good—no commuting. You can get to the gym more often, too. Lucky woman!

She'd boarded the R and gone home. What else to do? Having been—ah, there had to be words for it . . . having been where?

Somewhere i have never travelled . . . those lines from e. e. cummings, one of his weird love poems. *Gladly beyond any experience.* Having felt freed . . . *though i have closed myself as fingers, you open always petal by petal myself.*

Having been unresistant, curious, not wary.

Which was harder to believe: the jackpot or this thing with Roy?

3

Ellen, something's happened. It's Ennio, he fell . . .

Roy's tone was urgent, agitated.

Off the Balcony, at the gym. He's broken a wrist, maybe an ankle. Might have a ruptured spleen. He went up there by himself, I didn't re-alize—I thought he was behind the pile of mats in the corner, you know, where he usually hides out. But suddenly he was calling my name, and I looked up and there he was, dangling . . .

Off the railing?

No, off the track itself. He'd gone under the lower rail. His back was toward me. I yelled at him to wait, but someone slammed the Balcony door, the sound must've scared him . . . That's when he let go. I watched him drop— it was awful . . . they're checking his spleen now. Not sure about his ankles.

Is he talking?

He's pretty drugged.

Where are you, Roy, which hospital—Methodist?

Yeah.

In the background were voices, a phone ringing.

Ennio, my poor little guy . . .

Roy was weeping now.

4

It wasn't ruptured, the spleen. Nor was either ankle broken, though one was lightly sprained. Only the left wrist was broken, and they'd already put a cast on it. The doctors said it'd heal fine. Ennio was bruised all over, but it could've been much worse.

In the blue-ish light of the hospital hallway, Roy looked exhausted.

Let me get you something to eat or drink, Ellen said.

Thanks, I'm not hungry, I'm just waiting . . .

You've seen him?

Only for a few minutes. I'm staying here til they let me talk to him. But I don't think they'll let me into the room again til around five.

Want me to stay here with you til you can see him? Or is there anything you need me to buy? Meds, anything else?

He looked at her. What was in his gaze—confusion about what she'd just asked, or uncertainty about how to answer?

No, he responded after a moment. Gina'll be back soon, she went to fill some prescriptions. There's no need for you to stay.

Okay, but please let me know how Ennio's doing. And let me help. I can cover his medical expenses, okay?

Again that look, as though she'd said something that wasn't making full sense.

Yeah, he said. Thanks.

A nurse called his name, beckoning.

I'll phone when I know more, he said.

The kitchen counter needed wiping, the litter box emptying. How long had it been since she'd cleaned the apartment?

Or thought about Walter. *Full fathom five thy father lies* . . . a fathom was what, six feet or so? Christ, had Ennio actually dropped five fathoms?

Roy's expression . . . What he'd really needed was to be reassured, to be told *the kid's gonna be okay*. Not to be offered money.

How to get close to someone. Had she ever had the slightest idea? No, not like this; nor had she wanted to, really, til now. Which itself was worth . . . a great deal, unquantifiable.

Her linen shirt was soggy. Peeling it off, she rolled back and forth across the bed to mop herself off.

5

Win wasn't answering his cellphone. There was no voicemail on his land-line.

And it was already six o'clock. So Roy and Gina had probably taken Ennio home by now.

Get up, then. Shower, get dressed. Put on fresh clothes.

If Win was out and Maria was in his apartment, would she simply let the phone ring? Not that it mattered. Nor was there any sense in telling Win what'd happened to Ennio—he wouldn't give a shit about the kid's accident.

At any rate, he was probably making a vodka run right now. Or Maria wasn't answering. Or he and Maria weren't answering.

Try Dale instead. Text him about Ennio, say there was lots more to recount.

No, take it a step further—write a group email to all the nearest-and-dearest. Tell them about Roy. Say *I'm seeing someone.* Explain the situation. So guys, here's the thing: Roy's got a kid. Actually it's his half-sister's son, but he adopted the kid a few years ago, and I'm gonna help the boy get the therapy he needs since his biological father died in a train wreck and the kid's been acting out, sometimes he hides or he throws stuff—

—wait a sec, the nearest-and-dearest would say. The kid's father died *how?* The mother is Roy's half-sister? Roy is the kid's half-uncle and legal father at the same time? Why on earth are *you* paying for therapy for the kid?

There were only two options.

The first: let it all out—about the ticket, and about Roy. Beg the nearest-and-dearest to forget practicalities and listen, really listen, to what she was trying to tell them. It was new, this thing with Roy, really new, *somewhere i have never travelled*, and she'd have to take a risk, *love is a place* and *yes is a world*, and wasn't it high time she tried going there?

You're infatuated, Sophie'd say. Which is lovely, but you gotta be realistic. Ah, Anne would say, your situation sure sounds complicated, do things really have to be this messy? Just deal with the money now. *Cherie*, Giselle would say, remember that the child of a lover can be a very big challenge. Hey, Hank would say, how come this guy's a gym teacher, can't he do better than that?

As always, Dale would make the sharpest comment in the gentlest way. I wonder, he'd ask, how Roy imagines his own future. Have you talked with him about it?

The second option: stay mum about the whole shebang until the ticket was turned in.

If the beans got spilled now, the nearest-and-dearest would argue she was moving too fast with Roy and not fast enough with the money. They'd push her to deal with practical matters first. They'd tell her to get a team of lawyers, figure out the money stuff, don't even try to deal with Roy at the moment.

This thing with Roy. How did it feel, right here and now?

I were but little happy, if I could say how much.

Thank you, Shakespeare, you've nailed it.

Stay mum, then.

6

Dared him? How do you mean?

I mean, said Roy, that the woman got Ennio to go under the railing by taunting him. She actually dared him to try. Okay, Boy-Cat, off my lap now . . .

Roy put the cat on the floor, then slumped back on the sofa.

Man, I'm tired . . .

Of course you are. You've been through the mill.

He'd been up most of the night with Ennio. Though boy's spleen wasn't ruptured, the bruising had caused some internal bleeding. He'd need another day of monitoring.

How's Gina doing?

She's exhausted. I need to go relieve her soon, so she can get some rest.

Is Ennio in pain?

Not too much, thank God. He's sore and uncomfortable, and he says his body doesn't feel right to him. Which of course it doesn't. He got pretty banged around.

Can you take some time off?

I cancelled my classes today, but tomorrow I need to go to work. I can't risk losing my job. Plus I want to get to the gym at a decent hour tomorrow, so I can talk to a few people. Maybe someone will know who was on the Balcony with Ennio. Know what that person told him? She said he shouldn't be hanging out up there.

They had an actual conversation?

Yeah. She asked him if he knew any tumbling moves. When he said yes, she said he probably couldn't do this one thing—she called it a side roll, something like that, he wasn't sure. She showed him how to do it. She rolled over to the edge, went under the rail and grabbed it, wrapped her ankles around it. She said she could swing back and forth like a monkey. Of course that got Ennio's attention.

She swung herself away from the track? Like, out into the air?

Yep. Away from the track, then back under the rail, then away again. I didn't see it, but that's how Ennio described it. I bet you can't do this, she kept saying. Isn't that a dare? Ennio took hold of the rail and started swinging.

My God . . .

It was the noise that made him fall, just like I thought—the sound of the door closing. When he heard it, he let go of the rail. He said the noise scared him. If he hadn't managed to grab the edge of the track before dropping, he probably would've landed on his back.

What did the woman do when he fell?

She'd left—already banged the door behind her. My class was at the other end of the court; nobody in my group saw anything. And nobody at the front desk remembers seeing anyone rush out. She just disappeared.

How could someone walk away from a kid who's swinging off the Balcony?

Roy shook his head.

Can Ennio describe her?

Dark short hair. Not too tall. That's about it.

Did she seem to know him?

Nope. But that doesn't meant she didn't.

7

Frowning, distracted now. In some space of his own. Picturing something, seeing it in his mind.

I have a question for you, Ellen, and I don't like asking, but I need to. Have you been in touch with Maria lately?

Maria?

Yeah. Have you seen her, talked to her?

No. Why do you ask?

Is it possible the woman in the gym was her?

What makes you think . . . ?

Well, you've been trying to pull her away from your brother. Maybe she resents you for it. Maybe she wanted to get back at you.

Get back at me?

Yeah, using me—my son—as a kind of weapon.

Look, Roy . . . my God, even if Maria is upset with me for whatever reason, would she really put somebody else's *child* in danger in order to make a point? That's pretty crazy.

You're right, I'm sure . . . it's just a bad feeling I have.

Is there still some connection in your mind between Maria and your ex? What it is about Maria that keeps reminding you of her?

He exhaled slowly.

There's no physical resemblance between the two of them, he said. It's a subtle thing. Something about how withheld Maria seems . . . As for Gina—my ex—I can't help but feel it was her fault Renzo died.

Do you also feel she's the reason Ennio's your son now?

In a sense, yeah. It's like I'm blaming her for my family's bad luck and owing her for my good fortune at the same time.

Well, it's Ennio's good fortune, too.

I doubt he'll ever be truly glad about that. Not glad like I am, anyway. How could he be? He's lost the chance to grow up with his real father. Ennio will always believe the train accident was a fluke—which it was, of course, at one level. But my ex was the reason Renzo took that train back to London.

Actually, both Ginas were involved, weren't they? I mean, it seems Renzo was with your ex because he and your sister didn't get along well.

Yeah. But to me it felt—still feels—like my ex showed up out of nowhere to complicate things. I thought she was out of the picture, but she wasn't. Sort of like with Maria—she's shown up out of the blue, and now Ennio has an accident . . .

Okay, Roy, but listen, the woman on the Balcony had to be somebody else. It's way too much of a stretch.

You're right, dove. Of course you're right. I'm tired, let's stop talking about this. You know, I'm hungry, too. Haven't eaten much today. Can we grab a bite somewhere near the hospital?

Sure.

He reached for his jacket and pulled out his billfold.

Ah, crap, I've only got twenty bucks. I need to get to an ATM first, I forgot to stop off at the bank—

—don't worry, I'll cover it.

He put his wallet away.

I'm not comfortable with this, he said.

With what?

With your always paying for things and saying, oh, don't worry . . . I know, you've explained it. Sort of.

Please, Roy. I really am sharing my good luck with other people. Not just you.

He shook his head.

I don't feel short on luck, Ellen. And I can pay my bills. But it's obvious my bank balance doesn't match yours. I can't be generous with you in the same way you're being with me. This probably isn't the time to be talking about money, but the situation makes me uncomfortable. And since I'm about to benefit—or rather, Ennio is—I'd like to know where this windfall of yours is coming from. I don't see how we can go forward if we're not honest with each other about this stuff.

I agree. And I'll tell you all about it, I promise. Can you wait til the twenty-fourth? Just a week, okay? Things will be clearer then.

He nodded.

Okay. Now let's go eat.

8

They walked. He reached for her hand, his thumb pressing the center of her palm.

Oh, I didn't get a chance to tell you about Ennio's first therapy appointment. We went with him yesterday morning, before the accident. Which reminds me, I need to reschedule the next visit.

You'll tell me about the appointment while we eat?

Sure. Listen, I'm glad you're with me, dove, with all this stuff going on . . . it's not a lot of fun for you, I know.

I don't need fun, Roy. I want to be here with you, with all this stuff. You know, when I'm alone, it's often like I'm standing at a window, staring in.

At what?

At my life. As though it were somebody else's.

Still holding her hand, he swung her arm back and forth.

You could always open the window and climb in, he said.

You've no idea of the mess in there.

Is the mess recent?

Yes and no. About the recent part, I'll know more in a week. I can't predict how things will play out—too many variables.

Hm . . . mysterious. Meantime, I've lobbed a pretty big mess at you.

All that matters now is Ennio's health.

He'll heal up fine physically. But he needs a distraction to get him out of his thoughts—all this stuff about trains . . . he's got to let it go. He needs some other story to focus on.

Maybe I should write him a poem? A story-poem. With dogs or cats, maybe.

I bet he'd love that. Or something with birds, he's big on birds these days. Oh—as if yesterday weren't a long enough day, do you know what else happened when I got home from the hospital? Some woman rang my bell, wanting to take a look at Nadine's painting.

Huh? How'd she know you had it?

She'd seen it at the gallery in Park Slope. Someone there must've given her my address. I'll call them and tell them not to do that again.

Did she want to buy the painting?

Nope, just take a picture of it with her cellphone. She didn't talk, just stared at the painting and snapped a couple of photos. The whole thing took less than five minutes. A weird ending to a helluva day.

Among Animals

1

The parents were leaving phone messages. Having tried and given up on the cellphone, now they were using her landline. For a solid week, one message every day.

Blair, their voices said in unison, call us.

They were literally together when calling her. As if that would make a difference. As if it'd jolt her into responding to them. They probably wanted to know if she'd renewed the health insurance policy they'd each pushed on her, the year before. They'd offered to front the cost of the premiums; she could pay it back whenever, they'd said. They kept nagging her about it. No doubt because they didn't want to get stuck with big medical bills if something were to happen to her.

Forget it.

She hit delete on her landline's answering machine.

The real reason they were contacting her now was obvious: to make themselves feel better.

They'd say it was because they were worried she still didn't have insurance, but that wasn't why. They were calling so they'd feel less guilty about lying about Keith. They lied to save face with their friends. To gain sympathy with those women her mother played tennis with, the fake blondes with too much time on their hands. And the guys her mother's new husband worked with—investment bankers who bought five-hundred-dollar bottles of wine when they went out to eat, and flipped coins to see who'd pick up the check.

Now and then one of the blondes would come into the store, sent on a mission by her mother. Once, a woman pretended to be an artist and asked for help choosing stuff—the wrong stuff, like cheap acrylic gesso unsuited for oils. In the aisle she'd mumbled something like *sorry about your brother.* Trying to get a reaction, something to report back.

Foot-soldiers, Keith used to called the parents. Off to fight for merch at the mall.

In high school he'd been in a Marxist phase.

There'd been a teacher in junior year, an older man who'd taught Keith about Marxism. Keith had flunked that history class, but he'd talked about it with her. Only with her, because by that point he didn't have any friends. He wasn't political, but he liked Marx because Marx said animals too had become property, and all creatures had to be set free.

Animals didn't buy and sell, Keith said. They didn't wage wars. They made no pretense of family love; they just pushed their babies out of the nest when it was time. Some cats killed their babies if they were weaklings. That was better than allowing them to die slowly. Animals knew not to mewl about love.

Wherever he was now, Keith was alone. But there'd be animals around him, and he'd be taking care of them. It wasn't possible for a street artist to live like that, as he did, either in total solitude or with animals. She'd need to remain in the city. Alone as much as possible, visible yet invisible. An absurd creator.

2

That kid in the gym should've known better than to act like that balcony space was all his. He should've left when she told him *it's my turn.*

He'd taken her for a girl, easily scared off. He was one of those boys who had to learn, and she'd had to teach him the hard way. Keith would've taught the boy like that, as she did. Making him pay for it.

Keith had always known who she really was. His sister, but not really; in name only—a boy in a girl's body. He'd shown her he knew. This is how we do it, he'd said, and by *we* he'd meant *we boys.* My pup, he said, that's what you are. It hurt, she'd told him, but he said it had to, hurting was part of doing it. So she had to stay quiet, he said, and not tell the parents or anyone else. They wouldn't understand.

Of course they wouldn't. Only the two of them, Keith and herself, understood. Animals did whatever they wanted, with their sisters or brothers, whoever. To them it didn't matter. Animals didn't label each other's bodies. People were animals yet weren't allowed to be, and if they rebelled they were likely to get beaten up, or jailed. Or they silenced themselves.

That first time Keith was thirteen or so, and she was around nine. Afterward he told her he'd be leaving, as soon as he could. He'd already realized he had to go far away. And now he was by himself, among animals, where he needed to be. But what about her, his pup?

That kid at the gym was one of those boys who think they understand when they really don't.

She'd gotten out of there before anyone saw her. But she'd have to be more careful next time. The kid had fallen—she'd heard it—but he didn't seem badly hurt. He'd provoked it, anyhow. Asking *what's wrong* like that. Staring at her like he understood.

3

The parents were switching strategies now. A mailman had come to the door that morning, requesting her signature for a certified envelope. It'd been sent to the parents. They'd opened it, then resealed it. They'd crossed out their names and address and substituted hers. She recognized her mother's handwriting.

The envelope was official, from an office of the state. The Registry Office, whatever that was. Inside was a death certificate, dated six months earlier. Cause of death: heroin overdose. It was a faked document, for sure—the kind of bullshit they'd do. Their phone messages weren't working, so the parents were trying something else to get her attention. Trying to rouse her. No doubt they were lying to their friends about her, too—telling them their daughter was wasting her time working in some arts-supply store.

They'd say she hadn't gotten closure yet, and would have to be straightened out somehow. So she'd accept the truth about her brother.

But it wasn't true, any of it—couldn't be true.

If he knew what they were up to, Keith would laugh.

It'd help if he would get in touch.

But apparently there was nothing he could do. He'd had to choose silence. There had to be a reason for it.

Be the animal you are, he'd tell her if he were there. A pup.

Art's lonely, get used to it.

She had work to do. She'd have to lift another X-Acto knife from her workplace.

Nutshell

1

Win was swiveling back and forth on his bar-stool. There were dark half-moons under his eyes; his complexion was sallow. Had Maria given up on feeding him? For that matter, was she still living with him?

Hey.

He downed half his drink before speaking again.

Thought you'd forgotten our date.

No, of course not, Win. Sorry I'm late, the subways are a mess.

Wouldn't know, never take 'em. So I'll cut to the chase. I think you should go collect your money and travel around the world. I think you should toss dollar bills onto the street. Or open a publishing house, if you're not gonna write poems of your own. Publish other poets, at least. I think you should do anything but what you're doing.

Which is?

Waiting. For who knows what.

Uh, hello, it's nice to see you too, bro.

Come on.

No, really. Isn't waiting exactly what *you've* been doing ever since Mel died?

He turned away, silent.

How come you've thrown away your career as a composer, Win? How come you won't leave your apartment for anything but vodka? How come you won't take any money from me?

I'm fine with things as they are. I've been composing in my own way, but you haven't. You're a poet who isn't writing poems—all you do is read them. That doesn't feel too good, am I right?

Has Maria moved in with you? Does she pay rent, or just keep you in vodka?

Pulling out his wallet, he put a twenty on the bar.

I don't need to listen to this, he said quietly.

Don't leave. I shouldn't have said what I just said.

Yeah, you shouldn't. Take in your ticket, El—turn on the faucet and let things flow. Not just the money . . . because you never know when it'll all be cut off.

He stood and started for the door.

Hang on, Win. Please, I have to ask you something. Is Maria a decent person? I'm asking seriously.

He turned back.

Yes. She's Maria, not Mel; I'm not mixing them up. But yes, she's a decent person.

Okay then. I needed to hear it from you. Thank you for answering.

2

He took his keys from his pocket, rattling them in his hand.

Stop fretting about me, he said. All I need to do is keep sketching. The other day I thought to myself, I bet I could sketch that composition of Walter's—you know, the one he claimed I destroyed.

What brought *that* to mind?

I was thinking about Mendelssohn's lost cello concerto. He made just one copy of the score, and it fell off the stagecoach carrying it to the man who'd commissioned it. I used to wonder why Mendelssohn didn't just rewrite as much of the concerto as he could recall, and then re-score it. I know a composer who deliberately chucked a very long score and started over. It's a valid way of working.

Writers do that too, sometimes. Visual artists as well. They paint or draw over their work, knock down sculptures . . .

Right. The thing is, composition never really mattered to Walter. He didn't give a shit about process. When I lost that score of his, he couldn't reconstruct it or start over, because it hadn't ever mattered to him—not in itself. Just as a flag waved by his ego. I took down the flag by mistake, so I had to be taken down, too.

You read the score, but can you really recall it? You were only ten . . . Was it truly terrible? Or was it just that you didn't like it?

He shifted his keys from one hand to the other.

Yeah, I recall some of it. Walter wrote a lousy imitation of a song cycle by Poulenc. I remember the first song.

Poulenc, the French composer?

Uh-huh. Poulenc wrote a cycle for an excellent baritone named Pierre Bernac. I bet Walter wanted to prove he was better than Bernac. Like, not only could he sing, he could write his own songs, too.

If you were sketching Walter's music, would you use charcoal?

No, pencil.

Describe it—your sketch.

I'd scribble all over the paper til no white was left. Like one of those Ad Reinhardt paintings from the Sixties, remember, the color-field ones? Reinhardt did a canvas that looks all-black at first, til gradually you realize you're looking at a very subtle spectrum of tones. The canvas reflects the light and makes the black come alive, like it's moving. But with Walter's score I'd do something different—I'd make the black totally motionless. When you looked at it, you wouldn't hear a thing; the black would absorb all the sound. There'd be no music.

He stepped closer to the door, then spoke again.

You know, I always used to believe Walter had a terrific voice. Then one day Mel went to the public library and checked out a few of his recordings. She'd never heard him sing. When she came home, she told me I'd been listening to Walter's voice without really hearing it. Your father must've boxed your ears, she said.

He mimed the action, his keychain tinkling as he clapped his palms together.

If you do it hard enough, you can burst someone's eardrums. Of course

Walter didn't literally box my ears, that's not what Mel meant. She meant he'd boxed my belief in myself. When I lost that score, you know what he said to me? He told me I had perfect pitch but would never write anything good, because I had no feeling for music.

Christ, Win . . .

Yeah. You and Nola weren't around to hear that. It was just the two of us, a quiet little father-son moment.

Do you really believe musicians will be able to read your tinnitus sketches?

No one can play the music my tinnitus makes. My head's the instrument. My tinnitus sketches are variations on a theme.

Admit it—you're no longer composing. Not with those sketches, anyway.

With those sketches I'm no longer *notating*, El. I'm always composing.

Now he was right by the bar's front door, readying to leave. Yet still talking.

My tinnitus is getting more . . . insistent. I don't listen to music on my headphones anymore; I can't hear it clearly.

That's not good. What about your fugues, can you still hear them in your head?

Of course—I hear everything in my head. The fugues will be done soon, and they'll be played. I started out notating them, so I won't do sketches. I'll keep notating. But I've realized I couldn't finish the fugues til I met Maria. I had to hear from her first. About what she heard that morning, at the station.

What do you mean?

She told me that after the bomb exploded, Mel was able to speak. Only for a few moments, but she spoke. Maria told me what she remembers . . . I'll have to fill in the rest myself.

3

He gave his keys a toss, then another, juggling them.

Know what? In the sixteenth century, an Italian composer named Vicentino built a keyboard with thirty-six keys to the octave. It's called a microtonal keyboard; it lets you play intervals in any key. That keyboard freed him, like my sketching frees me. It's not that I think notating is pointless. It's just that I've needed another way of composing, a way that's new. New for me.

Again he rattled his keys.

You've been a deer in headlights ever since you heard the lottery news, haven't you? Afraid you'll be turned into a different person, and nobody will know who the old Ellen used to be—nobody will give a shit. You're worried this new super-rich person doing all sorts of new stuff will push you aside and take your place. But you're missing the point. Putting on a new identity will be as easy for you as writing a silly jingle is for me. Or as writing dumb lyrics for an ad would be for you. After all, you've spent years putting other people's thoughts into words. That's a cinch. It's your own words you can't spit out.

He pocketed his keys.

You know, not long after we met, Mel told me if I really wanted to keep composing, I'd have to do it without a parachute. She loved my work but always felt I could do more. She was the one who pushed me to sketch; she said whatever I heard shouldn't be limited by notation. And Mel talked with Maria about that, in Madrid—about my sketches—on that morning...

He paused, then added: And now I'm going home.

Is Maria waiting for you?

Waiting? No. But she cares what I think and do. She tugs on the string now and then—she says stop drinking, you've had enough. I think you should find someone who'll tug on *your* string, El. Or someone who'll play out the line and let you drift. That's what you need to do, but you've never let yourself do it. You're like Walter that way.

He put a hand on the door, his body pivoting as he added: Be more like Nola. Sing for yourself, even if you think no one's listening, or cares.

Blue Fairy

1

Ennio opened the door and grinned.

It's you! Hi!

His left wrist was in a cast that extended up his forearm; the flesh above his elbow was bruised.

Wow, Ennio, you took a real tumble, didn't you?

Not the kind Roy teaches!

That's for sure. How do you feel?

Kind of like a bird with a busted wing.

What kind of bird?

Um, a coot. I learned about them in day camp. There's this one kind, it's black with a white face, and it runs on the water before it takes off. The water's like its highway.

Gosh. May I come in?

Yeah, sorry! I want you to sign my cast. Mom's and Roy's names are on it already, plus a couple of our neighbors. When I go back to day camp, my friends will sign it.

Does anything still hurt?

This ankle, a little.

He lifted his left foot and planted its sole on the inside of his right knee. With his arm like a tucked-in wing and his head tilted to the side, he did look like a bird.

Roy's gonna be back by nine, he added. He's got a class.

Don't count on it, honey. He might be later than that.

Gina stood behind Ennio now, her face as blank as her tone.

Hello, Gina—I came to see Ennio . . . I'm so sorry about his accident.

I'm glad you're here, said the boy, 'cause now we can read another chapter of my book. Hey Mom, know what? Ellen likes reading aloud.

Gina gave a brief nod.

I'll go get my book, said Ennio. *She* gets tired of reading to me—he gestured at his mother—and Roy does too, sometimes. But that's okay. I like to read by myself, too.

Ennio, said Gina, go brush your teeth. Call me if you need help.

The boy rolled his eyes.

I'm fine. Hey Ellen, what was that thing you read to me last time? Jabber-something? A weird poem.

It's called Jabberwocky.

Ennio, said Gina, I think this might not be a good time for—

—oh, come on, Mom. You're bored, and Ellen can give you a break!

He handed a book to Ellen.

I'm partway through this, he said. It's really good. It's not *Harry Potter*, it's called *The Hobbit*. Roy said you told him I'd like it. You were right, I do! Good thing it was at the library, otherwise we'd have to buy it. Mom say we can't spend too much money on books—

—Ennio, let's go, you have to rest. The doctors said you need more sleep than usual.

The doctors are just trying to scare you.

Ennio, please . . .

Look, said Ellen, how about if I come back another time?

No, stay, please!

A half-hour, then, said Gina. Not more. Okay?

Okay. I'll meet you in my room after my teeth get brushed.

2

Just as Bilbo the hobbit was approaching the forest of Mirkwood, twenty minutes into the reading, Roy entered Ennio's room.

Hey, you two . . .

Ennio waved at him.

Roy, this story's getting really good! And Ellen's doing all the voices right.

She's a poet, remember? They're good with voices.

Yeah. I already know what book I want her to read next! And I can help her with the Italian names in it.

What book is that, En?

It's called *Pinocchio*. You know that guy you took me to talk with? He said I should read it.

Roy moved closer to the bed.

Dr. Rouse told you to read *Pinocchio*?

Yeah. He said it's famous in Italy. It's about this kid who's a puppet made of wood. Some animals and boys try to trick him, and he gets into trouble, I don't know what kind. But in the end, he turns into a real person. The doctor guy said it's a story for older kids. And adults.

Ennio paused, then added: He said it's for anyone who's lost a parent.

Well, said Roy, it sounds like a book we should get . . . Ellen, have you ever read it?

A long time ago. I can't remember all of Pinocchio's adventures, but it was a good story. The Disney movie isn't so hot.

Yeah, said Ennio, the doctor guy said the book's much better.

I can pick up a copy. There's a bookstore in my neighborhood.

Thanks!

Okay, En, that's enough. Lights out now. I'm taking Ellen home.

Home where?

Innocent, the question. Posed without worry.

Home here in Bay Ridge, Roy answered. My place.

So Ellen, if you'll be at Roy's tomorrow, you can come over and we can read what happens to Bilbo in that forest, what's it called?

The boy was looking at her, not at Roy.

It's called Mirkwood. Yeah, maybe we could finish that chapter.

Good!

Hey En, let's see what's up tomorrow, okay? I need to check my work schedule. And Ellen has stuff to do, too.

Okay. 'Night.

A quick hug for Roy, a wave for herself. Then Ennio curled on his side, his cast arm resting on a pillow. In a minute he was asleep.

Roy led Ellen to the kitchen; Gina was in the living room, watching TV.

Here, dove, have some water. You know, I'm surprised about *Pinocchio*. I mean, if Ennio reads it, is he gonna think he can't be a real boy til he finds his father?

I doubt it. Of course he'll think Pinocchio's lucky, since Geppetto doesn't die. But I bet Ennio will identify with the puppet—having to figure out what to do, who to trust . . .

Remember the Blue Fairy in the story?

Not really.

Let's say goodnight to Gina and take the dogs for a spin. I need to talk with you.

3

The dogs nosed their way down the street. Kay stopped to investigate a low hedge; Nine circled back to join her.

C'mon, mutts, keep it moving, said Roy. Ellen, look at those spooky shadows over there—those tree branches are like something in a fairytale . . . speaking of which, the Blue Fairy in *Pinocchio* is pretty great. I remember being struck by her when I was a kid and my grandma read me the story.

Remind me of her role?

At first the Blue Fairy is almost like a sister to Pinocchio. But then she disappears and almost dies, or seems to, yet she keeps turning into someone or something else. It's like she's there and not there. I mean, as you read the story, you never question whether the Blue Fairy exists, yet you also never know when she'll materialize. Still, she comes across as totally trustworthy. Pinocchio needs her, and she helps him figure things out. She's got his back, even though she doesn't want to be around him all the time.

His hand reached for hers now, bouncing it lightly in the space between them.

I sense, he said, you're a kind of Blue Fairy for Ennio.

Wait, Roy. I'm no good witch, believe me. And I'm no one's mother, either.

I know that. So does Ennio. But the Blue Fairy doesn't aim to be Pinocchio's mother. She has her own secret life. I think everyone starts off with a secret life; it's like the software of childhood, it comes pre-installed. But most people give up on theirs by the time they're adults. Ennio's starting to realize that, and he can see you haven't given up on yours.

His hand encircled hers now, seeking a reaction.

How to tell him what it'd been like, from childhood onward? Her own secret life had been hemmed in by a question no girl could avoid: *Do you want to have a child?* There'd been only three possible responses: yes, no, maybe. *Yes* got a girl off the hook. *Maybe* bought her time. But if she answered *no*, a girl couldn't escape the follow-up question: *Why not?*

I like kids, she said.

I can tell.

And I like Ennio. But not in the way you might be fantasizing.

Wait. Of course I hope you'll want to spend time with Ennio as well as me. But only as much as you're comfortable with. That's the only way it'll work. The important thing is, Ennio knows you'll tell him the truth.

About what?

Yourself. You know why Ennio asks you to read with him? Because *you* like reading aloud. He does, too, but that's beside the point. He knows I like it pretty well, Gina somewhat less . . . but you like it a lot, and he can sense that. He's looking for proof that people are actually able to be themselves. He's wondering if they're faking, a lot of the time. But he can tell you're trusty.

Trusty?

"My trusty steed"—that's a phrase in a story I used to read him. Recently I asked him what he thought "trusty" meant, and he laughed and said "my trusty steed," and then he answered my question. When someone's trusty, he said, you can tell who they are. I asked him, do you mean they're for real? And he said yeah, that's it, for real.

4

The dogs began prancing and snorting. Roy called them to his side; they sat, tails wagging, waiting for their leashes to come off.

Okay—almost home! There. Up you go . . .

The dogs dashed up the steps. Inside, Roy hung their leashes on a door-knob, then turned to Ellen.

I'm so glad you're here, he murmured.

Me too. But a bit scared.

Of what?

Right now, mainly of Ennio—his needs . . .

I am, too. More than you might think. He's my kid now, but not just mine. He's got his mom, and he'll always have his real father in his heart. It helps me to remember that. I don't have to be an open door for the kid every moment; it doesn't work like that. Not just because I don't want it that way, but because he doesn't.

He paused, then added: Don't worry, be trusty.

Uh, I think it's don't worry, be happy.

Whichever version you like—you choose. Might just be a matter of words, though. Seems to me they're basically the same.

A Wild Run

1

The job was going to end.

Her supervisor had given her two weeks. Something about needing someone friendlier on the shop floor—that was the supervisor's line, anyway. *Not the right environment for you, Blair.* The real issue was probably that they'd discovered some missing supplies and figured it had to be her.

Her final paycheck would come on Monday. She'd have to find a new job fast.

Where was Keith?

2

In the park at this hour—2:00 a.m.—nobody but herself. And chipmunks, squirrels, birds.

What kind of bird was it, the one in Nadine's painting? It looked like a dove of some kind. Keith liked doves. Once, he rescued a neighbor's ring-neck dove, a pale rosy-gray bird that didn't coo much. Keith said its cage was too small. On the day he rescued it, the boy who owned the bird was home alone, teasing it, poking through the bars of the cage with a lit match. The bird hopped and screeched in terror. When Keith heard the noise, he went in through the back door of the house and showed that kid he could never do it again, what he'd done to the bird. Taught him a lesson and made the kid promise not to tell his parents about it.

Hopping and screeching. Burn marks on the soles of his feet.

Keith released the dove outdoors. Even if it was killed by a predatory animal, he said, the bird would be better off.

3

The paint-over job was visible on the ceiling of the station where she'd put her slogans. Up there the cream color was slightly lighter. Though it'd been expunged, her project had still left a trace.

Where to get more cash? She jumped the turnstile and headed downstairs. No one was on the platform. No dollar bills or coins were lying around, either.

She walked the length of the Manhattan-bound side, then went back up to the mezzanine level and down to the Coney Island side. A train came in, a few passengers got off and climbed up the stairs—a nurse in uniform, a middle-aged couple, a drunk guy being tugged along by another guy who looked as though he were hauling a sack of trash. *Forget it*, the hauler said, *you're an asshole, why am I helping you?*

The train left, the people left. She was alone on the platform.

The only boy she'd ever wanted to help was her brother.

Just be a quiet pup, it's better that way.

The parents were still leaving messages. *Did you receive the certificate? Do you understand now? You need to move on, get going with your life.* Expecting her to be gullible. *If you need money*, the last message said—she'd deleted it, like all the rest—*be in touch, okay? Your brother made his choices, there was nothing we could do—don't put us through any more. Just let us give you some money.*

Hearing that, she'd felt a hard, sharp anger knife-twisting inside her.

No borrowing. No one on top.

It was time to take a bigger risk—make a wild run for it, like Camus said. She should do her next project in a subway car, with people all around. A kind of performance. An absurd intervention.

A work of art, said Camus, must make use of the dark forces of the soul.

A work of art, he said, is a confession.

She walked to the far end of the platform and sat on its edge, dangling her legs over, waiting.

She pulled up her legs a few seconds before the next train slid in. As it left, cool air from the tunnel swirled all around. She took out her phone and scrolled through the photos of Nadine's painting. That bird, those sparkles across its back and on its wings and breast—it was some sort of dove, for sure.

She slid the phone back into the rear pocket of her jeans. How much did she have in her wallet, maybe fifty bucks? Probably less. She'd have to get some more money, somehow. Soon.

Another train was arriving. The hiss of brakes, then a mechanized voice: *Watch the gap*. Doors opening, closing, shut. The train pulling out, gone now.

The tunnel's inviting darkness. She could just drop down there and crawl.

Her knees tingled as she pulled them to her chest, rocking back and forth, her eyes closed. Pup, pup.

Art's lonely, get used to it.

Countdown

1

Three days left. Today was Friday, mid-afternoon. Jesus—the day already half gone.

Did jackpot winners reach a point of simply not caring what time it was?

Roy's second class would be ending about now. He'd be picking up fish, fennel, and olives on the way home. Her assignment: a loaf of bread and a bottle of wine.

MetroCard and cellphone, where were they? There, in her bag's outer pocket. She pulled out the phone. Was her dentist's number in the contact list? That appointment for Monday the twenty-fourth would have to be cancelled. She scrolled down the list. So many numerals in a life, not just phone numbers but bank accounts, Social Security, PINs, the always-needing-to-be-changed passwords. An endless slew.

Trio, quartet.

And now a hot flash.

Rule one: breathe deeply, eyes closed. Rule two: find a distraction. Best thing was a phrase or line from a poem, something with easy rhymes and cadences.

How about Wallace Stevens: the bird's fire-fangled feathers dangle down.

Say it five times, silently.

The heat began to pass. The dampness took longer, as usual.

Fire-fangled . . .

And now just sit quietly, eyes closed, on this lumbering R train. Think about Roy.

After last eve's walk, lovemaking, then a midnight snack of blueberries, the two of them naked at the kitchen table. Moonlight dappling the dogs' fur.

A hot flash, too. Roy'd seen it; he'd handed her a cool glass of water. They went back to bed, to sleep, awaking just before dawn. Hands, tongues, the sole of a foot traveling the length of a leg. Roy careful, entering and moving very slowly inside, taking nothing for granted, making sure not to cause pain.

During breakfast, a phone call from Gina: the babysitter had just called in sick. Was Ellen there...? Roy asked if she could do it—stay with the kid. But more importantly, he said, did she *want* to? If not, he and Gina would find another solution.

She could, yes, but not for the whole day. She'd need a few hours for herself in the Slope, in the afternoon. Of course, he said, and Gina would come home after lunch; the morning was the challenge. And could she come back here for dinner, just the two of them? Good!

Now the R train was inching from the Slope toward Bay Ridge. Right beneath Sunset Park at the moment. Win's building was just a few blocks away, above-ground.

What was he up to? And Maria? Were the two of them together?

At last the train slid into Eighty-Sixth Street and shuddered to a halt. Win would draw the screech of brakes as a vibrating line that trembled on the page, like a wave of sound or heat. If Ennio were to look at it and be able to hear it, how would he react? Probably run and hide. Or yell—a big yell, first in Italian and then in English, or in some private language all his own.

2

Roy had already set the table. She opened the wine and sliced the bread as he served the fish.

So how'd it go this morning, dove?

It went fine. Ennio seems to be healing up well. He's got opinions on everything, by the way. I mean *everything*.

Yep! Here, have some fennel salad, it's good.

I got a lecture on the virtues and drawbacks of swing-sets.

That's one of his favorite themes. So what did you guys do? Did you get bored?

We read, played some cards, took a walk, went to that little park . . . I confess I got itchy after a bit. Like I always do with kids.

For me, it's not a matter of overcoming boredom, it's about moving through it. One minute I'm itchy, the next I'm laughing, or amazed. The weather keeps changing when I'm with that kid.

How much time will you be spending with him this weekend?

All day Sunday. Tomorrow he's at Gina's.

Are you looking forward to it?

Yes. There are moments with Ennio that just zap my heart. Of course there are always other moments when I want to run away and come back in a couple of hours. Sometimes when he's babbling away, I just want silence. And it's not fun when he's grumpy.

I don't mean to sound like I'm interrogating you, but . . . what part of Ennio's personality do you treasure most?

Good question, and hard to answer. I'd have to say his curiosity.

What's your biggest worry about him?

That he'll always be angry, but won't know why.

I think he has a pretty good idea why. While we were eating lunch today, he told me something about what happened in the gym.

Roy put down his fork.

Really?

Yeah. He said, you know that person who was there, when I fell?—I think she was mad. Mad at what, I asked. I don't know, he said. Then I asked, do you mean mad at something *you* said or did? And he said no, at something else. Plus she was sad, too. Sad about what, I asked. Same thing she was mad about, he said. I asked why he thought that, and he said, because I know how most bad things happen—they happen by accident.

Did he say more after that?

Nope. Changed the subject. What do you think was going on?

I can only guess . . . it sounds like right before he fell, he must've been thinking about Renzo's accident. And I bet he told you what he did because you didn't actually know Renzo. So he didn't have to worry about your reaction. You'd just listen. It felt safe for him.

He walked around the table and crouched by her chair, resting his palms lightly on her knees.

For Ennio, you *are* a kind of Blue Fairy, he said.

His gaze was steady, not pleading.

Look, Roy. Please don't expect things from me that I can't promise to deliver. Things I don't even know if I want to deliver.

It's fine. You're not supposed to deliver anything. I'm just struck by how much Ennio trusted you.

Of course I was glad—*am* glad—he talked with me. But I have to say it was unsettling. Like maybe I wasn't the right audience for it.

No right or wrong, dove. Thanks for being with my son today. For listening to him.

3

Saturday, 7:00 p.m., Tenth Street in the West Village. Midsummer early-eve sunlight burnishing the sidewalk, its color now pale gold.

They'd been in town all day. Roy had proposed the plan at breakfast: How about we divvy things up? You figure out the morning, I'll take care of the afternoon, and we'll improvise dinner.

Off they'd gone. The morning's entertainment was an exhibit of Gabriel Orozco's work at MOMA. Orozco used his notebooks as his studio— *evidence of process*, he'd called the notebooks. That phrase had charmed Roy. So if I get you a notebook, he'd asked, will you scribble something in it every day? Doesn't matter if it's poems or not.

Uh, she'd answered, it'll depend on the quality of the notebook.

I'll make it nice, trust me.

The start of the afternoon's entertainment was a brief nap in Central Park.

They'd sat on a bench near the Belvedere, propped shoulder-to-shoulder for a restorative half-hour. Then they'd strolled across the park to the C train, taking it south to Fourteenth Street for coffee and cake at Café Loup. After that, they'd meandered down Seventh Avenue.

And now, Mr. Organizer, she'd asked, what next?

Follow me.

At Tenth Street in the West Village, he'd stopped in front of a short, steep stairwell to a basement—Smalls, the place was called, a jazz club. There's a trio playing here tonight, he said. Let's take a chance on it. I'll see if I can get us tickets for the first set.

A few moments of solitude while he went down below.

Across the street an elderly man in jeans, sneakers, and gold-rimmed glasses walked slowly, his white T-shirt warmed by the sun's low rays. He looked absorbed, as though he were writing a poem in his head. What was it, the poem? Could she steal it from him, take it telepathically somehow? An hour earlier, holding her hand as they'd walked down Seventh Avenue, Roy had said quietly: *This whole thing feels good.* She'd offered nothing in response, though she'd had the same thought in that same moment. Yet it was easy, now, to embrace him as he emerged from Smalls waving two tickets in the air. Easy to slip a hand under his shirt at the base of his back and pull him toward herself, letting her body speak on her wordless behalf.

Evidence of process. Of moving in what felt scarily like the right direction.

Buy Me Love

1

Forgetting took practice. So did remembering, now that she'd gotten good at forgetting. It was a question of focus.

Now what was the guy's address . . .

Standing at the entrance to the R train at Fourth Avenue, Blair closed her eyes. She'd taken the R train. The guy's street was Eighty-Sixth—he lived right around the corner from its subway stop. But the apartment building, what was its number?

She closed her eyes. Yes: 345. And the apartment number was 7—the missing numeral in the sequence.

Good thing she'd picked a Monday morning. Everyone would be at work, the neighborhood quiet.

She walked down the side alley to the building's rear. The guy's apartment was on the third floor, she recalled; she'd taken the elevator up. The back of the building was partly ivy-covered, the windows fairly old. An external iron fire escape ran from the top floor down, ending about four feet above the ground.

A minute later, she was on the third-floor landing—an easy climb. The guy's kitchen window was open a few inches. She peered inside, listening. No sounds. Levering the window gently upward, she waited a minute, then removed her sneakers and slipped inside. Still no sounds.

As she sidled over to the hall leading to the front of the apartment, two dogs appeared. She remembered them from her first visit; they'd made a brief appearance, then retreated to the bedroom. Their ears were up now, alert.

Kneeling, she held out a hand. The dogs approached, nostrils flaring delicately—a male and a female. The male nosed her hand, the female her wrist. Were they siblings? During the first visit they'd sat quietly as she spoke with the guy, tracking her movements.

Good, she murmured. Good pups.

She stood slowly. The dogs' tails wagged a little as she made her way to the living room. As she'd expected, the painting wasn't heavy. It fit neatly into the gallery wrap-bag she'd brought with her—another item her supervisor at work would notice had gone missing.

Putting her sneakers back on, she moved to the front door. Anyone seeing her on the fire escape with the wrap-bag would be suspicious, but if she went out the front of the building like a resident or a visitor, there'd be no problem. Opening the door a few inches, she checked its lock to make sure it would shut behind her. Returning to the kitchen, she closed the window most of the way, as it was when she came in.

The dogs stood in the hallway, staring. She knelt again, both hands extended. The dogs came up and nuzzled her, then sat on their haunches, tongues lolling.

Happy, they seemed. Happy pups. But not free. Not with those things around their necks.

Removing each dog's collar, she slid them into her sweatshirt's pouch. Then she picked up Nadine's painting, opened the front door, checked the corridor, and headed for the stairwell. In under a minute she was on the street. There was a trashcan by the entrance to the subway; she chucked the dogs' collars into it.

2

An X-Acto knife was the best tool for the task, lightweight and sharp.

The canvas wasn't too thick. Carefully, Blair excised the dove. A gift for Keith, when he turned up.

She hacked at the rest of the canvas til it was fully shredded, then made a small pile of even smaller shreds. They were in shades of green, from forest to near-yellow: the colors of the ten-dollar bill in the painting. She tucked the shreds into the pouch of her sweatshirt.

The artist had died, and the rest of her work was gone. How or why didn't matter. Now *Buy Me Love* belonged to another artist, an absurd creator who'd make something new with it—the only person who could. The absurd creator who accepted that no creation could have a future. *To see one's work destroyed in a day while being aware that fundamentally this has no more importance than building for centuries*: Camus called this a difficult wisdom.

Traces: what the absurd creator's work would leave. To give the void its colors, said Camus. That would be enough.

End Game

1

The green suede clutch, of course. What better bag for the purpose?

Especially since she was wearing a chic pair of Armani flats and a handsome linen shirtdress, brand new, found in a secondhand shop on the Upper East Side—some rich woman's careless purchase, tossed in a closet and never worn.

Cool shoes, a new dress: all set. It never hurt to look like a million bucks, especially when retrieving a check for a hundred times that amount.

Unsnapping the front flap of the clutch, Ellen slipped a neatly folded hanky into its interior pocket.

The pocket's zipper was broken. Another thing for the to-do list, after the lottery-storm blew over. When she'd be able to luxuriate in time as though it were a bubble bath.

She snapped the flap of the purse shut, waiting for a bout of dizziness to pass.

The clutch would transport the ticket. Only the ticket, though. Nothing else, except for that cheerfully striped bit of silk Dale had gifted her a while ago—the hanky in which the ticket was folded. At lunch with him, she'd open the bag and pass him the hanky. The ticket would be cuddled inside, by that point merely a scrap of paper. A souvenir.

Daley, she'd say, what do you want for your housewarming? The sky's the limit . . .

2

At the Lottery Commission there'd be all sorts of forms to fill out—legal, financial, technical. They *would* let her retain the little scrap of paper as a keepsake, though? It was hers, after all. Bought and paid for.

Once signed, all the legal documents would go in her old brown shoulder-bag. That bag had a nice wide strap, good for comfortable carting. It was important to keep things separate—to mark a line she'd be crossing, between the old life and the new. Hence two bags: one for her usual stuff, the other just for the ticket.

How to get there? The R was the best train; its City Hall exit was closest to the Commission's offices. Or she could take the F, switch to the A, and get off at Chambers.

No, make this a direct flight. Take the R.

On the Fourth Avenue platform, a father was berating his teenaged son. Something about wearing dirty jeans to visit his grandmother.

What on *earth* were you *thinking*, the father kept asking.

I wasn't, the son kept answering.

Good lord, how did the kid manage that unruffled tone? Some people had a talent for not feeling shame. And what about the latest winner of the Pick Seven lottery: would she prance proudly home after collecting her prize, or would she slink back? Would she exult in her fortune and all it'd allow her to do, or would she stew her millions into a thick broth of self-recrimination? Would shame become for her like Win's tinnitus, shrieking in her head for the rest of her days?

Every jackpot winner was feckless. They all committed errors of judgment or action. She'd botch it somehow, too; the only question was how.

3

A train pulled into the station.

How strange—a D, pressed into service on the R line. And with lateral benches, too, rather than the R's paired seats. The interior was pretty clean, though. But this car was jammed cheek to jowl, even though it was already 9:00 a.m. Some signal-switch problem, no doubt.

Well, at least the air conditioning was working.

Entering the car, she used her elbow to pin her brown bag to her side. A schoolkid sidled past, bumping her with his knapsack.

C'mon, people, ordered the conductor, step lively!

The D's doors closed with the usual ding. On the bench opposite her was an empty seat. Another passenger headed toward it, a woman in her early thirties, dressed for an office. Pantsuit and blouse, pearls, lipstick the color of cotton candy.

Ah, let her take the seat. The poor girl's carry-all looked pretty heavy, as did her eyelids. Must be too stressed out to get some decent shuteye.

Nodding thanks, the young woman sat, sliding her bag behind her calves. Adjacent to her, an older guy glanced upward, then stood.

Here, he said to Ellen, gesturing, take my seat.

That's okay, you don't have to—

—it's fine, I'm getting off at the next stop.

Okay, thanks.

She inserted herself between the younger woman and a plump, rosy-cheeked man.

Packed like proverbial sardines.

At least nobody stank. Everyone was sitting quietly, too; reading, or gazing into space. After a minute, the younger woman pulled out her cellphone and began scrolling through emails. The plump guy was having his own version of a hot flash, his pudgy biceps pressing damply against Ellen's own.

She shifted a little, both hands on the green suede clutch on her lap. Her elbow connected with that of the younger woman on her other side.

Oh—sorry...

No problem, murmured the younger woman, her thumbs dancing across her phone's keyboard as she shifted in turn.

4

Elbows tucked, spine straight. Like a prim schoolmistress. The only position possible, really, given the tight seating. And no clutching of the clutch!

Why leave sweaty fingerprints on that nice soft suede? Just perch the thing on her knees like a docile kitten.

Seeing her so upright, Roy would laugh. And Ennio, what would he make of all this? Of course if he knew about the ticket, he'd want to come with her to redeem it. He'd squiggle next to her like an excited eel. As for Roy, he would sit on the other side of her with his eyes closed, working to steady each breath. Very still, he'd be, thrill and unease churning in his belly just as in her own.

At some point he'd open his eyes. They'd smile at each other like two bewildered climbers advancing toward the seat of happiness. About to get hit by—by what? An avalanche of cash, and what else? But wait . . . if he were sitting here with her now on this train, Roy would've already realized his privacy was about to drain right down the tubes. Sooner or later her name and face would be in the news, and if he were seen with her, his would be, too. So how would he react?

He'd reach for her hand. She'd take it. Seeing their clasped hands, Ennio would relax a bit. He'd lean into her shoulder, letting his legs dangle. The three of them would sit quietly as the train slipped through the tunnel.

Now the pudgy-biceps guy was really starting to sweat . . . was he gonna pass out? If he did, everyone would start flapping newspapers around his face. Maybe somebody would even pour a bottle of water on his head.

Ah, that'd feel good. Easy to imagine doing that to herself, but not with water. Instead, with a glass of chilly *prosecco*, which she'd buy as soon as she left the Lottery Commission.

5

This car on this train, what did it remind her of? The setting for a fairytale?

No, for a play—Prospero's island in *The Tempest*. What was Prospero's daughter's name? It started with an M . . . Mel, Maria? No, Miranda. Trapped on that island her whole life, Miranda was clueless about the mainland. Did Shakespeare think about alternative destinies for her, run a few ideas up his mental flagpole? What if, say, Miranda had been spirited off to Naples and installed in some opulent *palazzo*, where she'd hang out with dukes and princes?

Nope, that wouldn't have worked. In Naples she'd be thinking all the time about Ferdinand, the man who'd washed up onto her shores so unexpectedly. She'd want to return to the island.

After Court Street, the train began swaying slightly. It descended below the Hudson, steadied, gained speed, then slowed for the rise to the other side.

At Whitehall, a bunch of commuters got off and another group boarded. Ferry-riders, judging from the look of them—sunglasses propped on their heads, cheeks reddened by the wind. Now the train slithered more slowly. Christ, this stretch of track between Whitehall and City Hall had to be the twistiest in the whole system! The car's wheels made horrid screeches on each curve.

She covered her ears, pressing out the sound. This noise would kill Win, for sure. Thank God he was safe at home. And perhaps not alone. Not—go on, hope for it—without Maria.

At Rector the plump man got off and a young woman took his place.

Neither white- nor blue-collared. Not a professional, this girl. Artsy. Maybe self-employed, or out of work. In her mid-twenties. Wearing faded jeans and a sweatshirt with a kangaroo pouch—rather warm clothing for a day like this one, but with the air conditioning on these trains . . . her face was the blankest of slates. A bit tense, she seemed—hands on thighs, fingers slightly beaked, like she was readying to bolt. Maybe one of those people who hated being underground. Odd that she wasn't carrying a bag or knapsack. Actually, that wasn't so strange—plenty of people carried nothing but their keys, wallet, and cellphone. They just shoved stuff into their pockets. Purse-averse, was that a word?

More shrieking as the train slid toward Cortlandt Street.

Just two more stops. A major wave of dizziness. Wait it out; it would soon become an instant of the past. And the future? Right now, it looked like a mountain of dough.

6

Eyes closed, she uncovered her ears as the screeching and vertigo subsided.

Inhale, exhale.

Not so bad, this enforced sitting position—fingers entwined over tummy, knees together, eyes closed . . . better than sitting cross-legged, which was hard on the hip joints. Did the Buddha ever sit in meditation with an old leather bag strapped over one shoulder, or a suede clutch perched on his lap? Of course not. The Buddha needed none of that. The Buddha was whole and empty and fine with himself as he was, unlike people who were never whole and never empty and almost never fine with themselves, except in those brief instants when, unaccountably, they were.

As she herself was, right now.

Breathe. Just keep breathing.

A breath thou art, servile to all the skyey influences . . . What the hell, Shakespeare—if *skyey* could be a word, then couldn't *purse-averse* be one, too? Sure, why not.

It felt good to sit still, in any case. Eyes shut, body briefly untwitchy, the world's bad news held at bay. The subway car swaying like a cradle. Her plastic seat warmed by her butt.

The seat . . . good lord, this spot right here in a dark tunnel under the Hudson River, right here and now in late July 2005, might it actually . . . even though a war was on. And Walter was dead. And Win in who knew how much trouble. Might *this* be the seat of happiness?

7

At Cortlandt the doors pinged.

She kept her eyes closed.

Sounds of riders exiting, a baby whimpering. Jostling of passengers around her. Now some garbled mumbo-jumbo from the train's conductor: *Step aside, let 'em off, City Hall next, we're being held, moving shortly.*

The mind just had to sit back and breathe. That was all. If each and every mind in the world could just sit back and breathe, watching its thoughts pass like aimless clouds, there'd be no need for fretting.

But what if a person *wanted* to be subject to the skyey influences?

Oh dear, the Buddha would say. You've rather missed the point. But go ahead, do as you wish. Everybody's got to learn the hard way.

8

She felt her palms warm against her belly.

She blinked. The doors were about to close; any moment, the train would sputter back into motion. Where were they? The train had been held in the station a minute or so. She'd been in a patch of mental fog, almost dozing, eyes lazily fluttering open and closed. In that interval, what had taken place? She'd noted something, seen or half-seen it, registered it as peripheral. A hand rising from a thigh.

The seat to the right of her was empty.

The young woman in her sweatshirt stood at the open door of the subway car. With one hand she reached into her sweatshirt's pouch, pulled forth a handful of green stuff—something like confetti?—and tossed it in the air. Quickly she tossed out another handful, the colored bits gyrating downward til they littered the floor. Then she exited the train, slipping out just before the doors closed.

Ellen gazed at her lap.

An elderly man dropped into the vacant spot next to her. The baby's whimpering resumed.

What the hell's that stuff, said the elderly man, pointing to the stuff on the floor.

Ellen tapped her left side. The old brown bag was still there, its wide strap slung lightly over her shoulder. Had she put the clutch inside? No— it'd been on her lap the whole time. But it wasn't there now.

She stood, looked on the seat, under the bench, around it. She sat again, lowered her head, elbows on knees, dizzy. Only one thing to do:

stay aboard and ride it out—this wave that had crashed and was already receding, carrying off the past month like so much silt.

Next stop City Hall, barked the conductor.

She sat and rubbed her knees. Gone—as if it'd flitted off on its own. But a purse couldn't just flit off. She could picture it now: above-ground, in the grip of someone's hand. That person's other hand would reach inside the purse, feel around, and pull out a hanky, tossing it to the ground. Feel around some more and come up empty. Pitch the useless clutch into a garbage can.

Who steals my purse steals trash; 'tis something, nothing.

And the scrap of paper, released from the hanky and uplifted by a breeze, would flutter off by itself.

Elbows still on knees, Ellen squeezed her temples with her forefingers.

That girl in the sweatshirt—the one who'd littered the car with those colored green bits—it had to be her. She'd taken the purse. Slipped it under the kangaroo pouch, next to her skin.

Ellen lifted her chin and glanced at her watch. At her hand, trembling. Roy would be home now—maybe having some tea or reading the *Times*, one of his hands resting lightly on Kay's or Nine's head. The dogs had new collars; she'd bought them for him, and paid for a locksmith to change the front door's lock and install new closures for the rear windows. After the break-in, Roy had been distraught that he hadn't been more careful. For God's sake, he said, you don't let a stranger in to take pictures of something you own. What was I thinking? But why would someone take the dogs' collars, too? It doesn't matter, she'd told him, it's over now, the main thing is the dogs are fine.

He'd be checking his phone now, hoping she'd be in touch before he left for his afternoon class. Hadn't she told him she'd call or text after doing an errand downtown, before her lunch with Dale? He'd want to know how her day was going.

His lovely reedy voice. Those straight dark eyebrows.

I would not wish, confessed Miranda to Ferdinand, *any companion in the world but you.*

Her chin still resting on one hand, she let the other hand drop.

By her feet were a few colored bits. She reached down and touched them. Not paper, not plastic. Something else . . . cardboard, maybe? No, a slightly heavier material. Canvas of some kind, perhaps. The bits were in various shades of green, a little yellow now and then. Weirdly cheerful. Like a bed of grass with some dandelions mixed in.

On the subway floor, of all places. The thief left those bits there on purpose. Almost like an offering.

9

Just breathe. Because there was literally nothing else to be done.

The train was barely doing five miles per hour, but at least it was moving. Almost there—not at the Commission's offices but at Bouley, where she'd be having a nice lunch with Dale. Raising a glass to his new apartment. Fresh space, Daley, a fresh start.

About her morning she'd say nothing at first. Would celebrate his good news, share his high spirits, revel in his relief. Better to spring her own news on him at the meal's end. He'd stare at her as she spoke—first in puzzlement, then in disbelief. Wait, you won *what*? Are you *kidding*? And then your *bag* was stolen?

He would say nothing more for a good long minute. Then he'd shake his head, take her hands, grin, and utter something totally Dale-ish— *everything for a reason, huh?*—something in that vein, followed by a bunch of truly salty expletives. They'd order another glass of champagne. She'd make him promise never to tell anyone—not even the other nearest-and-dearest—or bring it up with her again, ever. To let it drop. And he'd agree, being the wise fellow he was.

Then she'd return to Brooklyn, feed the cats, and start looking for more freelance work. Detour over.

10

But wait. There was something else to do, something important, before picking up where she'd left off.

After lunch, instead of going home she'd go straight to Bay Ridge. She'd let herself into Roy's apartment with the new keys he'd given her when the lock was changed. He wouldn't be there, would already have left for his afternoon class. But when he returned, he'd be glad to see her—relieved, in fact. Everything okay? Yes, she'd say, everything's fine.

Then she'd ask him to call Gina and see if Ennio could come over for a visit. Once the kid arrived, she'd hand Roy a piece of paper. Well, well, he'd say, flapping it before him. Look at this—Ellen's written something for you, Ennio. I bet it's a poem. How great!

It's a prose poem, she'd tell the boy.

What's that?

Kind of a mix. A cross between a poem and a story.

About what?

Something that happened to me this morning, on the subway.

I wanna hear it.

Ellen, how about you read it to us?

Actually, I'd like to hear you read it, Roy, if you don't mind.

Not at all. Though I don't know how good a reader I am, especially of a prose poem I've never seen before . . . but I'll try.

He'd rustle the page softly, then clear his throat and begin. He'd read well, not rushing. It'd only take a minute or two.

Ennio would react immediately. Wait a second, he'd say, smiling and frowning at the same time. There's no *way* someone on the subway stole your bag with a jackpot ticket in it! You're trying to fool us!

I dunno, Roy would say. Anything's possible, right, En? I mean, Ellen's using her imagination. That's what she's supposed to do, she's a poet . . .

But Ellen, it doesn't make sense! Why would you have two purses with you—one on your knees and one on your shoulder?

Well, she'd tell the boy, I liked the one on my knees, the green suede one. It was really soft, like a cat. And it seemed like just the right bag for the ticket. It was small, so I could fit it inside the big bag if I wanted to. But actually, I felt like having it on my knees.

Like a cat . . . And you said the green purse was empty, right, except for the ticket. Which you'd wrapped in a *hanky*? Like, really?

Yep.

How come?

Well, the hanky was a gift from my friend Dale. I was going to have lunch with him today, so he was on my mind. I stuck the ticket inside his hanky, and put the hanky in the purse. That seemed like the safest place for it.

We'll get to meet Dale sometime, Roy would interject. I bet he's a nice guy. Did you and he have a good lunch?

Yes, we did.

But wait, Ennio would press. Wait a sec! Even if you liked having your green purse on your lap, and even if the purse did have a lottery ticket in it, there's no *way* the ticket was a jackpot winner. Why do you expect me to believe that?

Ennio, Roy would say, you're right. The odds of hitting the jackpot are ridiculously low. Still, isn't it fun to think Ellen *might* have had a jackpot ticket in her purse? This is a poem, remember?

Odds—what are they?

They're chances. When you play the lottery, you're buying a chance at winning. Everyone knows the odds of hitting the jackpot are super low. But everyone believes they might win, and that's how the lottery makes money—because people are willing to take a chance. *You* were, once, remember? And you lost a dollar.

Last time I'll do that!

Right. But you wanted to give it a shot, didn't you?

Yeah. And a dollar's not that much.

Right.

Just once, Ellen would say then. That's all it takes, Ennio.

At that, the boy would nod.

Then he'd say he liked her poem. And would add that it was actually a good thing her bag had been stolen. It would've been worse if it hadn't.

Really? Why is that, Roy would ask, chuckling.

Well, think how embarrassed Ellen would be when they told her, uh, sorry, you're wrong—you didn't win, those aren't the winning numbers.

Yeah, Roy would say, she'd feel pretty silly, wouldn't she? She'd be all like, oh man, what was I thinking? So it worked out fine in the end.

Well, but she did lose her purse, the one like a cat . . .

Yes, she'd say. I did, unfortunately. But I can get another purse. And what happened to me—it felt good, I have to say. Being the winner, I mean.

You know, Ennio would counter, you can do *that* whenever you want. You don't even need a ticket.

Do what? Be the winner?

No—imagine you've won.

That's true. So next time I'll imagine that I'll give *you* a big chunk of what I've won, and *you* can figure out what to do with it.

Hah! Yeah, I'll let you do that. And you can write another poem about it.

Then Roy would ask if he could hang onto her prose poem.

Sure, she'd say. But what about a notebook—for evidence of process, remember?

Of course I remember, he'd say. It's just that I haven't found the right notebook yet, dove. I'll know it when I see it. You'll get it soon, I promise.

One hand on his chest, making a vow. The other hand reaching for hers.

I'll wait, she'd say, we've got time.